MARGOT ARNOLD

Dirge for a Dorset Druid

A Penny Spring and Sir Toby Glendower Mystery

A Foul Play Press Book

The Countryman Press
Woodstock, Vermont

First Edition

Library of Congress Cataloging-in-Publication Data

Arnold, Margot.
Dirge for a Dorset druid : a Penny Spring and Sir Toby Glendower mystery / Margot Arnold. — 1st ed.
p. cm.
"A Foul Play Press book."
ISBN 0-88150-266-9
1. Spring, Penny (Fictitious character)—Fiction.
2. Glendower, Toby (Fictitious character)—Fiction.
3. Archaeologists—England—Dorset—Fiction.
4. Women anthropologists—England—Dorset—Fiction.
5. Dorset (England)—Fiction. I. Title.
PS3551.R536D57 1993
813'.54—dc20 93-40232
CIP

A Foul Play Press Book
The Countryman Press, Inc.
Woodstock, Vermont 05091

Printed in the United States of America

To Edward, Matthew, and Sarah Sweeney.
May their path to the light be joyful.

WHO'S WHO

GLENDOWER, Sir TOBIAS MERLIN, 1st Baronet [created 1992] Archaeologist. O.M., F.B.A., F.S.A., Knted 1977; b. Swansea, Wales, Dec. 27, 1926; s. Thomas Owen and Myfanwy [Williams] G.; ed. Winchester Coll.; Magdalen Coll., Oxford, B.A., M.A., Ph.D; Fellow, Magdalen Coll., 1949–; Fellow, All Souls Coll., 1990–; Emeritus Professor Near Eastern and European Prehistoric Arch., Oxford U. 1 dau., Sonya Danarova, m. Dr. Alexander Spring, 1991, 2 gr.ch. Mala & Marcus. Participated in more than 30 major archaeological expeditions. Author of several books, including *The Age of Pericles*, 1993; also numerous excavation and field reports. Clubs: Old Wykehamists, Athenaeum, Wine-tasters, University.

SPRING, Dame PENELOPE ATHENE, D.B.E. [Civil] 1992, Anthropologist. b. Cambridge, Mass., May 16, 1928; d. Marcus and Muriel [Snow] Thayer; B.A., M.A., Radcliffe Coll.; Ph.D., Columbia U.; m. Arthur Upton Spring, June 24,1953 [dec.]; 1 son, Alexander Marcus, M.D., 2 gr.ch. Marcus & Mala Spring. Lectr. Anthropology Oxford U., 1958–1968; Mathieson Reader in Anthropology, Oxford U., 1969–1993; Extramural Lectr. Oxford U., 1993–; Fellow, St. Anne's Coll., Oxford, 1969–. Field work in the Marquesas, East and South Africa, Uzbekistan, India, and among the Pueblo, Apache, Crow, and Fox Indians. Author of over 20 books including anthrop. classics *Sex in the South Pacific*, 1957; *Feminism in the 20th Century Muslim World*, 1978; *Modern Micronesian Chiefdoms*, 1989; and *The Fijians*, 1992.

Chapter 1

Sir Tobias Glendower gazed blankly out of the large windows of his All Souls study at a dismal grayness out of which a spiteful wind lashed unending raindrop tears against the glass. They were two weeks into glorious June and it had been raining like this from the beginning of the month, which had done nothing to raise his already-depressed spirits. He sighed heavily. He had so enjoyed writing *The Age of Pericles*—the only book he had ever really wanted to write—and now it was over, done with: newly published and received with rapturous scholarly acclaim and more unlooked for—and by him unwanted—honors from his peers. The present trouble was that he was hoist with the petard of his own success and was now being bombarded from all sides by people wanting him to do things, write things, talk about things he did not want to do and had no intention of doing—but he was fast running out of excuses.

He looked at the towering pile in his "In" basket and the emptiness of his "Out" basket and sighed again. He consulted his watch: five minutes had crawled by since he had last looked at it. He gazed mournfully at the silver-framed photo sitting on his desk: Penny and Sonya with Marcus and Mala on their respective laps, Alexander and himself standing proudly behind. Again he sighed. He had even run out of valid excuses to run over to New York to see his grandchildren.

His periwinkle-blue eyes fixed reproachfully on the grinning pixie face of their grandmother. "So typical of her not to be around when I need her," he thought. "Just because I was caught up in all the hoo-ha about the book and couldn't pay her any mind, she had absolutely no cause to go barreling off on that Australian lecture tour, and what she's doing now in New Zealand, God only knows. At her age, if she goes dashing around at this rate she'll drop dead in her tracks one of these days—and serve her damn well right!" This thought so shocked him that he hastily canceled it and groped for the comfort of his pipe. It was hot to his touch and he became dimly aware that the blue murk in the study was not so much due to the gloom of the day as to the enormous cloud of tobacco smoke that eddied above his knoblike silver-thatched head.

"Oh, damn," he thought crossly. "I've been smoking up a storm again. No wonder I'm so dry." He looked longingly at the cut-glass brandy decanter that stood on a small table by the wing chair near the window but then tore his eyes away. It was far too early for a drink, and he knew better than to start down that track to nowhere again just because he was down in the dumps.

"Dammit, *do* something," he charged himself and, getting up stiffly, ambled over to the window and opened it, heedless of the spitting rain. The blue smoke cloud surged out to battle the wind. He gazed down at the emerald green circle of the main quadrangle, empty of life, and at the ranked windows of his fellow scholars, all closed tightly against the elements. "Are they deep in their books or as bored as I am?" he wondered.

A flash of movement caught his eye as the porter's teenage son emerged from the lodge within the gate and scuttled lopsidedly across the quad, weighed down by a heavy leather satchel. Toby's spirits lifted slightly. "Ah, the morning mail!" he breathed. "Maybe there'll be something from Penny or the family." He shut the window and sauntered back to his desk, extracted a yellow pad from a drawer, and, grabbing a handful of letters from the towering stack, strewed them across the empty desk top before him and took pen in hand. With this satisfactory evidence of activity established, he settled back to await his mail.

When the inevitable knock on the door came, he roared "Come in, Ian," and the teen-ager edged into the room, groping in his satchel as he came. He was a sorry sight at close quarters, for the pink blotches of acne competed with plentiful brown freckles for possession of his pale face and clashed harshly with his carroty red hair, but his grin was wide and sunny as he produced a large handful of envelopes and dumped them on the desk.

"No rest for the wicked, eh, Sir Tobias?" he chirped. "Anybody'd think you was a film star the amount of stuff you get. Mind you, keeps you busy and your mind off this perishing awful weather, don't it? If this keeps up we'll all drown. Port Meadow's under water already, I seen it meself, like a ruddy lake it is. This better end soon or me love life will be down the tubes. I've only got me motorbike, y'see, and me bird don't like getting her feathers wet." And with this great thought, he was gone on his rounds.

Toby grinned slightly, shook his head in mock despair, and hastily leafed through the pile of mail. But there was nothing from New Zealand or New York so his spirits sank. He resifted the letters more slowly and one long typewritten envelope caught his eye, for it was marked "Urgent and Personal" and bore the superscription of the Dorset County Museum, Dorchester. He opened it, and, as he read, his round blue eyes behind his equally round glasses began to brighten.

"Dear Sir Tobias," it ran. "You probably do not remember me, but I am a former student of yours and have been Curator of the county museum here for the past 18 months. In July we are going to excavate a newly discovered henge situated right in downtown Dorchester, and it promises to be such an interesting and important site that I am about to ask a tremendous favor of you. Would you consider coming down here to act as consultant for the excavation? It would be a most tremendous help and honor to have you here.

"I only dare ask this because I know you have just published your excellent *Age of Pericles*, and so I am hoping to catch you before you launch into your next magnum opus. You are doubtless busy with many other projects, but I should emphasize that, once the dig is under way, you will in no sense be 'tied' to it, but, just now, while I'm still in the planning stage, I really need your expert help immediately and rather desperately. The site has some unique problems that I can only explain *in situ*, so would it be possible for you to come as soon as possible? Although the funding for the excavation is not entirely secured as of now, any expense incurred by you will, of course, be covered by me personally.

"Hoping against hope that I shall hear from you shortly," it concluded, "Sincerely, Stephen Farwell."

Toby leaned back with a contented sigh, clicked the appropriate switch in his photographic memory bank and brought up the face of Stephen Farwell on his mind screen. Oh, yes, he remembered Farwell perfectly: tall, dark, serious, and on the quiet side; had done a B.Litt. in Archaeology after his first degree in Modern History. Academically sound, but had a hard time of it financially, he recalled. Where had he gone after going down?—ah, Reading Museum, that was it. Had landed an assistant curatorship, which was no small thing in view of the limited opportunities of the archaeological world. So now he was curator of Dorchester, was he? He'd done very well for such a young chap. A slight wrinkle creased his high brow as it suddenly occurred to him that Stephen was no longer all that young—had to be at least 36 or 37. How time flew!

He sighed, then chuckled, and put the letter carefully aside, looking with triumph at his weekly desk calendar that had on its Friday page the ominous notation "OUP editor 11 A.M."

heavily underscored. Now he had something concrete with which to deter that obnoxiously persistent young man!

With renewed energy he quickly opened the rest of his mail, discarding most of it into the oversized wastebasket and dumping the remainder on top of the towering pile of his "In" tray. His desk cleared once more, he was just reaching for the phone when it pealed beneath his hand, causing him to jump. He picked it up and boomed, "Glendower here. What is it?"

"It's Campbell, sir. Sorry to trouble you but there's a gentleman here at the lodge wanting to have a word with you. I told him you'd probably be too busy and that he'd have to make an appointment, but he's being very persistent. Name of Farwell, sir, Stephen Farwell."

Toby's silvery eyebrows shot up in surprise. "Well, er, all right. A bit irregular, but I think I know what this is about and I'll make an exception. Send him right up, will you?"

"Ian just got back from his rounds, so he'll have him up in a jiffy," Campbell said and rang off.

Perplexed, Toby took up the letter again and looked at the date on it; it had been mailed last Thursday and today was only Tuesday. It made no mention of a possible visit, so why this sudden appearance?

He got up and went to open the door as footsteps clattered up the stone staircase. Ian's red head reappeared, followed by a dark one that towered above him. "Sir Tobias, it's Stephen Farwell," Ian panted.

"Come in, Mr. Farwell," Toby called as he retreated to his desk. "Thank you, Ian. I'll see Mr. Farwell out when we're through."

His first thought as Stephen Farwell advanced towards him was that the lad had surely grown, for he overtopped his own six feet by a good four inches; his second was that he was in one hell of a state, for a nerve jumped under his right eye and the sinewy hand that grasped his own with surprising strength was trembling. "It's extremely good of you to see me at such short notice, Sir Tobias," Stephen burst out. "But when I did not hear from you I just had to come in person to plead my cause."

His surprise growing, Toby decided to be soothing. "Sit down, Stephen. I must admit your visit is unexpected, particularly since I have only now received your letter." He plucked it from the desk and held it up. "You know, you only sent it on Thursday, and I suppose the weekend held it up a bit. Anyway, it just came in this morning's mail, and I was about to call you."

Something between a moan and a groan came from Farwell. "Only Thursday! Oh, damn, it seems so much longer than that. Anyway, now that I'm here will you please hear my case?"

"Of course," Toby murmured, settling back into his chair. "About this new henge? The field is yours, go ahead."

Stephen gave a convulsive wriggle. "Well, it's not exactly *new*. It was stumbled upon several years back by my predecessor when they were putting in the foundations for the Safeway shopping center between South Street and Acland Road, just off High Street in Dorchester. That's part of the ongoing problem. It's right in the heart of town and deeply buried under untouchable buildings. They couldn't hold up the construction back then, so all he could do was identify it and get a rough idea of its diameter. That's what's so staggering about the whole thing—from his figures it will be bigger than Woodhenge; possibly the biggest wood henge found to date and on a scale with Avebury and Stonehenge. What makes it all the more staggering is that its site is only 400 yards or so from the Maumbury Rings henge and only a mile or so, as the crow flies, from the Mount Pleasant henge. Do you know either of those firsthand?"

Toby nodded. "Yes, I dropped in on the Mount Pleasant excavations in their last season. Maumbury was before my time, of course, but I've seen it and the finds from it in your museum. If this new henge is also of the same date as the other two, you do indeed have a very interesting situation: why so many henges in such a small geographical area?"

Stephen's face lit up. "Precisely! My predecessor did not find any datable material, so this excavation will be crucial, not only in establishing the henge's dimensions but in dating it. What has happened now is that the Dorchester town fathers have decreed further house clearance to enlarge the parking lots in the adjacent area. You may remember that under one of the present parking lots nearby they found the Dorchester Roman baths and excavated those?"

Again Toby nodded as Stephen went on. "Well, the ex-curator fought like hell after the houses came down for the same deal, but all the council would agree to was to leave two areas fenced and unpaved for further excavation. He got so fed up with their shortsightedness that he quit and went off to Australia. When I came in and found out what was happening I took up the fight immediately, but I've met with a lot of local opposition and so looked for funding for the dig elsewhere and have it almost in the bag. If I don't go ahead with it now I'm afraid they'll just Tarmac the whole bloody thing over and it'll be lost forever. You'll have to see for yourself what's at stake. I desperately need you there on the spot."

"For my expertise or my clout?" Toby asked wryly.

Stephen's mouth twitched in an involuntary grimace. "For both," he admitted.

"Well," Toby said with a chuckle. "You could have saved yourself a trip. I was going to call you and say I was perfectly agreeable to your suggestion. It sounds very interesting. You mentioned a starting date in July, but I presume this will be late July after the colleges get out, right?"

"Right. I have a group of students coming up from Exeter University and another group from Southampton, and they have all dug before. About a week prior to that I'll have some local laborers clear the rubble and topsoil from the fenced areas, so that we can get right down to it from the start."

Toby pulled his desk calendar towards him, his gold pen poised for action. "So when would you like me to show up—the first week in July?"

Stephen's face was grim. "I'd like you to come back with me today—I need you *now*, immediately."

Toby put the pen down and fixed him with a stern blue eye. "You want me in Dorchester almost a month before anything is scheduled to start? There's something more to this, isn't there? What haven't you told me?"

Stephen's mouth clamped in a determined line. "Yes, there is something more, but I can only explain it in Dorchester. Please, I beg you!"

"You'll have to do better than that," Toby growled. He waved a hand at his towering pile of letters. "As you can see, I'm extremely busy. Do you seriously expect me to drop everything and go off at a moment's notice without the slightest notion what this is all about? Come off it!" His phone shrilled and with an exclamation of annoyance he snatched it up. "Glendower here—I'm busy. Call back later."

"It's Paul Berger at Oxford University Press, Sir Tobias. Sorry about interrupting and all that but just a minute of your time. I was wondering if we could move up our Friday appointment to tomorrow? I've had a couple of great ideas that I've tried out on my colleagues here, and I think you're going to love them. One—how about *The Age of Solon* as a follow-up to *Pericles*?"

"Good God, no!" Toby exploded.

"Then how about a definitive work on Plato and Atlantis?" the eager voice gushed on. "That would be a real zinger, and not so much work either."

"Certainly not," Toby roared. "And no, I can't see you tomorrow or on Friday. I'm going out of town on important business. I don't know when I'll be back, so don't bother to call. I'll call you when I return."

"But we'll lose the impetus from *Pericles*," the voice wailed at the other end. Toby hung up on him.

The interruption had given Stephen time to collect himself and he now looked calmly at Toby. "So you are coming?"

"Not with you, no. Obviously I have arrangements to make, but I will come," Toby said stiffly.

"I'd offer to put you up myself, but after my recent divorce I moved into a small bachelor apartment and there's very little room." Stephen sounded apologetic. "There's an adequate hotel at the top of High Street not far from the museum. I could book you in there, and I could set up an office for you in the museum itself."

Toby waved this aside and glared at him. "Look, I said I'd come and I will, but if you can't damn well come up with a very good explanation as to what is so goddamned urgent about my presence, I warn you I may just turn around and come right back here. I'll make my own arrangements."

Stephen looked wretched. "I can't explain here, I just can't. It would do no good, but there is an excellent reason, as you will see." In an effort to ease the strained atmosphere he indicated the family group on the desk. "While you were on the phone I noticed this—a very handsome family group." He peered more closely at it in growing surprise. "Er, isn't that Doctor Spring?"

"Yes, with our grandchildren. My daughter married her son," Toby explained.

Stephen's jaw dropped in amazement. "Your dau . . ." But seeing the steely gleam in Toby's eyes, he hastily went on, ". . . beautiful little girl, and I can see the boy is like you."

Toby preened. "Yes, Mala is a beautiful child. Poor Marcus lost out when it came to looks, but is a bright lad, thank God! Do you have children?"

Stephen shook his head sadly. "I'm afraid not. My ex-wife was very career-oriented. Just as well, as things turned out." A small silence fell.

Toby stood up. "Well, I've a lot to do, so why don't you get on back?"

Stephen rose and looked uncertainly at him. "You will come as soon as you can?" he faltered.

Toby relented. "Yes, if I can make it I'll be down by tonight; if not, tomorrow morning. Where can I reach you?"

The tall man groped in his pocket. "Here's my home phone, but I'll be in the museum until about seven-thirty this evening and back there at 8:30 A.M. tomorrow." His firm mouth quivered suddenly. "And please, Sir Tobias, be as quick as you can. I'm desperate." And he departed.

Toby leapt for the phone and dialed his housekeeper. "Mrs. Evans, I'm going out of town. Would you pack a couple of bags for me, and don't forget my digging clothes, eh? Oh, and doesn't your daughter run a B and B place in Dorchester?"

"Oh, yes, sir," the Welsh voice lilted back at him. "Woolaston Lodge she and her husband keep. Very well they are doing too."

"Is that in downtown Dorchester?"

"Yes indeed. Right by the old Roman baths, now a parking lot, it is."

"Good. Call her up and see if she can put me up, will you? I'll be back later to pick up the bags. Can't stay now but will talk to you later. Thanks, Mrs. Evans." Toby cradled the phone and dialed again, this time to Pitt Rivers Museum and his former nemesis, Ada Phipps, who still did all his typing. "Ada? Sir Tobias here. Look, I'll be bringing a pile of stuff in this afternoon for you and, er, any news of Dr. Spring's return?"

Ada, who sorely missed their sparring matches, was studiously noncommittal. "No, I've no idea about Dr. Spring's whereabouts or her plans. Why?"

"Oh, well, if she does get in touch and wants to find me, tell her I'll be down in Dorchester. She can contact me through the museum."

"For how long?" Ada demanded.

"I've no idea. See you later," Toby said, playing her own game and hanging up. He started to go through his pile of letters like a buzz saw.

Later, all arrangements made, his bags packed and stowed in the ancient Rolls, and the car headed due south on the A34, the energy born of his liberation started to ebb, replaced by mounting mystification. "What in the world could have put young Farwell in such a state?" he mused. "And what on earth am I getting myself into?" With a happy sigh he trod on the accelerator.

Chapter 2

It was still only a little after six when the Rolls left the London road and started to climb the steep hill to Dorchester's High Street, so Toby made a quick decision to go to his lodgings first and rid himself of his baggage and the car, whose size, as he had learned from long experience, made parking a major headache in any small English town. Taking a quick glance at the map Mrs. Evans had sketched, he turned off onto Church Street and carried on down Acland to the corner of Woolaston, where he pulled into the small paved courtyard behind Woolaston Lodge. Uncoiling himself stiffly from the driver's seat, he made towards the stone steps that led up to the main entrance of the house, and as he mounted them the door flew open and the evidently flustered Gwyneth Ap Jones surged out to greet him.

"Oh, Sir Tobias," she gabbled. "Good to see you it is, but I feel so terrible. The notice was so short, you see, and all we have is a little single room, not at all suitable in my opinion, but come you in and look at it and if it doesn't suit I'll find you something more in keeping elsewhere. The least I can do, seeing as how you were so good to us, having your lawyer help us with the buying of this place."

Toby had known this rosy-cheeked, plump, middle-aged woman since she was a toddler, and so was unfazed by this breathless greeting. "Good to see you, Gwen, and not to worry. I'm sure everything will be fine. All I need is a roof over my head, a bed to sleep in, and your excellent breakfasts. Shall I bring in my bags? And is it all right to leave the car there?"

"Oh, yes indeed, quite all right, and my Owen will see to your bags. But come you in first and look. It's mortified I am, but we're fully booked, you see, in spite of this awful weather." She shook her head in doubt as she led him down the hallway and up the stairs to the first floor. The room was indeed tiny, housing a single bed, flanked by a table with the omnipresent tea-maker tray upon it, a closet, a chest of drawers topped by a small color TV set, and an overstuffed easy chair jammed in between the foot of the bed and the window. Toby peered out of the window and noted that it overlooked the parking lot under which nestled the Roman Baths, and that diagonally across the road was a newer, raw-looking parking lot where he could make out the two fenced and weed-filled rectangles of the proposed dig.

"You see how it is," Gwen said dolefully. "Not suitable at all!"

Toby, whose style of living—apart from wine and books—had always verged on the Spartan, reassured her. "Couldn't be handier for my purposes. It'll do very well."

"You're sure?" she brightened. "There's a bathroom right next door and I'll put a 'Private' sign on it so you can have it all to yourself. And as to your breakfast, if you don't mind eating in our own kitchen-dining room, you can have that to yourself also. Me and Owen will have eaten and you won't have to be bothered with the tourists."

"Fine, fine," Toby murmured absently, looking at his watch. "But don't put yourself out on my account, Gwen. I don't even know yet how long I'll be here."

"One day or forever it is honored we will be," she assured him.

"Have you a phone I can use? I have to meet someone."

"There's a public phone in the hall, but no cause to use it. Use the one in our living room any time you wish day or night. I'll show you where it is and have Owen bring up your bags."

She ushered him downstairs and into a large room that ran across the front of the house and was comfortably and tastefully furnished with a mixture of Welsh and English antiques. A small and wiry sandy-haired man rose from the couch in front of a large-screen TV as they came in. Introductions were made before the Ap Joneses exited together, tactfully closing the door behind them as Toby headed for the phone.

There was palpable relief in Stephen Farwell's voice as he recognized Toby's. "This is very good of you, Sir Tobias. Come right along. I'll be at the front entrance of the museum waiting."

The pelting rain had eased off to a steady drizzle so Toby donned his raincoat and decrepit tweed hat before launching out. He crossed the road and made a quick tour of the fenced-in rectangles. "They certainly haven't left him much room to maneuver," he muttered crossly, as he turned his steps up the hill towards High Street. "Why the hell should they be so opposed?—doesn't make any sense."

He crossed the now almost-deserted High Street and turned left past the town hall towards the gray stone façade of the county museum. One half of the big double doors swung open as he came abreast of it and Stephen Farwell rushed out, grasped his hand in a bone-crushing grip, and exclaimed, "God, this is wonderful! Come on up to my office and we can get started."

"Well, I certainly hope it will be worth the trip," Toby grumbled, as they passed through the darkened museum and up the main stairs, their footsteps stirring hollow echoes. "I really don't appreciate all this mysterious mumbo jumbo."

Stephen didn't answer, but ushered him into the book-lined square of the curator's office. He indicated a green leather armchair by the desk for Toby and sat across from him, a green-shaded angle-lamp on the desk casting a harsh light on his stern, set face. "Bear with me," he said. "I'll have to do this in stages for it to make any sense." He extracted a slim pamphlet from a pile of papers in front of him and handed it to Toby. "First would you please read this?"

Toby's eyebrows lifted as he took in the demonic, horned face that dominated the first page under the caption "The Dorset Ooser." He hastily skimmed through it and looked up. "So?" he queried. "A wooden demon's mask probably used by the head of some ancient coven which has long since disappeared. What's this got to do with anything?"

Out of the shadows beyond the lamp's circle of light came a rustle of paper, and Stephen suddenly thrust an object into the light. Toby started, for the garish colors of the wooden horned mask, with its savage grinning mouth, its huge staring eyes, and the human hair on its pate and chin gave a singularly lifelike quality to the horror. He glanced quickly at the pamphlet and then at the mask. "It's not the same one," he stated. "This one is thinner and longer-faced and doesn't have a hinged jaw."

"No, it's this museum's 'ooser'—or at least it used to be." Stephen took up a heavy ledger. "This is our old accessions book. Under 1902—in other words several years after the disappearance of the Melbury Osmund 'ooser' in the pamphlet—there is this entry: 'A wooden demon's mask, a wooser, brought in by a God-fearing widow woman from Shipton Gorge. Found hidden in the rafters of her farmhouse attic. Does not know how it came to be there.' And there follows a minute description of the mask with measurements." Stephen shut the book with a snap. "Two days after this entry and before the mask was ever put on display, the museum was broken into through a small back window, now long since walled up. The only thing missing from the museum was this mask, which was never recovered."

"Then how . . ." Toby began.

"Please! Let me go on. I'm coming to that." Stephen's voice quivered with inner tension. "Last Wednesday, just before closing, I had taken a group of schoolchildren around the prehistoric Dorset exhibit up here, and the tour ran a bit late. The museum had been cleared and closed before we were through. After the children left, the volunteer on the sales desk, who went out after them, told me we had sold out of some of our Dorset monographs and needed to be restocked. I came back up here to pick them up and then decided to make a final check through the museum on my way back to the front desk." He stood up. "Would you come with me?"

Toby, feeling increasingly nettled, followed him out to the long gallery that ran around the main exhibition hall. Stephen fumbled for the switch and a dim light illumined the exhibits below. "I was standing here when I heard a noise from the Thomas Hardy exhibit enclosed over there—it's the contents of his study from Max Gate, his Dorchester home, which we've recreated just as he left it. I thought one of the school kids might have sneaked back and was up to some mischief, so I zoomed down the stairs," he suited the action to the word, Toby behind him, "and as you can hear that makes one hell of a noise."

"Not to mention you can't see a damn thing at that end of the room," Toby commented. "Were the lights like this?"

"Exactly," Stephen sighed. "So by the time I got up to it and got the lights on at that end there was no sign of anybody, nor any sign of disturbance, *but* on Hardy's chair behind the desk was a flat package with a note on top of it—addressed to me personally." He grimaced. "With all the IRA activity recently I must admit the first thing I thought of was a bomb, but when I read the note I knew differently. The package held nothing but the long-missing mask you've just seen." By this time they were gazing at the excellent re-creation of the Victorian study and at the Hardy bric-a-brac: eyeglasses, pens, inkwells, and blotter, strewn on the desk.

Increasingly mystified, Toby demanded, "And the note?"

"Let's get back upstairs and I'll show you," Stephen said with a little shiver. "Written on cheap, lined paper—the sort you can buy in Woolworth's—and the envelope ditto. The package was wrapped in a brown paper grocery bag from a local supermarket and tied with equally cheap string."

They reached the office and Stephen handed Toby the note from the pile of papers on the desk. The writing was a childishly laborious and illiterate scrawl. "You got your ooser back," it read, "Now you find out who done in our ooser and quick. We don't let nobody kill our oosers. You do it now or we tell the papers. We're awatching of you."

"What the devil!" Toby muttered. "Killing a mask? What the hell do they mean?"

"In Dorset witchcraft both the mask and its wearer—the head of the coven—are known as woosers. The Dorset dialect has trouble with the 'w' sound, so that 'wood' becomes 'ood' or 'ud,' and so on—hence 'ooser.' And I think I know what they mean. The Monday prior to the mask's return an old man, name of Job Squires, was found murdered on Eggardon Hill—you know the big Celtic earthwork a few miles west of here? His throat had been cut and a large old-fashioned scythe lay across the body."

A chill ran up Toby's spine, as past memories flooded his mind, of moonlight glinting on a scythe on the breast of a murdered man, and of all the horrors that had followed on the Dragon's Tongue. "There was a parallel case in Somerset back in the fifties," Stephen droned on, "so naturally the local papers and all the scandal sheets leapt on this one. You know the kind of thing—'Witchcraft Again Rampant in Dorset,' etcetera."

"So what did the police have to say about it?" Toby demanded.

"I haven't told them," Stephen said huskily. "You're the only one besides myself who has seen the mask and the note.

And, please, hear me out! There's more to come. I told you that I had to find funding for the dig from outside? Well, English Heritage came up with a grant, but they are so overwhelmed with similar demands that they could only give me less than half of what I needed to do the job properly." He swallowed convulsively. "Through an old friend I got in touch with a certain very eminent personage who is vitally interested in this kind of excavation, and he generously agreed to make up the rest of the funding provided that no word of its source gets out, since he has suffered much in the past from this interest and is understandably very shy of any publicity. If I had gone running to the police with what I have you can just imagine what the publicity would have been like: news hounds from all the rags besieging the museum, and every nut and thrill seeker converging on Dorchester. I haven't actually received the money yet—though it should be here within the next week—but, until it does arrive, I don't dare go near the police. My backer might get frightened off and then the dig would have to be scrubbed. The timing of this is so catastrophic for me that I even thought my opponents might have had a hand in it, so all I could think of doing was to get you down here as fast as possible, knowing your reputation."

"You mean as a *detective*?" Toby exploded. "Good God, man, have you completely lost your mind? What good can I do? I don't know beans about witchcraft or ritual murders—or Dorset life for that matter. How am I supposed to investigate the murder? I can't just stroll into the police station and say, 'Tell me all you've got on the Eggardon Hill murder. I've come to solve your case to please your local coven!' They'd throw me out on my ear."

"Just by being here you can save the day until the money arrives," Stephen said desperately. "You still haven't heard it all. You see, I received another note. On Saturday, when the museum is only open for a half day, the woman on the desk brought another envelope addressed to me. She had found it on her desk and had no idea who had left it. It is written by the same person and he asks for you by name." He handed the note to Toby. "We done right by you and you ain't done nothing," it read. "You get going quick or we tell. You need Merlin, find Merlin."

Toby's anger died and was replaced by raging suspicion. He looked coldly at Stephen. "What are you trying to pull? Outside of *Who's Who* and Debrett's my unfortunate middle name is not listed anywhere and is *never* used. Are you seriously asking me to believe that the almost illiterate rustic who wrote those notes got it from such a source? Or that he even intended to refer to me at all? In fact, who in the district but *you* would be likely to have such knowledge?"

"It only takes one person to dig out a fact like that and make it common knowledge," Stephen retaliated desperately. "I knew you would reject the idea, but you're wrong." Again he resorted to the dwindling pile before him and extracted a newspaper clipping. "You don't realize how newsworthy you've become over the years. This is from an article in a Sunday supplement of the *Dorchester Gazette* and relates, I believe, to your last venture in America. Note the heading!"

Toby scanned it and winced. "'Merlin' Glendower works his magic again and solves another murder," it declared. "Sir Tobias 'Merlin' Glendower and his partner, Dr. Penelope Athene Spring of Oxford University have successfully solved another 'insoluble' murder that had baffled the local police in Cape Cod, Massachusetts." He grimaced and did not bother to read on.

He put the clipping back on the desk. "Well, if your rustic correspondent reads the Sunday supplements, I suppose it is possible—but not probable . . ." he began, when suddenly the pool of light from the lamp swelled to a blaze and the devil's mask appeared to leap towards him. His head swirled with sudden vertigo and he started to black out.

He became dimly aware of a hand on his shoulder and Stephen's urgent voice. "Sir Tobias, what's the matter? Are you ill? Shall I get a doctor?"

With a tremendous effort of will he straightened up from where he had slumped upon the desk. "No," he said dazedly. "Just a giddy spell. Stupid of me. In the rush to get down here I skipped lunch, so I haven't eaten since early this morning. I think we'd better break this off for the moment and get some food and drink rather quickly. I've developed a tendency towards hypoglycemia of late. Is there somewhere nearby?"

"Oh God, I should have thought of dinner. I don't even have a drink here to offer you. But there are a couple of pubs up the street from here. We'll make for the King's Head if you feel up to walking, or I could get my car and drive you down to the White Hart at the bottom of the hill."

"No, I think some fresh air would do me good. Let's make for the King's Head," Toby said, getting to his feet uncertainly and taking deep breaths. His young companion whisked the mask and the papers out of sight and a lock clicked.

"Take my arm," Stephen urged, helping Toby into his raincoat then shepherding him in silence through the museum, shutting off the lights behind them as they went. Opening the massive front door, Stephen broke the silence. "As you can see, our intruder would have had no trouble slipping out the other night. It's only when the last person leaves—and that's usually myself—that the door is double-locked." They went out into another downpour, and as they hurried up the deserted street, revived by the pelting rain, Toby inquired, "You don't have a night watchman?"

"Can't afford one," Stephen said gloomily. "But we do have an alarm system wired into the police station. We have never had any trouble since I've been here." He whisked Toby across the street and into the beckoning lights of the pub. They passed through its saloon bar, which was crowded, and up some shallow stairs to the dining area, which was not. Seating Toby on a padded bench before a small, formica-topped table, he glanced at the blackboard on which was written the evening's menu. "There's roast chicken, with chips and peas, or beef stew."

"The chicken," Toby said, fighting to control the vertigo.

"I wouldn't recommend the wine here to a connoisseur like you, but they do have some excellent draft Somerset cider," Stephen went on.

"How appropriate!" said Toby. "I haven't had any decent cider since Brittany and my last ritual murder." Looking startled, Stephen went off to give their orders and returned shortly bearing two pint glasses of cider. Toby took a gulp of his and his eyes brightened. "Excellent indeed!" he breathed. "So, tell me about this local opposition you've run into."

Their food arrived, and, as Toby fell to voraciously, Stephen launched into a long and rather muddled account of the problems he had run into during his curatorship. "The infection even seems to have spread to the museum's board of governors," he concluded bitterly. "Some of them seem to think a curator should only curate and not dig at all, and I made it so clear when I took the job that I was a 'dirt' archaeologist and would be an active excavator."

"How many of them?" The re-energized Toby had finished his pint and was signaling their waitress for refills.

"Primarily three—unfortunately three of the more vocal and active ones—including Mrs. Westcott-Smyth, our current chairperson of the board." A dull flush appeared on Stephen's high cheekbones. "She is extremely hostile. Then there's old Colonel Orchard, but he's so whacko that no one pays him much mind. And, recently, someone I thought I could count on has changed sides and is equally hostile. You may know him, sir, because I believe he was up at Magdalen about the same time as you were—Silas Gulliver?"

"Hmm." Toby consulted his memory bank and a rather effeminate face surrounded by overlong fair hair popped on the screen. "Yes, vaguely. Rather an affected and effete young man. Read Modern History? Since I read Greats I didn't see much of him. Became a fellow somewhere. Let me see. Oh yes, fellow of Pembroke, but wasn't around there long, as I recall. What's he doing here?"

"I think he's retired, but he does a lot of writing on local history. Has a remote place near Colonel Orchard's in Stanton St. Gabriel, a little hamlet on the coast west of here, between Chideock and Charmouth. He was extremely friendly when I first arrived but now he's very much in Mrs. Westcott-Smyth's corner." Again Stephen flushed.

"Any idea why?"

"No, none," Stephen said shortly, but Toby suspected evasion, a suspicion confirmed when Stephen abruptly changed the subject. "All this other business aside, Sir Tobias, I meant every word I wrote in that letter I sent. I really need your advice on the excavation. I was wondering, if you feel up to it, whether I could drive you out to Maiden Castle first thing tomorrow morning to take a general look at the area?"

Toby gazed at him in mild astonishment. "I'm never averse to a trip to one of my favorite sites—but why the Maiden? It has nothing to do with the henge sites."

"From up there you can see the whole lot—Mount Pleasant, Maumbury, Poundsbury earthwork, and the new one. I'd very much appreciate it." Stephen was at his most earnest. "I'm afraid we'd have to go early, before the museum opens—say eight-thirty?"

"Well, all right," Toby agreed wearily. "But in that case I think we'd better pack it in now, if you're determined to drag me out at that ungodly hour. I've had quite a day."

Stephen suddenly became animated. "That's great, just great! Then I'll pick you up at around eight-twenty. Woolaston Lodge you said? That's right on the way to the Maiden."

Later, as Toby tumbled into his narrow bed, his unease about the young man's erratic behavior welled up again. "Tip of the iceberg," he muttered, as he snuggled into the downy softness of the duvet and listened to the rain at the window. "That young man has a lot on his mind, but I don't believe I've heard a tithe of it yet. Oh, well, sufficient unto the day is the evil thereof. It beats writing another damn book." And he fell asleep.

Chapter 3

A brief but vivid nightmare in which he was being chased around the Dragon's Teeth henge by a figure wearing the ooser mask and wielding a scythe brought Toby briefly out of his deep sleep. He awoke long enough to dispel his nightmare thoughts and to note that the rain had stopped before he sank back into downy slumber. He was next awakened by a tap on the door, followed by the comfortable figure of Gwen bearing a steaming cup of early morning tea. "Thought I'd best wake you, if you want to get off early, Sir Tobias," she said, putting the cup down on the tray beside him. "Haven't sugared it, but there's sugar in the bowl there if you take it that way. Breakfast'll be ready in 20 minutes, if that's long enough for you. Rain's cleared, so you should have a nice day for your outing. Might even get some sun by the looks of it. The wind's a bit brisk so dress warm."

"Splendid, Gwen, splendid," he answered sleepily, struggling up on one elbow and glancing at his watch. "I'll be down in time."

"No need to rush," she assured him, heading for the door. "I'll have it ready and waiting for you."

He gulped the hot tea and, invigorated, jumped out of bed, grabbed a quick shower and shave, dressed rapidly, and gave a hasty brush to his silvery thatch to complete his toilette.

Gathering up his binoculars, raincoat, and hat, and patting his pockets to see that he had his pipe, tobacco, wallet, and keys, he loped along the short passage and down the stairs. To his right came a low murmur of voices from the small dining room, but he turned across the main hallway and into the door on the left to the large kitchen which was redolent with the delicious aroma of sizzling bacon.

Gwen looked up from the large gas range as he came in. "Sit you down at the table. Right on the dot you are." She whisked a plate from the warming rack and started to pile food on it. "I checked with my mam on what you liked, so I've made you grilled kidneys, bacon, mushrooms, and tomatoes—is that all right?"

"Delicious," Toby said, as she plonked the heaped plate in front of him, along with a silver rack full of thin toast. "This will keep me going all day."

"I've some homemade blackberry and apple jam to go with your toast, if you like," she said anxiously. "Or there's marmalade."

"Oh, the jam, thank you. I'll tell your mother she'll have to look to her laurels. You're a great cook, Gwen," he flattered, attacking his food with zest.

Her round face dimpled with pleasure. "Tea or coffee?"

"I think I'll stay with tea. That first cup whetted my appetite for more. But, please, don't neglect your other guests for me."

"Don't worry. Owen's looking after that lot," she sniffed, turning back to the stove. "So where are you off to today?" she went on, as she filled his cup from the cosy-covered pot, putting the pot on the table by his elbow, and looking at him expectantly.

"Oh, just off to Maiden Castle with the curator of the museum here. We'll probably go on from there to some of the other local sites," he said.

"Would that be a Mr. Farwell?" she asked, crossing her arms

under her ample breasts and obviously settling in for a chat.

"Yes, he's an old student of mine."

"Really?" She giggled suddenly, her rosy face turning a shade rosier, as Toby gazed inquiringly at her. "Fine figure of a man, isn't he? Quite a one is Mr. Farwell, or so I've heard."

"How so?" Toby encouraged, pushing aside his empty plate and reaching for the toast and jam.

Her voice sank to a confidential murmur. "Well, quite a one with the *ladies* I believe. His wife left him, you see, and there was a *divorce*." Divorce in Gwen's book was evidently not the commonplace of life it had become in modern England. "And of course the Farwells have always had a *reputation* around here."

"You mean the Farwells are a Dorset family?" That Stephen was a local man had not even occurred to him.

"Well, yes, the Farwells of Chideock, isn't it? Famous for their smuggling and their goings-on in the old days. Clever as monkeys they were. Never got caught, so it's said."

Toby grinned faintly at her. "Tell me, Gwen, how did a nice Welsh girl like you, who's not native to this area, come by all this information?"

She looked surprised and a little shocked. "Oh, *I'm* not one to gossip, mind you. It's all from Owen. He runs an antique business on the side, you see, and he gets around all over the county, all the villages and hamlets. Rich pickings still to be had, he says, and of course he hears a lot on his rounds."

"Does he indeed," Toby murmured, making a mental note to better his acquaintance with the peripatetic Owen. As if summoned, the sandy head of her husband appeared around the door. "Three eggs and bacon, one bacon and tomato," he told his wife and grinned at Toby before disappearing.

With some reluctance she turned back to her stove. "You take your time now, Sir Tobias," she said. "No need to hurry."

Toby finished his tea and stood up with a satisfied sigh. "I've just got time for a pipe before my pickup. I'll smoke it out front and not smell up your kitchen. That was a delicious breakfast."

"I thought maybe a nice bit of smoked Finnan haddock and poached eggs for tomorrow?" Gwen said anxiously. "And if it's an evening meal you need I'd be more than happy to get it for you anytime."

"That's good of you, but I still am not certain what my plans are. And, yes, smoked haddock will be very nice," he said, making for the door and fumbling for his tobacco pouch.

Standing on the steps he lit his pipe and gazed up at the pale, watery sun fighting with the scudding clouds. What he had just heard had increased his unease at the motives of the young archaeologist. If Stephen was indeed a womanizer, it could well explain the apparent hostility of the chairwoman of the museum board, if she were one of the usual prim and proper matrons that ended up in such positions. Ditto for the old-fashioned and eccentric Colonel Orchard. From what he remembered of Silas Gulliver he would not have thought that sort of behavior would have upset him, but perhaps Gulliver had other fish to fry in this microcosmic power struggle. He was prepared to believe that Stephen needed him here, but for what purpose? To intimidate the rest by his lofty reputation? Or for some more devious reason? His cogitations were interrupted by the tooting of a horn and he looked up to see a small gray sedan moving into the open gateway of the courtyard. Stephen had arrived, and Toby determined to find out the truth of the matter in the course of the morning.

As he climbed into the car Stephen looked anxiously at him. "Are you all right now?"

"Quite recovered, thanks." Toby eyed Stephen keenly for he looked awful, his long face drawn and pale with dark circles under his gray-blue eyes. "But you don't look very well. Had a hard night?"

"Didn't get much sleep," Stephen muttered. "I've had insomnia for some time now, what with one thing and another."

He reversed the car out into the street and they sped down Weymouth Road past the Maumbury Rings henge, and then branched right onto the narrower road that led to Maiden Castle. The road ended in a large gravel-surfaced parking lot, over which loomed the massive convoluted walls of the huge earthwork. As Stephen drew into the empty lot he scanned the ramparts above them and said with satisfaction, "Looks as if we've got the whole place to ourselves—good!"

They toiled up the steep path towards the west entrance, but before they passed inside its sheltering walls Toby paused for a moment to catch his breath and to look behind him to where the ancient Ridgeway, laden with its prehistoric burden of long barrows, round barrows, and encampments, stretched towards the horizon, misty in the morning light. For a moment the past reached out and touched him.

An impatient voice summoned him back to the present. "Are you coming, Sir Tobias? I thought if we walked over and climbed the northern embankment we'd get the best overview." With a slight sigh, Toby obeyed the summons and went through the convoluted maze of the entrance to where Stephen stood gazing out over the huge expanse of flat, grassy sward within the earthwork that had once housed the Iron Age village of the Durotriges. In silence they crossed to the northern rim and, climbing the steep bank, looked down at the triple line of defenses erected by this tribe more than 2,000 years before. A brisk wind buffeted them as they reached the crest and looked northward.

Stephen began waving an explanatory hand. "Well, there's Mount Pleasant to our right, just beyond that newish housing development. If you can pick up the Conquer Barrow with your binoculars you can follow the main earthwork around to the east from there."

Toby obediently followed instructions and nodded. "Now, sweep west on that same line and you'll pick up Maumbury Rings down by the railway station," Stephen instructed.

Again Toby nodded. "Almost exactly on the same parallel, I'd say. Very interesting considering they were of the same date."

Stephen gave a little snort of laughter. "Our Colonel Orchard would love to hear you say that. He's potty about ley lines and such—writing a huge tome on them, I believe. You into that sort of thing?"

"Sacred geography you mean?" Toby pursed his small rosebud mouth. "I think a lot of modern archaeologists have gone a little overboard in ascribing too much complexity and significance to the sites, but, yes, I do think that men from the Neolithic onwards were aware of electromagnetic fields—after all you can actually feel and delineate them on some sites—and that they thought this had to be something special. Maybe they were right. After all we don't have the faintest idea what they signify, other than that they appear to be purely natural phenomena, like the magnetic poles."

Stephen gave another snort of disbelief. "Well, the new henge certainly doesn't follow that pattern. Backtrack to Dorchester South Station. Now scan north and a little to your right. Pick up the parking lots?" Toby nodded. "See a large, red-brick building just beyond them? That's the Safeway building under which the postholes of the wood henge and part of the ditch were picked up. If the figures on the henge are right, it might swing all the way over to the Icen Way, that Roman road heading towards High Street again to the right—which would make it of enormous size. So you see how vitally important this dig is."

"Indeed I do," Toby said, now training his glasses on the mist-enshrouded outlines of Poundbury Camp to the west. "Not so much for its dimensions as for its date."

Stephen followed the direction of his gaze. "Looking at Poundbury? I've often wondered why so many of the subsequent folkloric rites in the region went on up there and not here."

"When you consider the slaughter that occurred here when the Romans overran it, I'd say it was very understandable,"

Toby said tersely. "Folk memory is long and I don't suppose the small temple the Romans put up was sufficient in local minds to lay their ghosts."

Stephen shivered suddenly. "God, this wind is cruel! Let's get on down and away from it. Whilst we're here I'd like to get your insights into that old mystery of where the original inhabitants got their water supply." He skittered quickly down the embankment, and Toby, a little puzzled by this sudden change of direction, slid down behind him.

"Can't say that I've ever thought about it," he said, as he landed back on level ground. "What exactly is the mystery?"

Stephen started at a brisk pace towards the southern lines of the earthwork. "Well, when Wheeler dug this he didn't find any sign of Iron Age wells *within* the Maiden, and the nearest source of running water is the South Winterbourne, a tributary of the Frome that lies a quarter of a mile down in the valley south of here. In other words, it's one hell of a way to lug a water supply for what we know was a large village up here." His long legs ate up the ground as he angled towards a large square hole just beneath the inner southern rampart. "This thing *was* a well but was probably dug in the eighteenth century when they used this place as a sheep corral."

"Don't I remember a dew pond?" Toby queried, a little mystified by Stephen's growing enthusiasm for what appeared to be a totally unrelated subject.

"Yes, that *could* be ancient. No way of dating it, of course, but then it's very small and shallow and no way could it have served the village. It's been dry since recorded time. Come see for yourself. It's just over here." Stephen was off again, angling towards the center of the greensward and towards the low earth embankment that delineated the westward limit of the original neolithic earthwork around which the later massive Iron Age enclosure had been built. As they approached the round outline of the dew pond something gleamed white above its shallow rim, and Stephen halted suddenly and exclaimed, "Hello! What's that? Looks as if something has been thrown in it." He hurried towards it. "Oh my God! It's not some*thing*, it's some*body*," he choked out. "Jesus! I think it's a nun and she looks dead." He turned abruptly and covered his face with his hands.

By this time Toby was abreast of him and gazing down at what the shallow basin of the dew pond contained. It was a bizarre sight, for the white-robed body, with its flowing white wimple concealing the head, lay sprawled face down, arms outstretched in a parody of the Cross and, grasped in its right hand, an old-fashioned cutthroat razor with its blade glinting in the watery sunshine. Toby's eyes traveled down the body and his face set in grim lines, for protruding from the robe at the easterly end of the pond was a pair of very substantial men's boots. He bent down and felt for a pulse in the flaccid wrist, knowing it was hopeless. It was stone cold to his touch and the rigor mortis was already wearing off. With a grimace of distaste he gently and cautiously lifted the concealing wimple to expose a bluish face half-turned toward him, its bulbous blue eyes staring blankly under bushy white eyebrows, a bushy gray walrus mustache veiling its mouth, under which a ghastly neck wound gaped like a second obscene mouth—for both the jugular and carotid had been slashed. He drew a deep shuddering breath. "It's no nun," he said quietly. "It's an elderly man, and this getup, if I'm not mistaken, is that of a modern Druid."

Stephen gave a convulsive start and wheeled around, his eyes dilating, his face paling. "Oh, dear God, it's Colonel Orchard!" he gasped. "The old fool's finally flipped and killed himself. This is terrible! What are we going to do?" He started to shudder uncontrollably.

"Get hold of yourself," Toby charged, his eyes like chips of steel. "You've got to go and get the police here quickly. Go right for the top man—superintendent, chief inspector, whatever—and tell him what we've found. Tell him he'll need an ambulance, his forensic team, and at least two constables to guard the west and east entrances to keep people out of here. I'll stay and stand guard over the body until you get back. Do you know where the police station is?"

Stephen looked at him in a daze. "Police headquarters is on the Weymouth Road between Maumbury and the railroad station," he said mechanically. "Not far."

"Then for God's sake get going, and *hurry*!" Toby roared. "We don't want tourists wandering into this mess."

Stephen took off at a stumbling run and Toby watched him until he had disappeared through the west entrance. Then he turned back to the body and studied it. Something about its position just didn't ring true to him; there was something wrong. He circled the dew pond and stood by the feet, looking down at the body and trying to imagine the act—a man standing at the edge of the pond facing west, slashing his own throat, then falling forward with his arms stiffly outflung. He pursed his lips and shook his head. There were several inches of rainwater from the night's downpour in the dew pond, so the clothing of the body was soaked and heavy to the touch, but there was no reddish tint to the water, no sign of the blood that would have spouted so freely. In addition to this the boots were *within* the perimeter of the pond, not on the outside as would be expected if the man had simply fallen forward. He knelt down and gently edged up the robe, revealing, above the boots, the tops of red-patterned argyle socks that added to the incongruity of the garb. He examined the bare, hairy legs above the socks and let out a little sigh of satisfaction: there was well-established lividity on the backs of the legs, no sign of it on the fronts.

Over the years Toby had become something of an expert on forensic medicine, and he knew full well what this signified. The man had not committed suicide here, had not died here. He had been moved here several hours after his death, during which time he had lain on his back and the blood had settled in this unmistakable lividity pattern. This was a setup. And this, in Toby's book, made it murder, not suicide.

He retraced his steps to the head and, kneeling down, cautiously felt under the wimple to the sparse coarse hair at the back of the head. Again he nodded in satisfaction, for his questing fingers had encountered what he had anticipated: a lump on the back of the head. Solemnly he drew the veil back over the dead face. As he got up he became aware of a figure standing on the top of the embankment at the eastern entrance against the skyline, apparently watching him. He was about to wave away the intruder when the figure disappeared from the crest, and though he strained his eyes to see if it was approaching through the eastern gateway there was no further sign of movement.

Turning his back on the dew pond and its ghastly burden, he lit up his pipe and began to pace up and down. He was sorely troubled. What was he dealing with here? A second ritual murder badly disguised as a suicide? Or a well-thought-out, deliberate, and cold-blooded one to remove an awkward old man from the scene? There was one thought he could not push aside: he had been deliberately maneuvered, first to the site and then to the dew pond to make this discovery, and this brought him squarely to the troubled and overwrought Stephen Farwell.

He was sure that the student he *had* known would have been as incapable of murder as he was himself, but a lot can happen to a man in 15 years. The present Stephen Farwell was one great and mysterious question mark. Toby had come over the years to hate murder and murderers, and this time he was determined not to do what in times past he had often done. This time he would not hold anything back from the police. As soon as they got here, he would confide his findings to them and let the chips fall where they may. With this worthy purpose in mind he started to walk towards the western entrance to greet the forces of the law.

Chapter 4

After what had seemed an interminable wait, Chief Inspector Robert Hardy of the Dorset Constabulary came as an unexpected and very welcome surprise to the troubled Toby. Of medium height, his broad-shouldered figure gave an immediate impression of solidity and authority, an impression augmented by a serene long-nosed face and sparkling brown eyes that snapped with a quick intelligence. He had appeared at the head of a small phalanx of followers, the majority in the somber dark uniforms of constables. The only one in civilian clothes, a short dark man with a dapper mustache, bore the badge of his trade in the small black bag he carried. Over them all towered the tall form of Stephen Farwell; pale as a ghost, he was looking more wretched than ever.

After introductions had been made, Toby sailed desperately into action. "Inspector, Doctor, before proceeding to the dew pond, may I have a word with you alone? It is important."

The inspector's shrewd dark eyes searched the troubled blue ones and he gave an abrupt nod. "Certainly, Sir Tobias. I'll just secure the perimeter." He lifted his voice slightly. "Roberts, you guard this entrance and let no one inside until I say otherwise. Dickson, you get over to the east entrance and do the same." He eyed the stricken Stephen. "And, Mr. Farwell, if you would just give a brief statement on the circumstances of the finding of the body to Sergeant Wood here, we need not detain you any longer. Just be sure not to mention this to *anyone* until you hear from us further. All right? We will contact you at the museum."

Stephen reacted slowly. "But . . . Sir Tobias . . . I . . ."

"We'll see Sir Tobias gets back," Hardy interrupted. "You've had quite a shock, knowing the deceased and all, so if you don't feel up to driving, one of my men will take you back in your own car."

Stephen looked uncertainly at Toby and then away. "No, that's not necessary. I can manage," he muttered, and the rotund Sergeant Wood produced his notebook and led him away towards the southern embankment.

"The rest of you remain here for the moment," Hardy ordered and stepped briskly away from the group towards the northern rim, followed by Toby and the doctor. As soon as they were out of earshot he swung around. "All right, Sir Tobias, what is it?"

"It's murder, not suicide. And the murder did not occur here. The body was brought here several hours after death and deliberately placed in the dew pond," Toby stated bluntly. He looked apologetically at the doctor. "I am sure the doctor will confirm this as soon as he examines the body. I have not disturbed it in any way but I have looked at it," and he rapidly related his findings. "Furthermore," he concluded, "I think you will find that the body of Colonel Orchard was dressed in that absurd Druid's getup *post* mortem. For one thing, there are only faint blood stains on the front of it—doubtless from seepage—and if he had been wearing it at the time of his murder it would have been blood-soaked; for another, I located an abrasion on the back of the head under the headdress, and there was some gritty substance on it which needs to be analyzed. This would be impossible if the blow had been delivered *while* he was wearing it. There are some other factors, but you'll see those for yourselves. This, of course, indicates that the murderer not only knew the Colonel well enough to get close to him but also had access to and knowledge of his house."

The doctor was openly gaping at him, but Inspector Hardy's eyes were veiled, his mouth clamped in a thin line. "Quite a bombshell you've just dropped, Sir Tobias. Then let's get to it."

"Wait, there's one more thing." Toby's tone was urgent. "Apart from ourselves I feel it is very important that you should continue to treat this as a suicide."

"Indeed! Why?" The inspector eyed him curiously.

Toby cleared his throat. "Er, I understand that you have had another murder recently—within the Eggardon Hill earthwork? A man with his throat cut?"

Hardy nodded. "Go on."

"Well, although a clumsy attempt has been made by the murderer to make this look like a suicide, the elements and *modus operandi* are very similar: an Iron Age earthwork, the ritualistic trappings, the blood sacrifice angle . . ."

Hardy drew in his breath sharply. "Is that why you are here? For the Eggardon Hill murder?" he demanded.

"No, not at all!" Toby was alarmed. "I came down yesterday at Mr. Farwell's request to look over his proposed henge excavation plans. He's a former student of mine. He just happened to mention the murder in, er, casual conversation because he was upset by the unfortunate publicity it drew to the area."

Hardy seemed to relax. "Just asking. You see I am well aware of your reputation, Sir Tobias. I was at Scotland Yard during the Brighton Pavilion murder, though not directly involved. Moved back down here five years ago. I'm a Dorset man and the wife and I had had enough of London." He paused. "And I agree with you, until we know a lot more about this I do intend to treat it as a suicide." He looked across at the startled doctor. "Dr. Canfield, if your findings bear Sir Tobias out, I know I can depend on you to go along with this charade. The last thing we need here is more sensational publicity. Besides, if we've got a double murderer on our hands, it should lull him into a nice false sense of security."

It was Toby's turn to gape, as the inspector turned back to his clutch of constables and bellowed at the man bearing the rolled-up canvas stretcher, "Smith, I need you and one other at the dew pond. And when Sergeant Wood is through with Mr. Farwell, tell him to join us there. One of you others see Mr. Farwell on his way and the rest of you can get back to the station." He turned back to Toby. "Lead on! Thank God the early hour and the damp have kept the tourists away. At least it'll give us a short breathing space before the news breaks."

"Er, there was someone here," Toby confessed as they started off towards the dew pond. "Up on the top of the east entrance embankment. I couldn't make out if it was a man or woman—the sun was behind the figure. Whoever it was did not enter the enclosure."

Hardy cast a knowing eye over the terrain as they came up to the pond and its grim contents. "I'll send a man up to see what can be seen from there. Let's hope it isn't much." And as he and the doctor began their examination Toby turned away, lit up his pipe, and began to pace slowly. At the west entrance he made out Stephen's unmistakable figure going out with a constable and the tubby figure of Sergeant Wood advancing towards the pond. As the sergeant came abreast of him he halted and said in a rich Dorset accent, "Sergeant 'Ood, sir. Nasty business, eh? I always thought the Colonel a bit on the queer side, sure enough, but I never thought he'd be one to do himself in—him being a World War Two hero and all."

"You knew him?"

"Well in a manner of speaking I did. I'm a Charmouth man, and that being nigh Stanton St. Gabriel, y'see. Often had an official word with him about his goings-on, unofficially, if you know what I mean."

"Er, no," Toby confessed.

"Well, he was always out and about with them instruments

of his alooking for them ley lines, and some of the landowners thereabouts didn't fancy him trespassing y'see. Always leaving gates open and letting the animals out he was. So, knowing I was in the force like, they were always asking of me to have a quiet word with him. Didn't do no good. Always perfectly pleasant he was, but next thing you'd know he'd be at it again. Lived in his own world he did."

"Is there a family?"

"Colonel was a widower. But there is a daughter. Works over in Poole, I believe. One of those new fancy outfits over there. Not too close were the two of them, tho' she stabled a horse with him at St. Gabriel. Only times I ever seen her was when she came for the riding. Still, a proper shock to her it'll be sure enough." His amiable red face became owlishly solemn. "Even worse for the old couple who tended to him like. Been with him for years. Orchards too they are, but not close kin." His fount of information dried up suddenly as Inspector Hardy came up to them looking grim.

"Sergeant, I want photographs of the body from every angle before it's moved. Get Smith on it, will you? Bag the razor and take samples of the rainwater in the pond. As soon as you've done, get the body into the body bag and over to the hospital. Dr. Canfield is leaving now and will wait there to do the post-mortem right away. You stay with him until it's finished then bring the preliminary report and all Orchard's clothing back to me at the station for further forensic testing. Oh, and if anyone asks you anything, this is an *apparent* suicide. Is that all clear?"

"Yes, Inspector." The slightly puzzled Wood took himself off.

Hardy turned back to Toby with a sigh. "You were right on all counts by the looks of it. There's no doubt that Orchard was killed elsewhere and moved here later."

"Could the doctor estimate time of death?" Toby asked anxiously.

"What with all the rain and the cold we've had and the body being in water, he won't even make a near guess until after the post-mortem. By the amount of rigor left he guessed sometime late last night but warned me he probably wouldn't be able to narrow it down to a precise time. I'm not sure what we've got here—another fake ritual killing or a deliberate copycat killing. That bump on Orchard's head got Canfield very upset, since it conjures up a very ugly picture of the murder. The old boy was knocked unconscious first and then his throat cold-bloodedly cut—from the front, Canfield thinks; very nasty." He shook his head. "So, now suppose you tell me the rest of it, Sir Tobias, and I'll let you go about your business—whatever that is."

It jolted Toby. "I don't know what you mean," he stuttered.

Hardy's eyes were flinty. "Oh, come on! I don't know much about archaeology, but I do know the difference between a henge site and an Iron Age village. So how come you and Farwell so conveniently ended up here inspecting a dew pond that just happened to have a body in it? I know discovering a body is upsetting—though *you* seem calm enough about it—but I've never seen anyone quite as upset as Farwell. When he came bursting into the station he acted as if he was round the bend, and he looks as if he hasn't slept for a week. So what's up?"

The inspector had put Toby's own fears and suspicions firmly up front, but he was too uncertain and too upset to deal with them now: he took refuge in arrogant stuffiness. "The explanation is perfectly simple. We came up here because it is the best place to get an overview of the henge sites in the area—Mount Pleasant, Maumbury, and the new one. While we were here, as archaeologists often do, we got into a discussion about one of the unsolved mysteries of this site—the source of its water supply—and so naturally gravitated to the well behind us and then on to the dew pond here. That's all there was to it. As for Mr. Farwell's reaction, he's been under a lot of stress, because the upcoming henge excavation is an extremely important one and he's been having trouble finding the funding for it, which is why he came to me for advice. Also, after the many murder investigations in which I've been involved, some a lot more gruesome than this one, I have become inured to the sight of death, whereas I doubt whether Stephen has ever seen a body, and certainly not one he knew well, in such arcane circumstances. In his already-stressed state it was a final straw . . ." He suddenly decided to attack: "I also resent your implication that I am holding anything back. I have gone to considerable pains to give you what I discovered prior to your arrival, thereby saving you from the possibility of making an initial mistake in the matter and saving you a lot of time. And I *strongly* resent the implication that I am in Dorset for any other purpose than the archaeological project for which I was summoned."

His pomposity paid off, for Inspector Hardy promptly backed off. "No need to get on your high horse, Sir Tobias! I didn't mean to upset you. Now that you've explained it, it all sounds very reasonable. You have to understand that this rural area is usually a peaceful and law-abiding one, and now to have two grotesque murders in as many weeks has got me on the jump. In fact, I'm very sorry for that last crack of mine. If you were here to look into the Eggardon Hill affair, well, to be quite honest, I'd welcome your help, because I'm at sea on it. I don't want to call in the Yard if I can help it. Our chief constable is a prickly sort who doesn't like outside investigations; they upset a lot of the local bigwigs."

Toby relaxed: for his own peace of mind he needed to be in on the action and the quick-minded man before him had just issued a gilt-edged invitation. He made up his mind on the instant. "Since I am going to be staying here on the excavation business anyway, I'd be delighted to assist you in any way I can," he said. "In fact, one of your remarks intrigued me enormously. Referring to the Eggardon Hill murder you used the words 'fake ritual murder.' Does that mean that there isn't any Wicca or Satanist witchcraft going on in Dorset?"

Hardy gave a snort of laughter. "Never has been any of that modern claptrap down here, but witchcraft of the old kind?—plenty of that, I assure you. Ask any of our clergy, or go to the county library here. Shelvesful on Dorset witchcraft, they've got. I've been reading some of them myself. Always been a rare place for it, Dorset has, though, interestingly enough, more for its warlocks than its witches. It's the men down here that were the healers and the seers; some of the big families involved too." Hardy warmed to his subject. "Take the Gorge family now. Came over with the Conqueror and did very well for themselves around here. Owned big chunks of Dorset; Shipton Gorge, for instance, got its name from them, but their main holdings were around Bradpole, Powerstock, and Bridport, where I'm from. Warlocks, then alchemists, through the centuries they were, and, as so often happened, as the lord went so went the manor."

"I can see I have a lot to learn. Are they still around?" Toby demanded.

Hardy shook his head. "No, long gone as lords, but their influence stayed around until the beginning of this century."

"Then why don't you think the Eggardon Hill man could be tied in with this witchcraft?" With his own additional knowledge Toby was puzzled.

Hardy shrugged. "Well, I could be dead wrong, but old Job Squires was a no-account. In fact it was only by accident that he was identified as quickly as he was. At first we thought it was a hobo murder and robbery, apart from the scythe, but then one of our constables, who is from Shipton Gorge, identified the body for us. There was nothing *on* him, you see. All his pockets were cleaned out except for a few coppers. No identification at all. Clothing all old and ragged, he looked like a seedy old bum, and I believe *was* pretty much of an old drunk and layabout. Made his living, such as it was, at odd jobs—gardening, hedging, lambing in season, and so on—and lived alone in a tumble-down old cottage on the outskirts of the village. Sort of man you never notice until he dies."

"Somebody obviously did," Toby rumbled, deep in thought. "And why rob a man like that? There was absolutely nothing on him?"

"Nothing to identify him. We did find a wadded-up bit of paper in one pocket under the coins, but all it had on it was a couple of words written in pencil—'Mother Crowns'."

Toby perked up. "But surely that could be a witch name, couldn't it?"

Again the inspector shrugged. "Not likely. It wasn't written 'Mother Crowns.' 'Mother' was on one line and 'Crowns' was below it. I can show it to you, if you want. It doesn't really make any sense."

He was interrupted by the return of Sergeant Wood who wheezed, "All done, Inspector. Took all three of us to get the Colonel onto the stretcher, what with them wet robes and him being a big man and all. Oh, and I noticed something. I never seen the Colonel without a gold signet ring: always wore it on his right little finger. Well, it's not on him now, but he's still got his gold wrist watch on."

"Indeed!" Hardy turned back to the dew pond and gave it a final inspection. "Once you've got the body on its way, you, Smith, better get back here and go over the whole area to see if the ring is anywhere around. It may just have slipped off. Search the whole enclosure to see if you can pick up on it or anything else. When you've finished you can return with Roberts and Dickson. There's no further need to keep the place closed off."

He and Toby followed in silence as the men gathered up their heavy burden and trudged slowly off towards the west entrance. Heavy-laden though they were, their footsteps left no impression on the damp turf. Hardy heaved a dispirited sigh. "It was like this at Eggardon, not a hope of a footprint to indicate how many were involved or how they came and went."

"This time there must have been at least two," Toby said. "No single person, unless he were a giant with supernormal strength, could have managed the dead weight of a body that size. Again, that points to group action rather than a single murderer, doesn't it? Tell me, where do the local Druids fit in? Are they involved in local witchcraft?"

"I can see you like this *group* angle," Hardy muttered back. "But at this stage I can't be of much help. First time I've run across them. I know they exist. There was a piece in the paper the other day about the Dorset Druids and their proposed pilgrimage to Stonehenge for the midsummer solstice, which is coming up soon. Surprised me, because their spokesman was Colin Roper. He's a local estate agent and land developer and by all accounts as shrewd and hard-headed as they come: last person in the world I'd have thought would be involved in all this antique nonsense. Wood may know something about the Colonel's involvement with them . . ." he broke off. "Ah, here's Smith coming back, so I'd best be off to the station. There'll be a lot to do. I'll drop you wherever you like downtown—the museum?"

As they started to move towards the entrance and the hurrying constable, Toby thought quickly before answering. "No, with Farwell so upset, we'll not get much done today. Er, I was wondering, if you indeed would like some help, if it would be all right if I went over to Stanton St. Gabriel and took a look at the Colonel's house? I understand there's an elderly couple who looks after it, and it may be useful to find out his movements yesterday and where those robes were kept. I have my own car here and I'm staying at Woolaston Lodge downtown, so you can just drop me off at the station and I'll walk back from there."

Hardy grimaced. "A bit irregular, but in these circumstances, okay. I was going to send Sergeant Wood to break the news to them, but he'll be tied up for some time and we should alert the daughter first in any case. Tell you what. Come back to the station with me, and while you make a brief statement to go with Farwell's about the finding of the body, I'll make you out an official-looking chit to say I'm authorizing you to make inquiries. Country people can be very close-mouthed with strangers, so I suggest you don't tell them who you are, but say you're a friend of Wood's and are helping him out. I'll tell him what's happening when he gets back."

"Fine with me," Toby agreed, as they emerged from the west entrance to see a small gaggle of tourists gazing up curiously at them from the parking lot and a man with a large dog arguing with the constable on guard. He felt he was now in on the action and that was precisely where he wanted to be.

"Oh, just one other thing," Hardy said casually, as they climbed into his car and drove off through the gawking crowd. "Because of your remarkable reputation I am going out on a limb on this, and I trust that you will not put me through what you put Inspector Gray through on the Brighton case. I want to know *everything* you find and are doing, and if I see the faintest sign of flimflamming on your part, you will be *out* of it. Is that understood?"

Toby smiled grimly. "As you well know, I had very special personal reasons for acting as I did back then. Believe me, this time the only personal interest I have is to see justice done. You shall know everything I know. In all my other cases, if you look into them, you will find that I have always worked very well with the police."

Hardy gave a sudden chuckle. "Come to think of it, it's your partner, Dr. Spring, who has the reputation of being a major headache to the authorities. Where is she, by the way?"

"God only knows, for I surely don't," Toby said in sudden gloom.

Chapter 5

It was already afternoon before Toby set out on his quest for the Orchards', as a pleasantly fruitful delay had occurred after he had returned to his lodgings to pick up his car and his brandy flask, for which he felt an urgent need. The inquisitive Gwen was mercifully not visible, but as he let himself in, Owen's head popped out of the kitchen door. He was munching on a sandwich. "Anything I can do for you, Sir Tobias?"

Toby eyed the sandwich thoughtfully. "You couldn't make me up one of those, could you? I'm off on an expedition and don't know when I'll be back. Oh, and you don't happen to have an ordnance survey map of this area I could borrow? I'm told the place I'm after is off the beaten track."

"No problem. Let me take you up to my den on the top floor. You can browse through my reference books and take what you want, while I rustle you up a sandwich down here. Good bit of home-cured Dorset ham, and then maybe a bit of cheddar and biscuits with a noggin of Nut Brown to wash it down?"

"Sounds great," Toby agreed as he followed Ap Jones's wiry figure up the two flights of stairs to a small room that he realized was just above his own and was crammed with bookshelves. "Why this is a regular treasure-trove, Owen!" he exclaimed, examining the ranked reference books that included

Hutchinson's vast *History of Dorset*, a *Crockford's Clerical Directory*, an up-to-date *Who's Who*, an old *Burke's Landed Gentry*, a *Military Register*, and a multitude of maps and guide-books.

"I find it pays to know the people you're dealing with in the antiques business," said the canny Owen. "Help yourself, and when you're done, come on down to the kitchen and your lunch will be ready."

Toby struck out on the *Who's Who* and the *Burke's* but located the late Colonel in the *Military Register*. All he learned from the terse entry was that Orchard had been a product of Sherborne and Sandhurst, had earned a DSO as a captain in the closing days of World War Two, and had spent most of his postwar career in Austria and Germany, with a short stint at NATO headquarters in Brussels, and the remainder in England. From his given birth date Toby calculated Orchard to have been in his 75th year when he came to his gruesome end. He found the survey map he needed and descended to his impromptu lunch.

Owen had finished eating but had poured two pint tankards of ale and settled cosily at the table opposite Toby. "So you and Farwell are off on some more exploring?" he grinned.

Toby decided to humor him. "No, on a little of my own. I'm looking for Stanton St. Gabriel, St. Gabriel's House to be exact."

"Old Orchard's place? Oh, that's easy enough. Go right out west on A35 and halfway between Chideock and Morecomblake, just past Langdon Hill on your left, take the little side road to the left. Keep on it till you get to a cross-roads, then another left and it'll run you right up to the house. Can't miss it," Owen said quickly.

"You know Colonel Orchard?" Toby prompted.

"Bought a couple of things off him a while back. Doesn't have much, but I got a nice little Sheraton writing desk and matching chair and a Victorian chaise longue. Think they might have been stuff of his late wife's. Anyway he needed some quick cash for some of that seismic equipment of his. A bit batty, if you ask me, in a Colonel Blimpish kind of way. Don't get him on the subject of ley lines or he'll talk your ear off."

"I'll remember that," Toby evaded, getting up. "And thanks for your help, Owen. Now be sure to put this lunch on my bill."

"Oh, that's all right," Owen said cheerfully. "Nice to have a bit of company. Gwen's off doing the marketing and I'm stuck here until our next bookings check in, otherwise I'd have been glad to guide you. I know this area like the back of my hand."

"Well, thanks again. I'll certainly take you up on that sometime," Toby said as he went on his way.

Owen's directions were so exact that Toby reached the tiny hamlet before he was really prepared for it. He slowed down to a stop as he reached the T junction that signaled the end of the secondary road. Dead ahead of him was a pleasant, large-windowed early Victorian house that announced itself as "St. Gabriel's" on a discreet sign by a driveway slightly to his right. Postponing what he knew would be a painful interview and dithering in his mind about how best to approach it, Toby inspected the narrow lane that constituted the top stroke of the T: to his left it ended in what appeared to be the ruins of a church, huddled under the towering mass of Golden Cap cliff; to his right the road extended a little further, but the only other sign of habitation was the gray slate roof of a house behind a high hedge about halfway down it. Could that be Gulliver's house? he wondered, and craned around for any other sign of habitation. There was none. "Well, I've heard of remote, but this is ridiculous!" he muttered to himself, starting up again and turning slowly into the marked driveway.

As he curved around to the front of the house, he saw that it was flanked on the left by a large stable-barn that appeared of more ancient vintage than the house itself. Its doors were wide open and he could make out a jaunty little red sports car drawn up behind a very battered-looking Land Rover. The other half of the barn still held its original horse stalls, and, as he turned off the engine and climbed out, he could hear the gentle whickering of horses. Apart from this there was no sound or other sign of life. To the right of the house there was a narrow, freshly graveled lane apparently running down to the sea whose distant murmurings he could just make out. On the other side of the lane, a small cottage sat at right angles to the house, again of older vintage than the house itself. On closer inspection, both house and grounds had a slightly rundown look to them.

Nerving himself up, he strode over to the faded, black-painted front door and pulled on the old-fashioned wrought-iron bell pull beside it. Its tolling was unexpectedly loud in the silence but elicited no response, even when he tolled again.

Nonplussed, he stepped back and gazed up at the closed windows, then started towards the lane, intending to try again at the back. He was startled to see further down the lane a very new and shiny powerboat sitting upon an equally shiny and expensive-looking boat trailer. As he started off towards it, a door flew upon and a high, clear voice behind him said, "Were you looking for someone?"

He swung around to see the tall, slim figure of a chestnut-haired girl standing in the doorway of the cottage. She was dressed in riding clothes—jodhpurs, shining leather boots, a smart tweed hacking jacket, and white silk shirt; the impeccable effect was rather marred by the large Dagwood-type sandwich on which she was munching. "Er, yes, I was looking for Colonel Orchard's housekeeper," he volunteered.

"There's nobody home," she said between nibbles. "Martha and Joe are probably off to Lyme to see their ghastly granddaughter, who is always in some state of crisis. God knows where Father is—the car's here so he must be off somewhere, London probably. You could leave a message with me. I'll see Martha gets it. I'm Margaret Orchard."

Toby's round eyes widened in surprise, for by his estimation the girl was certainly not out of her 20s. "You are Colonel Orchard's daughter?" he queried.

"Yes, and you are?" she retaliated.

He was suddenly panic-stricken. "Um, Sir Tobias Glendower," he stuttered.

"My, my!" she drawled, stepping out of the doorway towards him. "Martha *will* be impressed. It's not often she gets knightly visitors driving up in Rollses."

He was in an agony of indecision. "Miss Orchard, have you, er, been contacted by the police this morning? We understood you were in Poole."

"The *police*? Why no, whatever for? Don't tell me you're a policeman! Have we had a burglary, or has some landowner given Father a horse whipping he probably thoroughly deserved? I only got here an hour ago and there was no one here when I arrived. I'm waiting around for a friend—a riding date." She seemed amused.

"Then, please, do as I ask! Please ring Dorchester police station and ask for Inspector Robert Hardy. He'll explain everything. I'm afraid it's bad news," Toby said desperately. "I'll wait out here."

"Oh, for Heaven's sake, come on in and sit down, do! Rapists don't usually drive around in Rollses and tell their victims to call the police!" She had sobered but her tone was exasperated. "In what era are you living, Sir Tobias?" And she stamped back inside.

After a moment of confusion Toby followed her in and perched gingerly on a chintz-covered wing chair. The girl sat on a matching sofa and dialed the phone on the pie-crust table beside her. Once put through, she listened intently, her long fine-boned face impassive, the only sign of tension a slow whitening of the knuckles on the long slim hand that grasped the phone. When she did break silence it came as another shock to Toby. "Think again, Inspector," she said tightly. "You've obviously got it all wrong. My father may have been a batty old man, but he's the last man in the world who would have taken his own life. You can talk until you're blue in the face, but you won't convince *me:* it has to be murder." Her eyes blazed over at Toby. "Yes, he's here." She thrust the phone at him. "This idiot wants to talk to you." She sprang up and stalked off into the adjoining room.

"I realize you can't say much, but how long has she been there?" Hardy's voice demanded.

"Not long. And the others aren't here," Toby said.

"She isn't buying it, is she?"

"Apparently not."

"We may have to tell her. Wood's just back with the preliminary. The doctor puts the time of death between ten and midnight. He can't narrow it further. From the lividity he estimates the body must not have been moved until at least three hours after death, in other words between one and three in the morning. I'd wager between two and three, after the rain stopped. She seems to be out of it so far as direct participation goes. She was at an office party over in Bournemouth last night until well after midnight and was in her Poole office briefly this morning. Does she seem a sensible sort, not the gabby kind?"

"Yes, so it seems," Toby murmured as she came back into the room and sat down in the vacated wing chair, her expression wooden, her eyes defiant. There were no signs of grief or tears.

"Then use your own judgment. If you think she'll keep quiet, tell her the truth and swear her to secrecy. I've just sent Wood out to give you a hand there. All right with you? Call me when you're through."

"Right," Toby said heavily and cradled the phone. He turned back to the impassive girl. "I realize this has been a most terrible shock for you, Miss Orchard, and I do not wish to add to the burden of your grief, but, if I tell you something in the strictest confidence, can we depend on you to keep silence and go along with what we have to do? It is of the utmost importance, I assure you, or we would not ask this of you."

Her brown eyes narrowed. "Yes, I can keep my mouth shut if need be. What is it?" Her tone was razor sharp.

"There is going to be an inquest on your father, as the inspector explained, and from the evidence that will be presented the verdict will be 'suicide while of unsound mind.'" He paused then went on softly. "But this is not so. You were correct. Your father did not take his own life—he was cold-bloodedly murdered, and our best chance of bringing the murderer to justice will be to let him think he has got away with it. In the end the record *will* be set straight, I promise you. So, will you help us?"

She let out a long sigh and sprawled back in the chair. "I knew it, I just knew it. Yes, I'll help. But who in the world would want to murder that old idiot?"

This so jolted Toby that he let out a small involuntary growl of protest and she looked up at him, a faint grim smile on her firm mouth. "That shocks you, does it? Sit down, Sir Tobias, and listen, for I imagine we'll be seeing quite a lot of each other from now on and it's important you understand. My father was nothing to me and I was nothing to him, and it has always been like that. He was in his late 40s and my mother just 40 when I was born. They had been married for 20 years and when a child did arrive it was too late and I was of the wrong sex, so my father simply ignored my existence. My late birth really took it out of my mother and she was a semi-invalid from then on. That's when Martha and Joe entered our ménage, but even with their help the combination of my father and me was too much for the poor soul. She died when I was six. After that . . ." her mouth gave an involuntary quiver, "well, I was packed off to boarding school and there I stayed, holidays included, unless some off-relative took pity and invited me to stay. He never visited, hardly ever wrote. I was simply a nuisance that had to be taken care of but otherwise played no part in his life." She sprang up suddenly. "I could use a drink—can I get you one? I have Scotch or brandy."

"Er, brandy, thank you," Toby murmured.

"Soda, water, ice?" she said, rummaging in a small antique corner cupboard.

"Soda, no ice."

With deft efficiency she fixed two tall drinks, handed Toby his, and resumed her seat. "When I became a teen-ager and somewhat harder to ignore, things got worse, not better. Not only was there the tremendous generation gap but my father was extremely old-fashioned in his ideas, more nineteenth than twentieth century. Women to him were purely domestic creatures who were supposed to look after men, produce children, and arrange flowers, if so inclined. He hated the very idea of a career woman. His plans for me—such as they were—ran along those lines. I was to get my O levels, go to a domestic science college to learn housewifely arts, have a stint as an *au pair* girl in France to polish my French, presumably to make me more attractive on the marriage market, and then either marry or, more likely, come and be his unpaid hostess and housekeeper until death did us part. Well, I had other ideas." Again a grim smile played on her lips. "I was lucky in that I had a very understanding and helpful headmistress. I've always had a flair for mathematics and an aptitude for computers, and she encouraged me no end. Somehow she managed to wangle it that he allowed me to stay and take my A levels, but then the balloon went up when I wanted to go on to college. No way was he going to pay for *that!* But," her face lit up, "in spite of him I managed it. I won a partial scholarship to Reading University and that, with a little money my mother left me, was enough to see me through; first a B.Sc. in mathematics and economics, and then I went on to get my CPA. My father was so furious that he didn't speak to me for years."

She got up again and, without even asking, replenished both their drinks, her face taut with remembrance. Sinking back in the wing chair, she continued. "I'm good at what I do and have done very well. I have a very good job with a great salary—for a woman." Her lips twisted in a wry smile. "I suppose you could say it was that which brought about a thaw in our relationship. Father hadn't any money to speak of. All his savings went into buying this benighted place, leaving him with only his army pension, and that doesn't go very far these days. Nothing came of his cracked idea to make the house into a B and B—who would want to stay in Stanton St. Gabriel? So, when I moved to Poole and offered to rent this cottage and stable my horse with him, he fairly jumped at it. I've always loved to ride—about the only one of my activities my father ever approved—and it suited both of us. That's the way it has been for the past two years. I came down here on my days off, and on the rare occasions we'd run into each other we both managed to stay pleasant. End of sorry tale." She sat up straighter, a defiant gleam in her eye.

Toby roused himself from the depression into which her pitiful account had plunged him, but he was also puzzled. "Yes, I do understand and I am very sorry," he said in embarrassment. "But I am hoping you can throw some light on your father's recent activities. Er, you did say your father was not very well off, and yet I noticed a new and expensive-looking powerboat as I came in."

To his surprise a sudden blush mantled her high cheekbones. "Oh that's not his, that's Nicholas's new toy; Nicholas Squires, the vicar of Charmouth. He keeps it here because our track has easy access to a good beach. He stables his horse here also; another of Father's 'renters.' That reminds me . . ." She glanced at her watch and the blush intensified. "He's unusually late. We had a riding date. Maybe I'd better call and see what's up." She headed for the phone, but after dialing, hung up and shook her head. "No answer, so he's probably on his way." She remained standing, looking down at him. "Is there anything else I can do for you?"

"Well yes, quite a lot, I hope." Toby did not get up. "Do you have a key to the main house? There is something I'd very much like to check on while I'm here. Perhaps you could show me around?"

"I don't have a key, but I know where Martha keeps the spare to the back door. I could let you in, but I've hardly ever been in the place myself so I wouldn't be of much help. We weren't on visiting terms," she said with a hint of impatience.

His heart sank. "Then is there anything you can tell me about your father's involvement with the Druids?"

This startled her and for a second she just stared at him. "The Druids! Well, yes, come to think of it, he did mention he was thinking of joining—quite recently it was. Something to do with Colin Roper? He was raving on as usual about those bloody ley lines and, yes, I remember now, he wanted to go to Stonehenge with the local Druids on Midsummer's Day; something about measuring to see if there was an added force to the field? It was all such nonsense I didn't pay much attention."

"Do you know where your father kept the paraphernalia?" Toby pressed.

"You mean his scientific doodads? Yes, they are in one of the stable stalls. He usually kept it locked."

"No, I mean his Druid's regalia."

"Never knew he had any. Not the faintest idea. What's that got to do with anything?" she began, when the door of the cottage suddenly quivered under a fusillade of knocks. "Meg, Meg, are you there? Please open up! I know I'm the last person in the world you want to see just now, but I have to see you. It's very important," a man's deep voice called urgently.

"Remember, whoever it is, not a word about murder," Toby warned.

With a startled glance at him, Margaret Orchard flew to the door and flung it open. The tall figure on the threshold, his hand still raised in the act of knocking, stood frozen as he gazed in at Toby: it was Stephen Farwell.

Chapter 6

After the poignantly intimate tête-à-tête that he had just experienced, Toby found himself firmly pushed into the background as a spectator in the ensuing action, which steadily increased in tempo. His own unexpected presence had so disconcerted Stephen Farwell that he had been well-nigh incoherent as he had mumbled out his condolences, none of which held the slightest indication of what the urgent import of his mission had been.

Margaret Orchard had also undergone a metamorphosis: from being the neglected waif/successful career woman of his interview, she had become, on the instant, the ultimate Ice Maiden, and Toby could not but admire her devastating performance. Stephen's own uncertainty had given her time to recover from the shock his appearance had so evidently given her. She heard out his stammered regrets in an absolute icy silence, until he had trailed off in despair and just stood gazing pleadingly at her. Then, in a few well-chosen sentences that dripped icicles from every word, she demolished him. She was perfectly polite, but the import was all too clear: she had no need for his condolences, no desire for his presence at this time, and the sooner he left the better off she would be; and, in the unlikely event that he should ever think of visiting her again, would he kindly call first as she did not appreciate impromptu visits when she was engaged with more important matters.

But Stephen's ultimate rout and precipitate flight came from another quarter. Once again there came knocking on the door and, with an offhand "Oh, that must be Nicholas," Margaret brushed past his frozen figure to open it, only to reveal the roly-poly form of Sergeant Wood, who touched his cap respectfully. "Good day, Miss Orchard. Sir Tobias told you I was coming? Thought you might like to know that we've contacted Joseph and Martha Orchard in Lyme and that they are on their way back, so you won't be alone at this sad time." His eyes slid past her to Stephen. "Well, well, and Mr. Farwell here too! Glad to see you all recovered from your shock of this morning. We've been trying to reach you at the museum but no one seemed to know where you were. So now I've found you."

Stephen roused himself from his dazed misery. "I am just returning to the museum, Sergeant," he said huskily. "Merely came to offer Miss Orchard my condolences and my help if needed, but it so obviously isn't that I'll be on my way."

He almost ran out of the door, as Wood called after him cheerfully, "Then we'll see you later."

The worst of it was that Toby could not make up his mind whether Stephen's pathetic performance was in his favor or another stroke against him, although the very fact that the young people knew or had known each other was another interesting lead for him to follow.

"Won't you come in, Sergeant?" Margaret, her cheeks still a becoming pink, said breathlessly. "It's started to rain again."

Wood glanced over his right shoulder. "Well, perhaps a little later, Miss, if you don't mind. I will have some questions about your father's affairs, but the Orchards have just pulled into the drive and I'd better have a word with them first. Fair upset they are. I'll be back to collect Sir Tobias presently, or would you like to come with me to the house?"

"I'm waiting for someone, but tell Martha and Joe I'll see

them later," she said and closed the door against the rain. She let out a little sigh and returned to the wing chair; a small, uncomfortable silence fell as she gazed unseeingly at Toby, who was searching his mind desperately for his next line of questions.

He was spared by another thunderous knock on the door. As Margaret sprang to her feet, it flew open and a rich, sonorous voice called, "Margaret, my dear, what on earth is up? The driveway is full of cars and I've just seen a policeman escorting the Orchards into the house. Has something happened?" The Reverend Nicholas Squires had finally arrived.

His appearance again came as a surprise and shock to Toby. Clad in riding clothes, he was a veritable oak of a man: tall and massively built, so that he appeared to block out the light as he towered in the doorway, his head was leonine and topped by a magnificent mane of gleaming silver hair.

As Margaret leapt to her feet and ran to him with "Oh, Nicholas, it's Father! He's dead," the massive head turned to her. In profile, with its high Roman nose and finely chiseled features, it reminded Toby of the matinee-idol actors of his youth: it was an outdated face, but of its time an incredibly handsome one.

But as Squires advanced into the light, one strong arm around Margaret's slim shoulders, Toby hastily revised his first impression, for the face that turned inquiringly to him bore the unmistakable signs of aging: a looseness about the skin of the jawline that in a year or two would become full-fledged dewlaps, slight pouches under the penetrating blue eyes that were just a little too small for the large face, and deep lines around the large mobile mouth. He was looking at a man not too far removed in age from his own. Though no psychologist, it only took him a second to conclude that Margaret had finally found the father figure she had always wanted.

His heart sank a little as she gazed confidingly up at Squires and said, "This is Sir Tobias Glendower, Nicholas. He came to

BCPL Discard/Damage Slip

Title: Dirge for a Dorset Druid

Barcode: 394777

Location: Media Type:

Staff
- o Discard ✓
- o Isolation
- o Patron Responsible
- o Damaged
- o Mend/Preserve /Bindery
- o Replace
- o Deleted
- o Processed
- o Problem

Dir. Notes
- o Promote
- o Book Sale
- o Donate/Send
- o Recycle

Other Copies/Locations of Title:

Replacement/Add. Info:

Damage Noted: STAINED

Patron Responsible:

Patron Barcode:

Donate/Send To:

Discard Note:

Date: 9/9 Staff Initials: E Dir. Initials:

your mom to read it over, but she's working late and won't be home in time to help.

Luckily, you can log on to Tutor.com:

By heading to Tutor.com/brookecpl

"Every single time I need help on my work, this ser-vice helps! It's like this little magical place where you can go and they help you understand what you're stuck on!"

—7th Grade Tutor.com User

math, science, languag
Prep, Microsoft Office

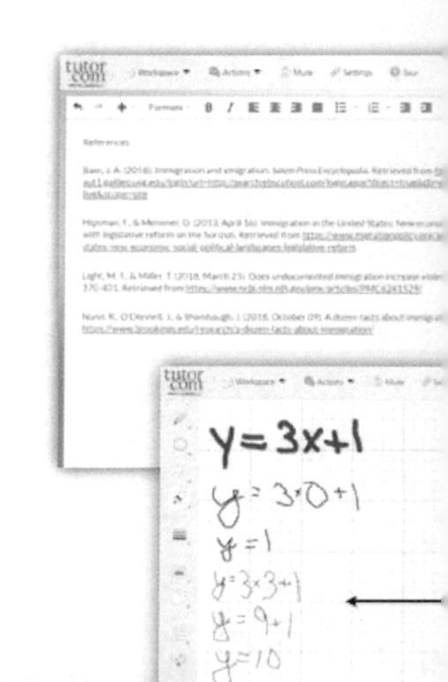

break the news and kindly stayed with me until you got here."

"Yes, I'm sorry I was so late, my dear," Squires said, as Toby uncoiled himself from the sofa and shook his meaty hand. "Some parish business came up at the last minute. But I still don't understand."

Toby cleared his throat. "I'm an archaeologist and was up looking at Maiden Castle this morning when Mr. Farwell and I made the sad discovery of Colonel Orchard's body. Er, I'm afraid it was a suicide."

This elicited a little choked exclamation from Margaret Orchard, who gazed at him wide-eyed. "Stephen was *with* you?"

"Oh, yes, very much so," Toby said blandly. "And very upset by it too. Well, now that you are here, Mr. Squires, I think I'll take my leave and search out Sergeant Wood." He reached into his wallet, extracted a card and started to scribble on the back of it. "If I can be of any assistance to you in any way at all, Miss Orchard, you can reach me at this address or phone number. I'll be staying in Dorchester for quite a while. Also, I repeat, in these unhappy circumstances you will probably be pestered for a while after the news breaks, but the less you say to *anyone* the sooner it will end."

"I understand, and thank you," she said faintly, as he went out. The rain had already stopped and the sun was struggling to break through the clouds. Toby noted a smart black Jaguar drawn up behind an old minicar and the sergeant's police car. Unless the Church of England had upped its pay scales one hell of a lot, he reflected, the vicar of Charmouth had to be a man of considerable private means.

He made purposefully for the back of the house and knocked at the back door, which was promptly opened by the sergeant, cup in hand. It revealed an old-fashioned kitchen and, seated at the white-scrubbed oak table, two old people partaking of that panacea for all English ills, a nice cup of tea. They were both of an age with the late Colonel; the little old woman hunched over, red-eyed and sniffling, the man dour-faced, his eyes downcast.

He was gripping his mug tightly with gnarled hands.

"Ah, there you are, Sir Tobias," Wood said cheerfully. "And here's Martha and Joe Orchard, and we can leave them to get over their shock like, while we check into things a bit." The old couple gazed dolefully after them as the sergeant led Toby out by a door on the opposite side of the room into a broad hallway that ran through to the front door; the house smelled of old age and stale tobacco smoke.

As soon as they were out of earshot, Wood began to talk rapidly. "Poor old devils, don't know what's hit 'em yet, so I haven't been able to get a lot out of 'em. I've made a quick check through the house, but there's no sign of disturbance or blood or anything, so I don't think it was here he bought it. The Orchards went off to Lyme about five yesterday and he was here and all right then, just pottering about. More trouble with that granddaughter of theirs, shoplifting this time. Proper little perisher she is and always has been: two illegitimate kids, lives off the State, and has been on booze and God knows what else since she was a teen-ager. Anyway, they called him last night about seven and he told 'em to stay there until they'd sorted the mess out and that he'd manage here. Always good to 'em he was."

"What about the clothes?" Toby interjected.

"Ah! Let's go up." Wood pointed up the stairs and led the way. "No mystery there, as you'll see, but I think you may be right about 'em. You could tell it puzzled Martha. Fair shook me it did when the doctor and the inspector explained the right of the matter, I can tell you."

"What puzzled Martha?" Toby was keeping his patience with an effort.

Wood led him into a pleasant, immaculate, and masculine bedroom. He indicated an open cardboard box that stood on one of the dressers. "The Druid doodads were in there. He only got 'em last week. What puzzled Martha was these." He indicated some neatly folded clothes on a chair by the bedside: an old tweed jacket, a flannel work shirt, and worn twill trousers. "You see, for a military man, old Orchard wasn't at all neat in his habits: always had a batman I suppose. So Martha couldn't get over how his clothes were folded up like that, 'cos he usually just dumped 'em all over the place and she'd pick up after him."

"Ah!" Toby was enlightened. "So whoever came in here took the robes, then, seeing the room was immaculately neat, folded the clothes he had taken off the Colonel himself. Did you find out who had keys to the house?"

"No, but I'm not sure that signifies." Wood shook his head ruefully. "Three-quarters of the time that back door was never locked. Not much cause to round here, you see. And half the time the Colonel'd keep the front door on the latch as well."

"I see. How about signs of blood on the clothes?"

"None, but his underpants and vest are missing. He was naked under them robes. So, looks as if he was knocked out, stripped down to his skivvies, then murdered and rigged out in them robes after. Nasty picture, eh?"

"Quite extraordinary!" Toby said. "Not only was it ill-done but why it was done in that bizarre way at all—it must have *some* significance. Anything on the razor?"

"No fingerprints other than his, but Martha doesn't think it *was* his, at least not to her knowledge: he used a safety razor. And the razor itself is nothing special, not fancy, no initials or anything like that. Sort that was as common as dirt around here 60 or so years ago. Lot of the farmers still use 'em for cutting twine, so they're often lying around in people's barns—just like the old scythe we found on Job Squires." He sighed heavily.

"You were at Eggardon Hill?" Toby queried. "Mind telling me about it?"

"Oh, yes, right on the spot I was. Poor old bugger. There was no doubt that *he* got it right there where he lay. Clothes were soaked in his blood and there was some on the scythe, but the doctor soon twigged it wasn't used in the murder. At the time he said it was done with something like a razor—could have been the same one that did the Colonel, come to that. Never did I see an expression on a dead face like Squires had. He looked so surprised!"

Toby was busy on his own train of thought. "You've so much valuable local knowledge, Sergeant. Tell me, do you know if there's any kinship connection between Job and the vicar of Charmouth?"

A strange expression flitted across Wood's bland face. "Ah, the Reverend Nicholas Squires!" he said. "One of a new breed he is, not like the clergy in my young days. I know he bears a local name, but he's only been around these parts a couple of years. A latecomer in all senses, you might say. After his last wife died he went to some kind of school the C of E has for latter-day parsons like him, and when he got out of it this was his first posting, or whatever they call it."

"Last wife?" Toby was puzzled.

Wood smiled grimly. "He's had three, each one richer than the last, so the story goes. Was some sort of businessman in the Midlands before he took the cloth. Very popular with the ladies is our vicar. My wife has been to church more in the past two years than in the whole of her previous life. Doesn't want to fall behind the crowd, y'see."

"What do you think of him?" Toby was blunt.

Wood was silent for a moment, then he said carefully, "I think the reverend is a man who knows exactly what he wants and doesn't stop till he gets it. He may be a man of God now, but in my opinion he is not a Godly man. But, so far as being connected with Job? No, I don't think so. If you're looking for a connection, more likely there's one right downstairs. Martha was a Squires from Chideock, where there have been Squires as long as Orchards—and Farwells, come to that." He slid an inquisitive glance at Toby. "I can ask her, but Job was not the kind of man that anyone readily claims as kin."

"Er, in your investigations did you see any indications that Job was involved in any kind of witchcraft?" Toby persisted.

"Funny you should ask that," Wood ruminated. "But I wouldn't be at all surprised myself. The inspector, when we found out about the scythe being a sort of prop, wasn't buying any of that, but, well, I looked over the shanty Job lived in and there were some things there that struck me as odd. For one thing: though the place was such a mess it was hard to say for sure, it looked as if it had been searched, but of course since we didn't know what he had, there was no way of telling if there was anything missing. But there were a lot of herbs there, both growing and dried, and a lot of booze bottles filled with various concoctions. I recognized one of 'em by its smell because one of my old grannies used to use it. It was weslic."

"Weslic?" Toby echoed blankly.

Wood grinned. "Yes, it's an old herbal liniment. According to my gran it'd cure anything from sprains to pneumonia. When I'd get bronchitis as a kid, she'd slap it on my chest first thing. Ponged something awful and burned even worse, but it worked every time. Dorset healers have always used it and, if Job was a healer, well, he may have been into other things as well."

"Hmm, very interesting." Toby looked around him, suddenly restless. "Is there anything else up here?"

"Not that I could find, but come on down to his study." For the first time Wood looked uncomfortable. "I took a quick run-through of his papers, and there's a couple of things." He led the way downstairs and into a very cluttered room to the left of the front door. There was a large desk covered with papers in the window, and an enormous table in the center of the room piled with papers and maps. "As you can see, this is going to take a lot of going through. All the stuff on the table is to do with that there book he was supposed to be writing. Can't make head nor tail of it myself. The desk here has his personal papers. I couldn't find a will, and Martha and Joe say that, to their knowledge, he never made one. But I did find this . . ."

He selected a long envelope and held it out to Toby, an unhappy expression on his face. "It's an insurance policy for 25,000 pounds taken out just after his wife died, which, if my memory serves me right, is about 20 years ago. His daughter is named as sole beneficiary."

Toby skimmed through it quickly and handed it back to him. "Are you thinking this could be a motive for murder?" Wood nodded miserably. "I know people have been murdered for a lot less than that," Toby observed, "but in this case I very much doubt it. For one thing, although 25,000 may have been a goodly sum back then, it's not a significant amount nowadays. Miss Orchard has a very good job and I'd be willing to bet she makes almost twice as much in a year. Granted, if he died intestate, she'll inherit everything, but everything, apart from his pension that dies with him, is apparently just this house which, I imagine, will be more of a burden than an asset, considering its remote situation and the present depressed real-estate market. So, no, I can't see this as a very tenable motive. We'll have to dig deeper than that, I'm afraid."

Wood looked relieved, but then saddened. "Put like that I see your point, but it leaves those old 'uns in a pretty pickle, doesn't it?" He jerked his head towards the kitchen. "I doubt the girl will even be able to keep the place going, let alone want to. So they'll be left without a roof over their heads and not a penny piece of the Colonel's to help them get one. What's to become of 'em?"

"I don't know, but at least it removes all suspicion of his murder from them," Toby replied grimly, "since they had the strongest motive for wanting him alive."

He was interrupted by the opening of the door. The lugubrious figure of Joseph Orchard marched in. "There's been a theft," he croaked and jerked his head. "Come and see." They exchanged startled glances and herded out after him, as he marched through the kitchen, where Martha was now hunched over the ironstone sink washing the dishes, still sniffling. He headed out the back door for the stables.

"What's missing, Joe?" Wood called, puffing along beside Toby, but only getting another jerk of the head. They gained the stable, which smelled of a curious mixture of hay, horses, and gasoline, and Toby noted with distaste that two of the horse stalls stood open and empty: in spite of death, the riding date had still gone on.

Their guide halted before the very last stall and jerked his head at the padlocked door. "Padlock's been broken," he said in an even richer Dorset accent than Wood's. "'Ooever done it put it back, but it's open and it warn't like that yesterday when I left." He demonstrated and swung the door open. "Colonel kept all of his stuff in 'ere and some of it's amissing."

"What's missing?" Wood asked, whipping out his notebook.

"Don't know," Joe growled.

Wood was red in the face. "What d'you mean, you don't know?"

"Don't know what that stuff is or does," Joe retaliated. "But I say some of it's amissing." He pointed a gnarled finger at what appeared to be large metal detector. "Something like that, but smaller. Came with a little black box and that's gone too. Colonel only had it a month or so. New it was."

Toby looked at Wood in consternation. "This does rather tear things. Suppose the Colonel came upon someone in the act?" he asked. "Maybe you'd better get some men out here to search around the stable to see if there's any sign of a struggle or blood—though with all the rain it'll be a slim hope . . ." He shook his head in perplexity. "But that doesn't make any sense either, no sense at all—why then the robes and the setup at the Maiden? Nothing fits together and nothing makes sense. God, I'm confused. Not only can't I see any light at the end of the tunnel, I can't even make out where the tunnel is!"

Chapter 7

Toby's state of confusion was not helped by the events of the next three days when nothing worked out quite as it was supposed to. Hardy had been forced to retreat from his wished-for and contrived suicide verdict, partly due to Dr. Canfield's unwillingness to fudge the medical evidence and partly to the coroner's unwillingness to condone the police's strategem. They had had to settle for an "open" verdict, "pending further police inquiries."

"At least it has *some* compensations," a resigned Hardy said to Toby when it was all over. "We can pursue our inquiries about the Colonel more openly and not have to use that senseless theft as an excuse."

Toby's own presence as witness at the inquest had not helped matters, for it had brought the reporters out in swarms: "What was he doing in Dorchester?" "Had the police called him in to assist them?" "Was this a murder investigation?" The old Toby would have fled, cringing before such pointed and pertinent questions, but the new Toby calmly stonewalled and went on about his archaeological reasons for being in the area at such ponderous length and interminable detail that even the most avid of the reporters dropped off in exhaustion or sheer boredom.

"I find if I can be boring long enough, it works every time," he had confided to Hardy, who openly admired his performance. "But I think I'll keep a low profile for a few days just to make sure they are off my back. I've plenty in mind to do during that time."

"I would like you to show up at the funeral and go back to the house afterwards," Hardy said anxiously. "Everybody who was closely connected to the old boy will be there, like Roper, the museum board members, and so on. I've already spoken to Margaret Orchard about it and she's all for it. Sergeant Wood and I will go to the funeral, but we can scarcely go back to the house. People shut up like mussels if we're around, but you'll get to meet them all and may pick up something useful. It's on Tuesday, interment in Charmouth and then the funeral reception at St. Gabriel's. She's gone back to Poole until then to finish up some business and arrange for leave. Not exactly heartbroken, I'd say. Do you think she will keep her mouth shut?"

Toby shrugged. "I certainly hope so, but I wouldn't guarantee it. She seems pretty close to the vicar."

"Well, if she spills to him that should be safe enough," Hardy said comfortably. "Vicars are used to keeping their mouths shut, and he's not connected in any way. Witches and Druids are scarcely in his line, and what motive could he possibly have?"

"None I suppose," Toby sighed, but brought up a question that had been niggling at the back of his mind. "Have you had any trouble with smuggling around here in recent years?"

Hardy looked at him in amazement. "Smuggling what? Dope? No, it's a problem we've mercifully been spared. Oh, like everywhere else these days there's a certain amount of drug *users* in the bigger towns who account for a lot of the petty crime, but Dorset is too far off the beaten track to make it a good target area. It's not like the southeast coast or the major ports."

"Not necessarily dope." Toby was clinging stubbornly to his vague idea.

"Then what else? With the Common Market in full swing, all the old standbys like booze, Swiss watches and such aren't worth the risk anymore. Whatever gave you that idea?"

"We are looking for a *motive* for Orchard's murder, and it did strike me that with St. Gabriel's being so remote and with easy access to a good beach it would be an ideal place for it. And the vicar of Charmouth does have a big powerboat sitting there."

Hardy just laughed at him. "In the eighteenth century and the era of brandy and French lace, you might have had something: it *was* a choice smuggling area. But now? And powerboats are common around here, the latest status symbol for the ones with enough lolly. No, you can forget that. The motive has to lie a lot closer to home than that. By the way, how are Farwell's excavation plans coming along? Did quite well at the inquest I thought."

Toby tensed slightly, for this sudden change of subject was uncomfortably close to home and he wondered if Hardy's own suspicions were veering in that direction. "Yes, he did," he agreed, "and there are still a lot of arrangements to be made on the excavation plans, but then we still have a month to go."

In actual fact he had scarcely seen Stephen since the fiasco at Margaret Orchard's. Farwell had not contacted him and this had suited Toby well enough. Until he had more information and could make up his own mind about Stephen, he felt direct confrontation was best avoided. They had had a brief encounter prior to the inquest at which Farwell had been apologetic about his neglect, pleading pressure of museum business and trips to London concerning the funding. Although still haggard he appeared somewhat calmer and had indeed given a good showing at the inquest itself and with the reporters after it, parrying their questions as deftly as Toby himself had done. He had appeared to be as puzzled as they were about the "open" verdict.

Toby had tackled him on one subject that was very much on his mind. "Have you received any more anonymous notes?"

Stephen flushed. "No, not a thing. You haven't, er, mentioned any of that to the police?"

"Not yet, but the Eggardon Hill affair is still hanging fire, so as soon as your funding comes through I intend to do so, although it would be much better if you told them yourself. It may be a very valuable lead."

"Oh, I will. I will indeed," Stephen said. "I couldn't help wondering if poor old Orchard's suicide wasn't somehow connected with it."

"Quite possibly. After you left to get the police there was someone at Maiden Castle watching me," Toby returned. "It did occur to me that it might be your anonymous correspondent 'awatching' our activities."

"Really!" Stephen seemed genuinely impressed. "That may explain why I haven't heard: they know you're here. That's splendid!"

"Splendid" was not the word Toby would have picked but he let it pass. "I had not realized that you were so deeply rooted locally," he probed. "I don't think you mentioned that."

"Me?" Stephen was startled. "I'd never lived in Dorset before I came here as curator. Oh! I expect you've heard of the Farwells of Chideock. Yes, well, I am *descended* from them; my grandfather was a country doctor there and worked himself into an early grave at it. My father got out as soon as he could: couldn't stand country life and had a chronic itchy foot. We lived all over the place, but not here; anywhere but here." This remembrance appeared to unsettle him.

"The Orchards also being an old Chideock family and the fact that you and Margaret Orchard evidently know each other, led me to think your connections were closer than that," Toby persisted.

Stephen shot a quick glance at him and flushed. "That was long ago when we were both at Reading." Toby continued to stare steely-eyed at him, so that after a moment's pregnant silence Stephen went on. "Oh hell! I might as well tell you, since it has nothing to do with present events. We were close, very close at one time and I didn't treat her at all well." He sighed heavily. "I met my ex-wife not too long after Meg and I . . ." he gulped. "She was older than Meg, more sophisticated, and a lot more determined, so we got married. I was so wrapped up in Helen then that, well, poor Meg . . ."

"In other words you dumped her," Toby said coldly.

"God forgive me, yes," Stephen muttered. "She was just a kid and I was old enough to know better. She took it very hard. It was all wrong and I'll never forgive myself, never."

"Exactly how much of an age difference was there?"

Stephen looked wretched. "Ten years. I'm 37; she's 27 now. She was 19 then."

"But you have met since?" Toby queried.

"I've seen her at museum affairs a couple of times with the Colonel—at a distance. After Helen and I broke up I tried to mend fences but got right royally, if understandably, snubbed. As you saw for yourself, she can't stand the sight of me."

"I see," Toby said, regretting that another of his possible scenarios had gone up in smoke. "Will you attend the funeral?"

"In my official capacity I have to show up, even if I'm not welcome," Stephen said stiffly.

"Then I'll see you there." Toby was coldly dismissive. "If you need me before that you know where to leave a message. I trust the funding will be available shortly so that we can get things moving on the other business." On that note they went their separate ways.

Apart from a daily phone call to Hardy to keep up with any developments, Toby stuck to his intention of keeping a low profile and applied himself to what he did best—research. He spent many hours in the pleasant reference room of the county library and learned far more than he really wanted to about Dorset witchcraft, the Dorset Druids, who to him seemed even more half-baked than the main branch from which they had split in the sixties, and smuggling.

The more he learned, the less native witchcraft and the late-coming Dorset Druids appeared to be connected. To his utter frustration they were on two parallel and separate lines that, even if they did eventually meet in infinity, had nothing to do with each other now, nor, apparently, did they have any areas of conflict. His research on smuggling he found more interesting and rewarding in that it unearthed several items which piqued his curiosity. From the seventeenth through the mid–nineteenth century the area between Chideock and Lyme Regis had been a positive hotbed for it, particularly in the late eighteenth century. Farwells and Orchards figured prominently in the records, notably in the latter period when a formidable gang had operated, headed by a mysterious and never-identified leader called "The Colonel," and in which the church of Stanton St. Gabriel had figured as one of their clearinghouses for French contraband. Another name that had leapt out at him from the records was one Isaac Gulliver, known as "The Gentle Smuggler" because he had never used firearms and was credited as being one of the best and most successful organizers in the business. Since the name was a rare one, he was positively looking forward to renewing his acquaintance with the effete Silas Gulliver to find out if there was a link with the notorious Isaac. A further titillating item was that in the early eighteen eighties the vicar of Charmouth had been the head of one of the local smuggling syndicates and had indeed used his own church as a warehouse for his contraband. When this colorful character had been found out, he had fled the country, abandoned the cloth, and had ended his days as a pirate in the Caribbean. Unfortunately, as interesting as all this was, it did not advance Toby's knowledge of the present murders one whit.

Indeed, the only advances were coming from official sources, although there Hardy himself was facing multiple frustrations. The late Colonel had had no use for lawyers, so there was no handy solicitor to apply to for knowledge of his business matters or dealings. The local bank that had housed his account, in the manner of banks, was very reluctant to disclose any of his records until considerable official pressure was applied. On the whole they revealed little save an old man's struggle to make ends meet on a limited income, but there were two items of considerable interest. Some six weeks before his death the Colonel had deposited 3,000 pounds in cash. The added balance had not stayed in the account for long because a week later 2,800 of it had been withdrawn, again in cash, so there was no indication of either its provenance or its destination.

"Margaret Orchard knows nothing about it," Hardy confided to Toby over the phone, "so I was wondering if you'd go over to St. Gabriel's with Wood. He'll have a go at Martha, and, if you would, you go through Orchard's papers to see if you can find any receipts for those amounts, or come up with any clues from that damned book. We've had the study sealed off, so if there *is* anything it should be there still."

Thankful for a change of pace, Toby hastily rendezvoused with the amiable sergeant and they descended on St. Gabriel's. "I made sure Joe would be out of the way," Wood confided as they drove up to the house. "Martha's a lot more communicative when he's not around. A regular sourpuss is Joe."

Communicative was not the word; Martha was positively garrulous, and over an obligatory cup of tea in the kitchen before he slipped off on his own appointed task, Toby found her stream of confidences interesting. His respect for Wood's competence grew as the placid sergeant let her have her head, but deftly kept her on track and, with the occasional interjected question, got far more out of her than a more official approach would have done.

They were treated to an entire history of the Colonel's involvement with his mania, which had started in a small way during a German posting not long after his wife's death where he had become interested in water dowsing and had found he had a gift for it. Then he had gone on to metallic ores and on retirement had even thought of setting up as a professional dowser. "But nothing came of that, poor soul," Martha sighed. "No call for it in England, y'see." It had only been after they had moved to St. Gabriel's some eight years ago that his growing passion for dowsing had fixated on ley lines. "Oh so excited he was! Started out at t'other end of the county following the lines from them big places in Wiltshire, them with the big stones," she explained earnestly. "Followed them all over the place, he did, and when he got around here a couple of years ago he got even more excited. 'Martha,' he sez to me, 'Golden Cap is a very special place, a . . . focus.'" She brought out the word doubtfully. "'We picked the right spot,' he sez to me, 'a place of power.'" And it was after this confidence that he had gone on a buying spree for more elaborate equipment than the hazel wands, pendulums, and copper rods that had been his stock-in-trade until then.

"Notice any change in him in the past six weeks or so?" Wood broke in.

Martha pondered. "Not to speak of. Y'see the longer he went on, the more excited he got, you might say. In high spirits he was, like a schoolboy looking forward to a treat." Her lips quivered suddenly. "It's why I just can't make out why this awful thing has come upon us."

"Can you remember if he made any special trips?" Wood asked hastily to prevent another tear storm, and he named the day before the cash deposit.

Martha shot him a reproachful glance. "'Course I can. That'd be the day he went up to London. Took him to Dorchester station, Joe did. Stayed in his club and came back the next day. Joe picked him up again."

Wood gave a satisfied grunt. "Did he take anything with him?"

"Not that I know of. Just his briefcase and a little bag for overnight. Packed it myself," Martha said.

He named the date of the withdrawal. "Any trips around that time?"

Her wrinkled face wrinkled further in anxious thought. "Not that day, no, but the next he took the Land Rover and drove somewhere. When he came back he had that thing that's amissing. I remember him apatting of it and saying how our lives would be a lot better for it soon. Tickled pink he was."

Wood looked triumphantly and meaningfully at Toby, who hastily gulped the last of his tea and stood up. "Thank you for the tea, Mrs. Orchard, but I must get to work now."

"I'll unlock the study for you." Wood rose with him. "Be back in a second, Martha. Could stand another cup of the brew if there's one left in the pot."

As he let Toby in he muttered, "Looks as if we're really on to something, don't it? Any receipts or anything with those dates we'd appreciate, Sir Tobias. Good hunting!" And he hurried back to his talkative hostess.

Toby started with the jumble on the desk, but a thorough search yielded nothing. Discouraged, he turned his attention to the large table and studied the Colonel's master map of Dorset before diving into the rest of the intimidating piles. The whole map was so crisscrossed with lines that the Colonel's mania, not to mention his imagination, was readily apparent, but he did note with interest that a whole mess of them radiated from Golden Cap. Orchard had not been a diary keeper, but Toby felt he had hit pay dirt when he unearthed a meticulous log of his journeyings and observations. Flipping through it he noted that in the past two months Orchard's explorations had been confined to the immediate area of Stanton St. Gabriel, and that a month previous to that he had been at Eggardon.

Putting the log aside for further study, he turned reluctantly to the task of sorting the scattered papers and books into some sort of order, but again nothing emerged from them that gave any clue to the Colonel's cash windfall. As he worked on he noted that Orchard had had one of his own absent-minded habits—that of sticking envelopes, cards, or scraps of paper into his books as markers.

Thoughtfully he turned back to the desk in the window and the small bookcase that stood adjacent to it. It was crammed with books on dowsing and ley lines. He began pulling them out one by one and extracting all the markers and almost immediately hit pay dirt: a long envelope bearing the imprint of a Southampton marine supply firm yielded a receipt for 2,850 pounds and a three-year guarantee for a "super-sensitized metal detector," and it bore the date of Orchard's Land Rover trip. Pocketing this, he went on with his search and his eyes lit up when another book yielded three business cards, all from London jewelers who offered free assessments of Victorian and antique jewelry. He had just straightened up from his painful crouch when the door opened and Wood came in looking crestfallen. "Joe's back, so that's the end of that," he announced. "I'll not get anything out of Martha with him around. Find anything, sir?"

Toby showed him his finds and explained his thoughts on them. The sergeant's face lit up. "Now that's real helpful. Gives us something concrete to check on, and now we know what that thing that's amissing is, we'll get right on it." His round face crinkled up. "But what in the world would anyone want to take a thing like that for 'round here? No metals here in Dorset of any kind."

"Not the faintest idea." Toby shook his head helplessly. "Is it all right if I take this logbook along with me?" But here he ran up against Wood's cautious conservatism.

"Sorry, sir, can't authorize that I can't, not without the inspector's say-so. Maybe if he okays it you could pick it up Tuesday when you'll be coming here. Now, if it's all right with you, we'd best be getting back with these things."

"Right, but I've not quite finished," Toby said. "You go through the rest of the books in that bookcase in case there's anything else, a receipt or whatever. I have something else to check." Quickly he went back to the logbook and made some rapid notes on the last three months of entries before Wood announced he'd finished the bookcase. The room was again locked and sealed and they let themselves quietly out the front door.

Wood dropped him off at Woolaston Lodge, where a huge pile of forwarded mail awaited him: to his deepening depression there was nothing in it from Penny. After a morose session with his brandy flask, he made up his mind. The Ap Joneses were out, so he made for their private phone and dialed. "Ada," he boomed uneasily, "any word yet from Dr. Spring?"

"Still in New Zealand so far as I know," Ada said curtly. "Why? Do you want to leave her a message? Is there something wrong?"

"Yes, there is," he said testily. "Two murders in fact."

"Oh Lord, Sir Tobias, you're a regular magnet for them," she said with sweet sarcasm. "Wherever you go these days it seems bodies start popping out of the woodwork. So what message did you want to leave for Dame Penelope, *if* she gets in touch?"

Toby swallowed his pride. "If you know where she is, Ada, for God's sake find her. Tell her I need her here—urgently."

"I'll be sure to do that, *if* I hear," Ada said and hung up on him. After that minor triumph she sat at her desk and rapidly consumed six chocolate creams from a paper bag, her placid brow wrinkled in thought. Finally, with a deep sigh that set her ample bosom quivering, she muttered to herself, "Suppose I'd better. She'd never forgive me if anything happened to the old devil." Cramming two more chocolate creams into her mouth, she picked up the phone and dialed. "Overseas operator? Oh, is that you, Gladys? Good, it's Ada. A person-to-person call to New Zealand for Dame Penelope Spring at Roamora Lodge, Wairoa, North Island." She rattled off a string of numbers. "It's a family emergency. How long will it take? 'Bout twenty minutes? You'll put it through to Pitt Rivers here? Good." With a satisfied sigh she put down the phone and helped herself to another chocolate cream; she had done her good deed for the day.

Chapter 8

Toby met with Hardy and Wood in the parking lot of the Queen's Arms Inn in Charmouth before the funeral, partly to avoid the parking congestion at the church, partly for him to be briefed on new developments and to get the study key from Wood.

"No word from London yet," Hardy said, "but the manager at the Southampton store was helpful, if not too enlightening. It seems this gadget was a special order to oblige Orchard; normally they don't stock such equipment. According to him it's a brand-new type of metal detector, hence the stiff price. It works somewhat along the lines of a Geiger counter and it can sort out the types of metal it's detecting, iron from tin, gold from silver, and so on—something to do with their atomic weights. He hasn't seen it in operation himself so has no idea how good it is, nor did he get any idea from the Colonel as to why he wanted it. Unless we can find the damn thing I don't think we'll get much further on that line."

"Don't seem to have much connection with them ley lines, does it?" Wood put in.

"Unless he stumbled across some kind of metal deposit when he was looking for his ley lines with the other metal detector and wanted to find out more about it," Toby said, as they trudged up the hill towards the church. "We know he was at Eggardon three months ago and frequently on Golden Cap, which has some Bronze Age burial mounds on it, I believe."

"You mean treasure-trove of some kind?" Hardy queried.

"The Bronze Age Wessex culture was heavily addicted to gold jewelry and so were the later Celts, and the Durotriges around here were a rich tribe. During their final clash with the Romans they might easily have buried some of their wealth. It's a distinct possibility," Toby mused.

Hardy gave a low whistle. "Wouldn't that be something! I sent one of my blokes up to London yesterday to check on those jewelers, so if he comes back with any gold transaction, well, we *may* be in business. What a motive!"

"I doubt whether it will be that easy," Toby went on. "For one thing it would be considered treasure-trove and the Colonel would have known that from his museum activities. There has to be an inquest on treasure-trove. For another, Celtic and Bronze Age gold jewelry is very distinctive, and I can't see any reputable jeweler buying it for hard cash. Of course it could have been melted down into small ingots, I suppose." This thought depressed him considerably.

They reached the parish church, which sat close to the main road that ran parallel to its long axis. There was still no sign of the funeral cortege, so they took a turn around the graveyard. Hardy stopped suddenly. "Hallo! Here's a Gorge. Remember I was telling you about them?"

"Oh, that's old Digory, Inspector," Wood chipped in. "More than 50 years he were Parish Clerk here. Rare old character he was. Started off under the smuggling parson as a young man he did, but managed to keep himself in the clear just like his great-grandfather Digory before him, though *he* was up before the Assizes for aiding smugglers. He got off."

They looked at him in amazement. "How come you know all this, Wood?" Hardy asked.

The sergeant preened a little. "My wife's granny was a Gorge. Daughter of his son Thomas," he nodded affably at the headstone. "They knew their roots they did, all the way back."

Toby was fascinated. "Are they connected with the Bradpole Gorges? The warlocks?" He raised his eyebrows significantly at Hardy.

It was Wood's turn to be startled. "Oh, I don't know about that. First one I knows of is old Digory of West Hays back in the early sixteen hundreds. Always kept to the same names they did."

"Where's West Hays?" Toby asked.

"Why, Stanton St. Gabriel to be sure! Farm's still there and in operation, the old farmhouse too."

"And still a Gorge farm?"

"Oh no, not for centuries. Name's gone too. No Gorges round here now."

Hardy let out an exclamation. "I see the cortege has arrived; we'd better get on in. Let's sit right at the back." They hung back until the main party had entered the church and then went in to witness a rather odd spectacle. The first three rows of pews were filled by the funeral party, with the slim navy-clad figure of Margaret Orchard accompanied by Martha and Joe in the front pew, together with a burly, fair-haired man. Then there were several rows of vacant pews, but the back rows were completely packed. They were forced to settle in the middle of the church as Wood muttered, "Quite a turnout! That lot back there are part curiosity seekers, but mostly the vicar's fan club."

On the other side of Toby, Hardy muttered, "That's Roper in the front pew with the Orchards—going to say a few words I'm betting. The museum board is in the pew behind them."

"Is Silas Gulliver among them?" Toby asked. "He was at Oxford with me in the long ago."

"Yes. See that rather large woman on the aisle end? That's Mrs. Westcott-Smyth. He's next to her, the one with the yellowish-gray hair."

Toby would not have recognized the somewhat rotund figure, but noted that Silas still favored overlong hair. He could see no sign of Stephen, but as the vicar of Charmouth made his entrance, looking even more magnificent in his black cassock and white surplice than he had appeared in riding clothes, Toby saw Stephen slip into a vacant pew on the opposite side of the church.

The service got underway, and he could not help admiring the performance of Nicholas Squires, for a performance it truly was, and it crossed his mind that before his many marriages and shadowy business career the vicar must have had some theatrical training. When Roper got up to deliver the eulogy it was a definite anticlimax. He had a surprisingly reedy voice for such a large man, was evidently nervous in these unaccustomed surroundings, and he seesawed between an owlish hushed solemnity that rendered his words almost inaudible and a jarring and out-of-place breeziness which Toby suspected was his normal business manner. As he piped on about Orchard's wartime heroics, his services to his country and to archaeology, and his sterling, forthright character, there was an audibly growing restlessness, particularly at the back of the church, which quieted down immediately when he faltered to a stop and the vicar took center stage again. The pallbearers collected the coffin that sat in front of the altar, and, with the vicar leading the way, mellifluously intoning the 100th Psalm, the congregation herded out after the funeral party into the graveyard. As the main participants took up their positions around the newly dug grave, Toby noted that Stephen had managed to work himself through the throng and had taken up a position close to Margaret Orchard. Flanked by Joe and Martha, she stood serene and impassive as Squires, at the opposite end of the grave, intoned the final words of committal, and, as the coffin disappeared out of sight, she patted the sobbing Martha on the shoulder and shot an enigmatic glance at the towering Stephen.

Toby had purposefully distanced himself from the two dark-uniformed police officers, who were drawing their share of curious stares from the crowd, and covertly studied the group himself for anyone who appeared to be interested in him, but there was no one. He decided to slip away before the crowd started to break up and, once out of the churchyard, headed back down the hill with long strides, lighting up his pipe as he went and diving into the welcoming open doors of the Queen's Arms to browse through a pint of their best cider while waiting for the coast to clear. The cider was so good and he was so unwilling to face up to the upcoming party that he treated himself to another and listened idly to the pleasant rumble of Dorset voices in the bar.

Some overheard sentences caught his attention. "T'vicar is going to have his work cut out for him now with the old one gone. The young 'uns 'round here'll be sniffing around right quick, you mark my words. Nice little piece like that. He'd best work fast if he wants her."

"My money's on the vicar then. Don't know what the old perisher has, but I wish I had it. T'wife is fair crazed about the old bugger." Enlightened, for this idea had not even occurred to him, Toby reluctantly drained his glass and went forth to do his duty.

The funeral party was in full swing by the time he got to St. Gabriel's House. Joe was standing guard on the front door and ushered him into the large drawing room on the left where French doors giving upon the adjacent dining room stood wide open, revealing two large tables laden with baked meats and silver punch bowls. After greeting his hostess, who was embedded in a group of cheerful young people of whose provenance he hadn't the faintest idea, he made purposefully for the nearest punch bowl and was helping himself to a glass when his arm was seized and squeezed in a firm grip. "Oh, Sir Tobias, what an honor to have you here!" A husky female voice breathed in his ear, and as he swung around, startled, the largebosomed, full-figured woman of uncertain years grasped at his free hand and pumped it vigorously. "Brenda Westcott-Smyth, chairwoman of the museum board. I am *so* pleased to meet you at long last. Of course I know *all* about you."

"Er, how do you do," he stuttered in growing alarm, as she retained her grip on his hand and gave it another squeeze.

"Although this is such a *sad* occasion we really must have a heart-to-heart talk," she said, surging up against him and literally backing him into a nearby corner.

"Er, what about?" he gasped, vainly trying to disentangle his hand.

"Oh, so many, many things! We have so many interests in common: art, archaeology, the preservation of our glorious English heritage, the Celts—I have Celtic ancestors myself, you know—and I've read every single one of your books on them. So thrilling!" Her moonlike and overly made-up face yearned up at him.

"I have never in my life written a book on the Celts." With a determined tug Toby got his hand back. "I'm afraid you must be confusing me with my father. He wrote several," he said stiffly.

She was not in the least disconcerted. "Oh well, as they say, like father, like son," she said with a little titter. "You're down here about the Celts aren't you? And I simply must insist you come and have dinner with me at the manor at your very first opportunity, and we can have a lovely tête-à-tête. How about tomorrow?"

"Impossible, I'm sorry. Other engagements," he gulped, and saw with overwhelming relief Silas Gulliver making purposefully towards him, a concerned expression on his long, thin face. "You'll have to excuse me now, I must have a word with an old acquaintance of mine."

She glanced over her shoulder but did not budge an inch. "Oh, it's Silas," she said with a girlish titter. "He's *so* possessive. Naughty boy!" she chided with elephantine playfulness, as Silas reached them. "No need to be jealous, you know. Just having an archaeological chat with our eminent visitor."

Silas nodded at him. "Hello, Glendower. It's been a long time. Brenda, Roper is looking for you and wants a word. And Squires just arrived."

"Oh yes, poor Colin, I must see him," she said, with a resigned roll of her bulbous blue eyes. "I'll leave you in good hands, Sir Tobias, and remember we have a date as *soon* as you are free." And with some reluctance she ceded her place to Silas and hurried into the next room.

"So what brings your eminent self to our neck of the woods?" Silas demanded with a faint sneer as soon as she was out of earshot.

Toby studied him before answering. The years had not been kind to Gulliver; the rather girlish good looks of his youth had faded into a seedy and peevish-looking age, which was even reflected in his shoddy and rumpled clothing. He had all the earmarks of an academic gone to seed. He decided to go on the attack. "I came down to give Stephen Farwell, a former student of mine, a helping hand on this important henge excavation. I was surprised to learn that there has been opposition to the dig and that you were in the opposing camp. How come?"

Silas was taken aback. "Well, no, that's not quite right. I'm not against the excavation, but I haven't liked the way Farwell goes about things." He took a hurried glance over his shoulder and went on. "Look, there's a lot going on around here you ought to know about, but we can't talk here. Can you come to my place for dinner tomorrow evening—just the two of us? We've a lot of catching up to do and I can fill you in on what the situation is. I live just down the lane at East Hays Farm."

This suited Toby well enough. "Yes, I'd appreciate that. When?" he demanded.

"Oh, say seven-thirty for dinner at eight? Mine's a bachelor establishment so don't expect too much, but I expect I can cajole the old crone who works for me into getting us something edible." Silas seemed astonished by his easy victory. "At least I can offer you some fairly decent wine."

Toby unbent a little. "Sounds splendid," he murmured. "So what have you been doing with yourself all these years? I understand you've become a local historian of note. I'm afraid I rather lost touch with your activities after you left your fellowship at Pembroke."

Silas looked uncertainly at him. "It was Oriel, actually, and I found I was suffocating among the bunch of old fuss-pots there so I had to get out. Went to Canada for some years, then a short spell in America." He gave an affected shudder. "God! Those Americans were frightful. So I wandered back to Europe. Always liked French history, y'know. Was a visiting professor at Exeter for a while. Came into a bit of money and decided to pack teaching in and settle here, where I'm a medium-sized frog in a very small puddle. End of unilluminating story, but then we can't all be the gilded darlings of the academic world, can we?" He bristled slightly.

Toby let it pass. "I'll value your local expertise," he said. "Outside of its ancient monuments, I know little of this part of the world and it appears to be fascinating. I shall look forward to tomorrow evening. Do you know much about Dorset Druids?"

Silas was again startled. "Not my line at all. You might like to talk to Colin Roper about them."

"Yes, I'd like to meet him," Toby hinted.

Silas seemed relieved. "Come along then. I'll just see if the coast is clear and Brenda has moved on to fresh pastures. You mustn't mind her, she's a bit of a lion hunter but quite harmless." He started off across the room.

More like a man-eater, Toby thought gloomily, as he followed him out, but noted with grim amusement that the unquenchable Brenda now had the Reverend Squires firmly pinned in a corner of the drawing room and that, after Silas had introduced him to Colin Roper, he too wandered off towards them as if bent on another rescue mission.

He had correctly summed up Roper, who proved breezy in the extreme and on back-slapping terms with the few middle-aged people who were present. On the Dorset Druids he proved garrulous without being at all enlightening, and it was only when Toby put in a pointed question about Orchard's membership that he dried up and appeared disconcerted. Roper lowered his voice and darted a quick look around. "This is hardly the occasion to bring this up, but since you ask, well, the Colonel was neither the age nor the type of person we would normally allow in our group. But he was such a harmless old boy and he *seemed* so keen that I hadn't the heart to turn him down. Believe me, I was quite appalled when I heard he'd been found in the regalia. I know he was always a little bizarre so I suppose he just flipped out, but that kind of negative publicity is the last thing we need, I assure you."

"Has your sect experienced any problems with local witches?" Toby persisted.

Roper looked at him in blank stupefaction. "Witches! Why no, why should we? The Dorset Druids are an all-male organization and have nothing to do with witchcraft, local or otherwise."

"But there are male witches," Toby continued. "Maybe one trying to infiltrate your group?"

Roper grew indignant. "Certainly not! For one thing—not that I know much about it—I believe local witchcraft is confined to rustic hicks, who wallow in those ridiculous old superstitions and are not even in the same league with us. We Druids are educated people from the middle class, a few even upper class, and are preeminently a religious group. No, what small troubles we have had come from some fanatical church and chapel groups, and they belong in the Dark Ages . . ." He was interrupted by a man who came up behind him and slapped him on the back, and to whom Roper turned with almost palpable relief. "Hi, Bill, I found just the right thing for you," he fluted. He turned back to Toby. "If you'll excuse me, Sir Tobias?" He fumbled in his pocket and produced a business card. "If I can give you any further information, please feel free to call me at this number. Nice to have met you."

Left to his own devices and seeing the party was beginning to thin out rapidly, Toby decided it was time he consulted the logbook in the study. Fumbling in his pocket for the key, he crossed the hall and then stopped abruptly: the police seal on the door was ripped across and when he tried the handle it gave under his hand. His heart pounding, he slipped into the room and halted in consternation. The large table in the center of the room had vanished and the papers and books he had so carefully sorted out where piled in disarray on the floor in one corner. Glancing out the window he saw Joe Orchard perched on the hood of a car smoking a cigarette, and, boiling now with anger, he went storming out, banging the door shut behind him. "What the hell has happened here?" he roared at the old man. "The police seal is broken, the study open, and the Colonel's papers in chaos. Who did this?"

Joe glowered at him. "We needed the table for the buffet. Martha said 'Ood and you were finished in there, so we took t'table out."

"But the door was locked and the room sealed!" Toby cried. "Surely you knew you were not supposed to go in? And how the hell did you *get* in?"

"Drawing-room key—one fits t'other in this old place," Joe growled. "Arter this is over we'll put it back and lock up. No need to get so riled up. Nothing worth taking in there anyways is there?"

"By God, you'd better hope that is so or you're in big trouble," Toby growled back, and rushed back inside. Kneeling before the piles he sorted feverishly through them, then, with a little groan, ran frantically through everything again. When he had finished his face was grim: the logbook was gone.

Chapter 9

"*Diamonds*!" Toby's deep baritone soared an octave in surprise. "Did you say diamonds?"

"Indeed I did." Hardy's voice, heavy with frustration, came over the phone. "Seven unset diamonds of variable quality, six of them with marked flaws, antique cut and of no great value, but the seventh a flawless five-carat solitaire-cut white. That's why he got the 3,000 quid."

"But . . . but . . . did he have any explanation for them?" Toby spluttered, once more in total confusion.

"A very reasonable one, or at least one that satisfied the jeweler. Said they were his late wife's and that since the settings were old-fashioned he'd taken them out, thinking they'd be worth more that way. He'd already told the same story to one of the other jewelers on our list who had only offered him 2,500 for them." A heavy sigh floated over the wire. "Checked with Margaret Orchard and, as usual, she knew nothing about anything. Couldn't remember her mother wearing any diamonds, but then she was only six when Mrs. O died, and her father had never mentioned them to her. So there goes your treasure theory and it appears to be another blind alley. This case is driving me up the wall. Every time we get a promising lead it just blows up in our faces, and we're right back where we started."

"Not quite." Toby had regained his composure. "The very fact that the metal detector and the logbook have been stolen has to mean *something* and in my opinion the theft of the latter narrows the field down, namely, to someone at that funeral reception who seized an unforeseen opportunity to grab the book."

Although the police had been just as upset as he had been and had grilled the Orchards unmercifully after the party, it had yielded no result, for neither of the Orchards had seen anyone hanging around by the study and there had been so much coming and going both before and during the reception that it was impossible to pin down either the time of the theft or a likely perpetrator. In one respect the theft had greatly eased Toby's mind: Stephen Farwell was the one person who could not have been involved in it, since he had had no part in the pre- or post-funeral activities.

At his last remark Hardy snorted sarcastically. "Oh, that's great, that is. Just 50 or 60 people to check out, that's what that gives us."

"I think you can narrow it down a lot further than that." Toby was blunt. "It seems reasonable to suppose that whoever took the detector also took the logbook, and that means an intimate knowledge of both the Colonel and his habits. That rules out all the young people from Margaret Orchard's office, his few army buddies who turned up, and even those members of the museum board who only knew him casually from board meetings. In fact I'd go out on a limb and advise concentrating on the people in the closest geographical area who were on visiting terms with Orchard."

"You pointing the finger at Gulliver?" Hardy was equally blunt.

"Not just Gulliver. There's Roper for one, Mrs. Westcott-Smyth, whom I learned resides nearby in Chideock Manor, and, for that matter, Wood's charismatic vicar."

"Oh come *on*!" Hardy was irritated. "Can you honestly see Squires sneaking around indulging in petty theft?" He stopped abruptly. "Unless," he went on, "he is under the spell of the winsome Margaret and all this is just flimflam to get us chasing around in circles. After all, when it comes to *cui bono*, the only one who benefits even to a small degree from Orchard's death is his daughter. No one else does. We know she's out of it so far as the actual murder is concerned, but it doesn't mean she isn't behind it."

"I find that very hard to believe. I mean what possible connection could she have with the Eggardon Hill murder?"

"Then you show *me* how the two murders are connected. We have no proof that they are other than the method, and the Colonel's might have been a copycat killing. It's happened plenty of times before," Hardy retaliated.

"I am going to find that connection." Toby was at his most stubborn. "Since the logbook went, I am more convinced than ever that they are linked with the Colonel's research, and that once we find the key to that we'll have the real motive. And it would also put Margaret Orchard in the clear, because she would have no need to steal those items, since they belong to her anyway. I'm hoping my meeting with Gulliver tonight will give me some new ideas."

"You seem to have plenty of ideas already, Sir Tobias, but what we need are a few concrete facts," Hardy said drily. "But you go your way and we'll just plod along on ours. We've impounded all the rest of Orchard's papers and my fingerprint team now has the unenviable task of going over them page by page. It just might turn up something and it's about all we have left." On that pessimistic note he hung up.

Another call, however, lifted Toby's spirits. This one was from Stephen Farwell, who sounded jubilant. "The funds are in and we're all set to go. I'm off to the police now with the file and the notes on the mask to get those off my mind. The only truth I'm going to fudge is that I've only just told you about this and you advised me to go straight to them. It occurred to me your fingerprints would be on the notes and they just might test them. Is that okay with you?"

"Well, er, yes." Toby was a little uneasy about that, but at this stage did not wish to jeopardize his good relationship with the Dorset police and with Hardy in particular. "You'll probably have to see Inspector Hardy eventually, but, if possible, try and get hold of Sergeant Wood first. I think you'll find him more receptive to the witchcraft angle and less likely to probe deeply about the dates."

"Oh, fine!" Stephen said airily. "And can we get together tomorrow at long last so that you can go over what I have in mind for the dig to see if I've made any goofs? How about lunch at the King's Head about one and back here after?"

"Yes, I can do that," Toby agreed and, heartened, went off with Owen Ap Jones on what had become something of an afternoon ritual. They had been scouring the neighborhood pubs starting from Shipton Gorge and fanning out from there trying to pick up any scraps of information on the activities of the late Job Squires. Thus far their gleaning had been meager, for the very sight of Toby, who was a complete stranger, had been sufficient to dry up rustic garrulity, particularly if they had broached the subject of witchcraft. He had been at the point of bowing out of this particular activity and letting Owen, who, while still an outsider, was on chatting terms with the villagers, go on alone, when they had come across an ancient farmhand who had been a longtime drinking companion of the late Job. Several pints of free beer had loosened his tongue and they had picked up some things that to Toby were very significant: Job had been a frequenter of Golden Cap, "a rare place for agathering of his herbs;" in season he had worked as a hedger for Orchard, and, most significantly of all, in the past three months had been uncommonly flush with money and had stood rounds at the pubs. The old man had no idea of the source although Job had hinted there was more where it came from. He had dried up when the subject of witchcraft had been introduced and had stared blankly when Toby had asked whether the names Mother Crowns or Merlin had been mentioned by Job.

But this encounter had heartened both him and Owen, for the old man had mentioned another of Job's favorite watering places in Chideock, and it was there they were currently headed in hopes of finding another talkative ancient. Wednesday was evidently an off day, for, apart from two dedicated and silent darts players, they were the only patrons. Owen, in his easy way, made the best of a bad job and started up a lively chat with the bartender, leading him gently into the subject of Job. But beyond confirming that he was "a regular old character" and had indeed been spending money freely at the time of his murder, the barkeep had nothing more to add. Owen then switched to his own line in antiques, introduced Toby as a buyer from London, and wondered audibly if they'd find any good stuff for sale at the manor.

Then the barman waxed eloquent. "Not likely," he sniffed. "All show and no substance up there, if you ask me. Not the real article at all. Westcott-Smyth indeed! The old man made a pile in plumbing supplies, and my bet is that he was just plain Smith back then. Bought the manor when he retired and tried to play country gent, but not for long. Dropped dead in his tracks in Bridport the year after they came. The merry widow's been playing the same game ever since, when she isn't busy chasing the nearest thing in trousers. 'Course she musta been 20 years or more younger than the old 'un, so she's been making up for lost time. Not all that choosy either, even went after one of her gardeners and him half her age. Real shocker she is *and* a bad payer. Maybe the old man wasn't as flush as we all thought. Leastways, of late, it's like getting teeth pulled to get any bills paid by her." At this point a party of American tourists had swarmed into the bar and Owen and Toby quickly slipped away.

On their way back to Dorchester Owen seemed thoughtful. "You know, when you mentioned Merlin to that gaffer the other day, it rang a bell with me, but I can't for the life of me bring it to mind. I've seen that name or one very like it 'round here somewhere recently, and somewhere odd, but I'm damned if I can think of where. Is it important?"

Toby shrugged. "I don't know. Possibly. Anyway if it comes back to you, let me know. And Owen, if you're still up for it, I think that you're so much better at getting people to talk than I am, that you'd do better on these expeditions without me along. You know all the questions to ask now and I just seem to put a damper on things."

"Maybe you're right," Owen said with unflattering alacrity. "And with us getting so busy now, I can just dodge off when I have a free moment and we won't have to worry about getting together." And on this businesslike note they parted.

Before setting off for his dinner date, Toby went over the sparse notes he had made from the logbook and fretted silently. Which was the important site—Eggardon or Golden Cap? Three months ago Orchard had been at Eggardon; three months ago Squires had started to be well-supplied with cash; was it hush money, blackmail, a payoff? Or had both murdered men stumbled across something and had to be silenced? With a sigh of frustration he put away his notes, got out the Rolls, and headed for Stanton St. Gabriel.

It came as no surprise to him that Silas Gulliver's home reflected the same seediness as its owner. Easy Hays Farm was a dark, drab place, badly in need of paint both inside and out; its sparse furnishings were unpolished and shabby, with a generally uncared-for look to them. Only in Silas's study was there a degree of creature comfort, with two leather armchairs drawn up before a small coal fire in the open grate, which had been lit against this rain-chilled evening.

As host, Silas was being anxiously affable, and over their predinner sherry, they got through the inevitable whatever-happened-to's of sundry classmates. As eight o'clock came and went with no sign of dinner, Silas excused himself to see what was happening to it, and as his absence lengthened, Toby made a tour of his bookcases that were neatly categorized and mostly what would be expected of an ex-professor of history. Most of the books were much worn, but when he came to the section on French history Toby noted a whole shelf of brightly jacketed new books, including one massive and expensive tome in French on the French Crown Jewels. He was just reaching for this unlikely book when his host announced triumphantly that dinner was served and ushered him out into the chilly gloom of the candlelit dining room.

Cursing inwardly at the dim light that effectively prevented him from observing Gulliver's face at the opposite end of the table, not to mention what he was eating, Toby, over the substantial vegetable soup, sailed right into action. "So, you were going to fill me in on the opposition to the henge dig and to Stephen Farwell," he prompted.

Silas immediately plunged into a long and rambling tale of the local scene that appeared to have precious little to do with either. He complained long and loud about the ex-curator who, he claimed, had put up the backs of all the city fathers of Dorchester with his demands, as they were already very wary of archaeological digs, due to the long drawn-out previous excavation on the Roman baths that had held up their much-needed parking lot. The compromise they had worked out with him had not even satisfied him; he'd complained of the museum board's lack of support, both moral and financial, and had quit. "I honestly thought Stephen Farwell would be a great improvement, being of a younger generation and from Oxford," Silas said peevishly. "But he soon showed his true colors, and the way he has behaved—well, quite beyond the pale!"

"How so?" Toby said, as his soup plate was whisked away by a shadowy crouched figure and replaced by an already laden plate of roast lamb, roast potatoes, and fresh garden peas.

Again Silas lapsed into vague generalities about Stephen's "skirt-chasing" activities and his divorce. "Of course what he

did with his personal life was his business," he said grandly, pushing the claret bottle down the table to Toby. "But after the way he treated Brenda, well, that was just *too* awful. I don't care how good an archaeologist he may be, I'd be glad to see him out of here."

"How did he treat Brenda?" Toby said mildly, refilling his glass with what he considered a very tolerable Medoc.

Silas again went off on a tangent. "You have to understand that she's been so vulnerable since Westcott-Smyth died, and I fear men have exploited her shamelessly. Take Roper, for instance. He sold them the manor originally for a frightfully inflated price and as soon as the old boy died was fawning all over Brenda. I consider myself one of her true friends and I warned her at the time to watch out for him, but of course she wouldn't listen. It was all Colin this and Colin that, quite sickening. She needed to sell off some outlying land to pay off the death duties. Colin conned her into selling it to him for a fraction of what it was worth and then dropped her like a hot brick after he got what he wanted. Serves him damn well right that the real estate market has slumped and that now he's in trouble," he added viciously.

"I'm afraid I don't see what this has to do with Farwell," Toby murmured.

"I'm getting to that," Silas snapped, reclaiming the bottle and refilling his own glass. "Brenda is just too big-hearted for her own good. I mean it was the same story when Squires arrived here. She took him under her wing, introduced him all around to everyone who is anyone, and was quite wrapped up in him. But as soon as he had his ties established, well, he was also 'too busy to see her.'" He snorted angrily. "But I've noticed he's never too busy to go riding with Margaret Orchard or to take her out in that ostentatious boat of his. She's young enough to be his daughter; disgusting I call it, though I think another motive for keeping his horse and boat here may well be that he doesn't want to flaunt his wealth before his down-at-heel, ardent parishioners." After this bit of vented spite he added surprisingly, "Not that he isn't a good chap on the whole." He paused as the shadowy silent figure reappeared bearing dishes of cherry cobbler topped with thick cream and, seeing they were still not finished, simply plonked the dishes on the table beside them and went its silent way.

Silas continued, "Brenda had been so depressed that when Farwell came I was quite relieved when she took such a shine to him." Toby felt a surge of sympathy for Stephen. "She did for him what she'd done for Squires, introduced him to all the right people, supported him a hundred percent at the museum; couldn't do enough for him. I know a lot of people criticized her for not including his wife in these parties, but, as Brenda said to me, the woman was simply not the right sort: one of those hard, modern women, all flash and feminism. She just didn't fit in, you know?" Toby's surge became a tidal wave of sympathy for Stephen as he got the picture. "And what thanks did she get?" Silas went on. "A most appalling public scene! Farwell—who has a filthy temper, by the way—telling her at the top of his lungs in Dorchester High Street to leave him alone and stop pestering him, that she had caused him enough trouble already, and that he wasn't interested in her aging charms. I was all for bouncing the bounder out and so was she, but we couldn't get sufficient support. Lot of ingrates."

"Except for Orchard," Toby put in quietly. "I take it he was equally of your opinion."

Silas let out a startled little laugh. "Well no, not exactly. Orchard was pretty switched off when it came to personal relationships. No, he was against the excavation because of his silly ley lines. Thought the dig might 'disturb' the network of magnetic fields he claimed to have found between Maumbury, Poundbury, and Mount Pleasant and would lead to all sorts of local problems."

"So you just cut off Farwell's funding, is that it?" Toby demanded.

"Fat lot of good that did," Silas said peevishly. "I've heard he got the money after all." He peered down the table with sudden suspicion. "Did you put it up?"

"No, not a penny." Toby was bland. "I am here solely as an advisor and will continue as such."

Silas once more became the concerned host and, their cobblers and the bottle finished and his offer of cheese and biscuits declined, suggested they retire to the study for coffee and brandy. The coffee proved appalling but the brandy very good, and in this cosier ambience Toby led Silas, skillfully he thought, into the relationship with the neighboring Orchards. This yielded little of substance. They were not on dining-out terms, though Silas had occasionally dropped into the big house for a drink, and the Colonel likewise had dropped in on him from time to time. "To be honest, although he was the right sort for a neighbor—unlike that surly bastard at West Hays—a little of Orchard went a long way. He was a bit of an old bore," Silas admitted. "I enjoyed dropping in on Margaret for a chat far more. Poor kid, when she came down there was nothing much in the way of decent company around here." But on the important question of Orchard's local explorations he avowed complete ignorance.

Toby switched to Gulliver's own writings that soon had him pulling slim volumes and pamphlets from the bookcases, along with lengthy explanations. "Ah! I see you have one on local smuggling," Toby exclaimed. "I was wondering if by any chance you were any kin to the famous, or is it infamous, Isaac?" This startled Silas, who hemmed and hawed a little before answering. "Well, yes. Distant kinship only. I'm surprised you've heard of him."

"I find this an interesting area," Toby said, "and have been doing my homework."

"It was lively enough in his time, but there's nothing lively about it now," Silas said with sudden vehemence, and hurriedly returned to displaying his works.

The room was warm, the brandy mellow, and a comfortable Toby let Silas ramble on and on until he realized with a start that it was almost midnight. With a muttered apology for his late stay he got to his feet, thanked his host for a delightful and informative evening, and made a vague date to return this hospitality. Silas seemed loath to see him go and followed him out to the car, babbling on about how nice it was to have some erudite companionship for a change.

The rain had stopped but had been replaced by a sea mist that appeared to be gaining density by the second, so, after a hurried farewell, Toby started to edge cautiously back down the narrow lane to the T junction. He was surprised to see the haloed lights of a car coming towards him, and even more so when it suddenly turned into the driveway of St. Gabriel House. Intrigued by this unusual late hour for a visit, he drew the Rolls up just past the entrance to the house, slipped out of the car, and silent-footed it back to the misty driveway. As he peered down it, the rear lights of the car went out, there was the muffled slam of its door, and the door to the cottage flew open. The slim figure of Margaret Orchard was silhouetted against the light within. An unmistakable figure joined her and the two shadows merged in a passionate embrace: it was Stephen Farwell.

Chapter 10

Toby passed a wretched night, and morning found him hollow-eyed and mired in despondency. For the hundredth time he went over the discovery that had apparently condemned the two young people to whose strange behavior over the past week, he admitted to himself now, he had willfully turned a blind eye simply because he had not wanted to believe it. Hardy had to be right after all: the only person who benefited from Orchard's death was his unloving and unloved daughter, but she must have had help, and what better source for that help than a guilt-ridden ex-lover with an ax of his own to grind? It explained everything: all the fake occult trappings and settings; the phony thefts; all those red herrings carefully planted by a clever young man who knew how to con an old fool like himself and send him chasing after shadows, and the police right along with him.

The only thing that gave him pause was the strange gut feeling he had had all along that the murders of the old wooser and the old dowser were somehow linked, and whichever way he juggled the evidence he could not see how Job Squires had fitted in to all this playacting. He would have staked his life on the authenticity of the wooser mask and those notes, and, if Stephen *had* been playing a part in their first meetings, he had to be a greater actor than the late Laurence Olivier. It was the one thing that made him unsure.

Over a silent breakfast he made up his mind what to do. He would keep his final rendezvous with Stephen where, in fairness to the police, he would give no hint of his suspicions, then he would write up everything that had transpired, *everything*, leave it with Hardy and return to Oxford this very night. The case would take its course, but without him. It would not be the first time that a would-be murderer had called him in, but this time he had no stomach to see that murderer brought to justice: that would be up to the law.

He went upstairs, thankful that the Ap Joneses were so rushed off their feet by their houseful of guests that they had not noticed his inner misery. He got out his suitcases and started to throw things in, then changed his mind and sat down to begin his report. After a while he abandoned that also and went off in search of the phone to call Stephen. "Do you mind if we move up our appointment to noon? I have to get back to Oxford today," he said tersely."

Stephen sounded surprised. "Well, er, yes certainly. See you at the King's Head at noon then."

Toby returned to his report, and as he covered page after page in his small neat handwriting he realized what a damning document it was: motive, means, opportunity were all there. It took him all morning, and, bracing himself with a hefty slug of brandy against the upcoming interview, he went off to seek the Ap Joneses to announce his imminent departure. He could find neither of them and, since it was almost noon, abandoned that idea and set off for the King's Head, rehearsing his own roleplaying.

He need not have bothered, for the relaxed and happy Stephen was so bubbling with his own news and so enthusiastic as he talked over their ploughman's lunches and cider that Toby scarcely had to say a word. After the quick lunch they went back to the museum, where Stephen had all the plans efficiently laid out for inspection, and, apart from a few suggestions on the tricky question of dumping the excavated soil and the best disposition of his work force, Toby could find nothing to add. "It all seems to be in excellent shape, so I'll take my leave of you and get back to Oxford," he said stiffly.

"When will you be back?" Stephen asked.

Toby eyed him coldly. "I won't be back."

"But I thought you were helping the police on the Eggardon Hill murder!" Stephen burst out.

"I have done all I can on that and am about to pass it on. The rest is up to the police."

"But you will be back for the excavation?" Stephen exclaimed.

"Possibly, if circumstances allow," Toby evaded.

"Oh, please do! You don't know what a wonderful help you've been and I can't thank you enough. I'm sorry to have involved you in all this other wretched business, but even there something good has come out of the bad." Stephen gave him a sudden radiant smile. "There's something I *must* tell you. No one else knows because, well, the timing isn't right, but something wonderful has happened—Meg and I have made up. Everything's all right again and I feel like a new man. What with the dig all set and now this, I've never been happier in my whole life, and I owe most of it to you."

This staggered Toby, and once again he was confused. Could any cold-blooded murderer be *this* good an actor? For the innocent look of radiant joy on Stephen's face was authentic. At a loss for words, he said gruffly, "Well, congratulations, but I must be off." And he strode back to Woolaston Lodge in a state of high perplexity.

As he let himself in he could hear the Ap Joneses talking to each other in the kitchen. Before he faced them, he decided he needed to think things out again, so he slipped quietly up the stairs and opened his door. He stopped transfixed on the threshold, for on his bed and sound asleep was a woman: it was Penny Spring.

The surge of overwhelming relief at the sight of her was so strong that he swayed dizzily and had to steady himself by grabbing the door, which slammed back against the wall. The figure on the bed stirred and opened one hazel eye. "Hmm, so there you are. You look dreadful. You've been boozing it up again I'll be bound. I probably look worse. God, this jet lag is awful!" She struggled up, ran a hand through her already-towsled mouse-colored hair, and smothered an enormous yawn. "And what's all this?" She waved a hand at his half-packed bags.

"I was leaving, going back to Oxford. I'm not going on with it," he said.

She was off the bed in a bound, bristling. "You are *what*? I've come posthaste three-quarters of the way around the globe because Ada made out you were in dire straits, and you have the nerve to tell me you're quitting! What the hell is going on?"

"You don't understand," he protested weakly. "Things have take a most unfortunate turn and I cannot face what I think is the inevitable outcome." He grabbed up his police report and held it out to her. "It's all in here. I was going to hand everything over to the police and go home."

The hazel eyes glinted furiously at him. "I'm not going to read any damned police report. You're going to tell me every last thing that has happened here in sequence, step by step, and I don't care if it takes the rest of your life—which might be short."

"Well, if you insist," he grumbled, fumbling in his pocket for his pipe. "It all started when I heard from . . ."

"Whoa!" She held up a tiny imperative hand. "If you're going to smoke, we'll not talk here." She looked around the small confines of the room. "For God's sake, is this the best you could do? For a millionaire baronet this is not exactly the Ritz!"

Toby looked around him in amazement. "What's wrong with it? It's all I needed," he spluttered. "And the Ap Joneses have been very kind."

She snorted. "Well, I'm not going to listen to you encased in a blue cloud, so let's go to the park. It's a lovely day."

"Is it?" He had been so absorbed in misery that he hadn't noticed, but, as he looked out the window, sure enough the sun was shining brightly in a cloudless blue sky. "How extraordinary! What park?"

"Oh really Toby, you've been here God knows how long and you don't even know there's a municipal park three blocks away?" she said, putting on her sneakers. "Nice little park—bowling green, tennis courts, playground, paddling pool, town clock, and a bandstand. Lovely flowers too. I booked into a B and B place on Cornwall Road that runs beside it, because I didn't know whether you were in so deep that I'd have to play it separately. I called Gwen from there and she sneaked me in to wait for you."

"You know Gwen?" he said dazedly.

"Really, you are getting positively addled!" she chided. "Gwen used to babysit Alex for me when she was a teen-ager, don't you remember? Do come on!"

He was so delighted to see her that if she had told him to roll over and bark he'd have done it, so he followed her meekly out and along the South Walks Road that followed the lines of Dorchester's Roman wall. They took a turn up West Walks until they reached the park gate. "You want the bowling green or the bandstand?" she demanded, waving an explanatory hand. "Plenty of benches in the sun."

"The bandstand, so long as there's not a band in it," he said, puffing peacefully away, so they settled on a blue bench opposite the bandstand, its wrought-iron pillars gaily painted in the same shade of bright blue. "All right now," Penny commanded, "take it from the top and don't leave anything out."

The telling took a long time, as a gentle breeze ruffled the bright flowers around them, and Toby's deep rumble was counterpointed by the shrill shrieks and laughter of children playing in the playground beyond the mercifully empty bandstand. Penny listened intently without interrupting. She took no notes, as he would have done had their positions been reversed, for her many years of field work had trained her to tape record in her mind the spoken word for instant replay thereafter. It occurred to her as he rumbled on that she was going to need a great deal of this facility in the near future. He had finally arrived at the events of the day and ground to a stop. "So you see why I was getting out," he said. "What do you think of it?"

They sat in silence for several minutes, he in a relieved peace, she in an agony of concentrated thought, her pixielike face screwed up in concentration. Finally she said, "You've made a case, but not a good one in my opinion. In fact I think you've got yourself into such an emotional stew that you've gone off half-cocked before you've got all the facts you need. Over the years how many times have your gut feelings turned out to be correct? Almost always, I'd say. And yet your scenario about Farwell and the Orchard girl doesn't fit in that first murder anywhere, and, if you feel the two are linked, then they probably *are* linked and we are looking for a very cold-blooded murderer. From what you've told me, and given the crafty old drunk Job Squires so evidently was, I'd say he'd been paid to keep an eye on the Colonel's activities by someone they both knew very well, a friend in other words, and when Job had something substantive to report and asked for more money on the strength of it, that someone had no further use for him and just offed him. No wonder he looked so surprised!"

"I never even thought of that," Toby confessed.

"My dear, you're terrific on research, but when it comes to people . . ." Penny shook her head sadly. "And it seems to me that you have a whole host of suspects, all money-hungry, and far more likely to want Orchard out of the way than a young man to whom he was at best a minor nuisance, and a career girl who probably thoroughly enjoyed rubbing the old boy's nose in her own success after the way he had treated her."

"But what did he *have* that they wanted?" Toby cried. "He was hard up too."

"He had those diamonds. And I don't for one moment buy

that story about taking them out of their settings," she came back at him. "It would never have occurred to a man like him, and how many career colonels' ladies without private means have five-carat diamonds anyway?"

"She could have inherited them," he protested.

"Possibly, but then he'd have cashed in on them sooner, not 20 years after her death. And you haven't even checked to see if she *did* come from monied people. No, I think he found them, just like you previously supposed he may have found a Celtic gold trove. I *like* your smuggling theory. He may have stumbled on a smuggler's cache."

"But there *is* no smuggling going on around here. I checked that with Hardy." Toby was growing testy.

"You were talking of smuggling *in*, how about smuggling *out*?" Penny retaliated. "I understand there is quite a brisk trade in stolen antiques and objets d'art between England and the continent. Friends of mine had their Regency house in Brighton almost stripped of antiques by thieves, and the police calmly told them that probably their furniture had been on a boat out within hours of the theft. Have you checked on recent diamond robberies in the West Country?"

"Well, no, that didn't occur to me," he confessed. "But I can find out soon enough."

"So you're not going back to Oxford, not giving up?" she queried.

"Now that you are here, no," he admitted.

She grinned at him. "Good! For if the answer had been yes, I'd be out of here tonight to carry out my original plan of visiting the family on my way back, and *you* would have damn well paid for my ticket."

He chuckled. "Fair enough! So who are we looking at first?"

"Take your pick—Gulliver, Roper, the sex-pot widow, Squires . . ."

"Squires isn't hard up. He seems to be very well fixed," Toby interrupted.

"He *appears* to be rich," she corrected. "And anyway, I find a clergyman who's had three wives and is working on a fourth definitely fishy, especially since, as you have pointed out, he's the only one we know of with that indispensable smuggler's tool, a boat. What we need most," she went on, "is a pipeline into the local scene, someone like that sergeant of yours but not in the police. Ap Jones, as you've already discovered, is very useful because he knows the area, but he's still an outsider. What we need preferably is an outsider, who will talk to us, married to an insider. Rural communities tend to be the same the world over, and it would take more years than we have left to break into what really goes on in Dorset village life, take it from an anthropologist! So that's where we have to start, and maybe Wood can help us find someone, but first," she sprang to her feet, "I've got to be fed. I'm absolutely ravenous. Where can we eat?"

Toby looked at his watch. "But it's only 5:30!" he protested. "It's far too early for dinner."

"Not for me it isn't," Penny declared. "My stomach is still on New Zealand time."

"The tearooms will be shut by now, and the restaurants won't be serving dinner yet," he said. "We could try the pubs. There's a good one, the King's Head, at the top of High Street."

"Then let's go, go, go," she urged. "I'll show you where I'm staying on the way." They walked across the gardens and exited onto Cornwall Road. "The one with the red door on the corner there," she pointed out as they went by. "Don't have the telephone number yet but Gwen knows it if you need it." They branched right on a road that led them to the roundabout at the Top o' the Town and turned right again onto High Street toward the King's Head.

There he settled her at a table and returned with a large gin and tonic for her, cider for himself, and the bad news that the pub did not start serving dinner until 7:30. "Two hours!" Penny exclaimed. "No way! Anyway I see from the board that their special tonight is roast lamb, and I had enough lamb on my Antipodean trip to last me a lifetime. We passed a place on the way down here that starts frying at 5:30, so I'm heading back there. I could just fancy a nice plate of fish and chips. Drink up!"

"A fish and chip place? Good Lord!" he exclaimed in horror, as she swigged down her drink. "It probably doesn't even have a liquor license."

"Then you stay here and drink and I'll go there and eat," she said with determination and stood up.

"No, I'll come with you," he said, desperately gulping down his own. But when they got to the small shop that advertised a restaurant in the rear and where the front frying-bar was presided over by a very fat man and an almost equally fat woman, the combined odors of hot oil, rich batter, and fish were too much for Toby and he said feebly, "I think after all I will leave you to it. I'll be waiting for you in the bar when you've finished."

He returned to their table in the pub and waited. An hour and a half went by. "She must be eating the place out!" he muttered into his glass. "Or has keeled over and died of acute indigestion. I'd better go and see." He hurried back up the road.

The fat couple had been replaced at the busy bar an by acne-faced youth and a young pudding-faced girl. "Er, I was in earlier with a small lady who was dining here. Have you by any chance seen her?" Toby inquired nervously of the youth.

The boy nodded and jerked his head. "Back in the restaurant there with me mum and dad."

A little mystified, Toby went through the glass door in the rear and found himself in a long narrow dining room where only three tables were occupied. At the one nearest the door he spotted Penny's mouse-colored head bent in deep and earnest conversation with the enormous proprietor and his wife. As he loomed over the table Penny looked up, her eyes dancing with delight. "Ah, Toby, sorry to have been so long, but you've missed the best fish and chips in the West Country. Meet my excellent hosts, Bill and Vi Cox—Sir Tobias Glendower." As the couple grinned and nodded at him, she went on. "Bill here is a true Cockney, born in the sound of Bow Bells, but Vi's a Dorset girl from Whitchurch Canonicorum, with a sister in Charmouth and a brother in Chideock. Tomorrow is the day she always visits her sister, so I'll be driving her over." She gave him a meaningful grin. "They've been so interested in what I had to tell them and would like to give us a helping hand. Isn't that nice?"

Chapter 11

"I just couldn't believe I'd get that lucky so fast," Penny enthused. "When I heard that Cockney accent it sounded like a heavenly choir, so I went right to work. He's as shrewd and sharp-witted as they come and tumbled immediately to what I was after. She's an amiable sort, if a bit blank, but with them on my side I should get results fast."

"I only hope to God you didn't let on about the second murder," Toby growled. "The police would have a fit." They were back at the King's Head, and for the second night in a row he was facing a plate of roast lamb, roast potatoes, and green peas, while Penny browsed happily through a double helping of apple dumpling crowned with Devonshire cream.

"Country people may not have had the benefits of an Oxford education but they aren't stupid. I didn't tell *them* about the murders, they told me. What's more, they've already decided what it's all about even if they haven't settled as yet on the murderer, and they've been thinking along much the same lines as you did at the start: namely, that Job was murdered because he was a warlock and that Orchard's was a retaliatory murder because he was a Dorset Druid and that there's a private war going on between the two groups."

"Good Lord!" Toby exclaimed. "Don't tell me we're back to that idea."

"No, of course not. They don't know what we know, but it does show how clever the murderer is. With that idea firmly planted in local minds, the police aren't going to get one hell of a lot of cooperation. If I can get on an inside track tomorrow, see how the wind blows, and convince them I'm on their side, then you'll just have to trust me when it comes to telling them the true facts about Orchard's death. Once I can show them it was all a carefully planned charade, I think their anger will redirect itself into the right channels and they'll open up more."

"Well for Heaven's sake be careful," he said automatically, and they went on to map out their separate plans of attack for the morrow.

"I shouldn't have had that second G and T," Penny said at length with another huge yawn. "I've had it. I'm going to totter back to my bed and flop. Where and when shall we rendezvous tomorrow?" If clear, they would meet at the bandstand; if wet, Toby would seek her out at her lodgings. They set the time at 5:00. "Vi has to be back by then to start the frying," she explained with a grin.

First thing in the morning Toby set about his appointed tasks. He strolled over to the police station and had a long interview with Hardy, who was rather taken aback by his long list of requests. On the diamonds Toby was sadly disappointed; there had been no recent diamond robberies in Dorset or its surrounding counties, although Hardy had shown himself more open to the idea of outgoing smuggling than he had of the incoming. "Come to think of it, there has been a rash of robberies in the smaller country houses around here," he admitted, "and mostly small stuff taken. The bigger places haven't been touched because they have good security systems. No particular pattern to the thefts and none of the stuff has ever shown up. Even Mrs. Westcott-Smyth had one about a year or so ago, a Tiffany lamp and some pieces of Lalique crystal. Got the insurance money for them of course, so she didn't appear too upset."

"Indeed?" Toby said. "Is there any way you can get an idea of the financial standing of all the people I've mentioned? It might help to find out who is hurting the most for money."

On that Hardy was inflexible. "Sorry, not possible. You've seen how difficult it was in the Colonel's case, so unless you can give some concrete reasons why any of them should be investigated, we simply can't pry into their private affairs. Being hard up isn't a crime; after all, most of us are these days." However, he did have one further bit of interesting information on the diamonds. "When I talked with Martha about them, she did confirm what Margaret Orchard had said; she never recalled Mrs. O wearing any and remembered only a small diamond and sapphire engagement ring and her gold wedding band. That was it. So then I got back to the jeweler and he had some interesting things to add to his original statement. He had the lesser diamonds looked at by a jeweler friend who specializes in antique jewelry. It was his opinion that the stones were cut prior to Victorian times, eighteenth century or possibly even earlier, and that the way they were cut indicated they'd been used in something like a parure or a tiara, where their flaws would not be apparent but where they'd supply a lot of glitter. Again that doesn't sound too much like the late Mrs. O, does it? I checked her background out, as you asked, and it seems she was an army nurse and that her father was a Methodist clergyman, so that doesn't sound like money either. You may be onto something with the diamonds."

"How about on Orchard's side?" Toby asked.

"Not much money there either. You've seen Martha and Joe. Well, most of the Orchards are more like them than him. His branch was a bit better fixed, grandfather was a country solicitor and his father a civil engineer who spent a lot of time in the colonies. Had enough to send him to a decent school and then Sandhurst, but no real wealth or any land behind them."

It was much the same story on Colin Roper. The family had ancient roots in Dorset, but Colin's father had been a real-estate agent in Bridport, and Colin had first worked in and then inherited the business and moved it to Dorchester. "Did very well for himself in the real-estate boom of the seventies and eighties, but now? I'd say he was hurting pretty bad. Land poor he is. Bought up a lot of land on spec for development, and of course there's no development going on now. On this Druid business, well, he *might* be sincere, but I think while the boom was on he also found it mighty handy for business contacts."

This took care of the native born, and on the "outsiders" Hardy was even vaguer. "According to Westcott-Smyth's records, which I checked, he was born in Birmingham and inherited his business from dear old Dad: nouveau riche he was. Made a packet out of supplying rebuilt bombed areas of the Midlands after World War Two. Mrs. W came from much the same background. Her father owned a small chain of hardware stores in the Birmingham area, though, unlike her husband, she got a degree in history from Birmingham University. Married money so never has worked," Hardy observed with a sniff. "As to Gulliver, you probably know more about him than I do. He seems innocuous, and to my mind Nicholas Squires is also a nonstarter. Now you've brought up this smuggling thing again and Squires does have a boat, I will check and see what I can get on his background, *very* quietly. All the people you seem fixated on have certain local standing, so I'll have to tread warily."

"Fair enough," Toby said, and stood up to take his leave.

"Half a sec more," Hardy said, and flipped open a folder on his desk. "What do you make of all that stuff Farwell brought in? He told me you'd seen it."

"Added to what I've found out about Job Squires I would say that he *was* the wooser referred to in the notes, that the mask and doubtless other paraphernalia were removed by other members of his group after the murder, and that whoever did murder him knew he was a warlock and so arranged those fake trappings."

Hardy was only listening with half an ear. "And this 'Find Merlin, get Merlin' note, has that anything to do with you being here, Sir Tobias? Merlin *is* your middle name isn't it?" he said softly.

Toby winced, for the inspector was now treading on treacherous ground. "No, pure coincidence. After all Merlin is a name connected with witchcraft since pre-Roman times. It could well be the name of another coven head just like Mother Crowns might be. Or it could even mean a Druid, for Merlin *was* one. I don't feel it has much to do with anything concrete."

"And you don't think Orchard's murder might have been a retaliatory gesture?"

"No, I don't." This time Toby was very positive. "For one thing, why pick on Orchard, whom very few people would have known as a Druid because he had joined so recently? And if you're thinking *he* might have killed Job, I consider that out of the question. He may have been eccentric but he was no homicidal maniac. His murder bears all the same phony trappings as Job's did, so to my mind is by the same hand."

Hardy sighed and nodded. "Yes, I must say I agree with you, but why, by all that's holy, *why* were they killed?"

"I don't know, but I intend to find out," Toby said as he took his leave. He mooched back to Woolaston Lodge and once again applied himself to the phone. He called one of his All Souls colleagues, Barnaby White, an emeritus professor like himself and a former fellow of Oriel, seeking more information on Gulliver.

"Phew! Going back a bit, aren't you?" White exclaimed on hearing his request. "Fancy old Scrounging Silas turning up after all these years!"

"Scrounging Silas?" Toby echoed.

"Well, that's the main thing I remember about him. Always at it. Touched everyone in the college at one time or another. You know the kind of thing—'Lend me a tenner till Tuesday'—but of course no one ever saw a penny of it again. Other than that all I remember is some vague scandal about pinching some of old Vincent Carruthers's—remember him?—valuable books. The old boy was very absent-minded by that time, and Silas claimed he had returned them so nothing could be done. He left Oriel not too long after that, and when some of the books turned up subsequently in a rare book shop in London, Carruthers bought 'em back. Gulliver was a pretty sleazy type I'd say. If he hasn't improved, watch your pockets!"

"So you don't know where he went or what his special field was?" Toby persisted.

"Sorry, no idea. Just dropped completely out of sight. Wasn't a particularly friendly type, so I can't think of any old Oriel hands who could help you. What's he up to these days?"

"Oh, local Dorset history mainly, but also seems keen on French history," Toby said.

"Odd sort of combination," White sniffed. "And not too financially rewarding I'd say. Wonder who he's scrounging off now. Anyway, sorry not to be of more help, Glendower. You on another of your cases by any chance?"

"I'm helping the police," Toby admitted.

"Bit of a change from Pericles, eh? Well, I'll ask around about Gulliver and if I find anything I'll let you know. Where are you?"

Toby told him, rang off, and went out intending to seek out the library and a more up-to-date *Crockford's* than Ap Jones's, hoping to find more on the Reverend Squires. As he passed the kitchen, Owen popped his head out. "Oh, two things, Sir Tobias. You've had a number of calls from a Mrs. Westcott-Smyth," he grinned meaningfully. "Wants you over for dinner, preferably tonight, and would you call her back as soon as possible."

Toby shuddered. "No, thank you! If she calls again tell her you haven't seen me and don't know where I am."

"Righto! The other thing is that I *think* I've remembered where I saw that Merlin name," Owen went on. "It was on a tombstone, and I'm almost certain it was in Whitchurch. I could get away for a couple of hours now. Want to go and hunt for it?"

Toby consulted his watch. "Why not? I can go to the library later."

The village of Whitchurch Canonicorum snuggled cosily, sheltered by low hills, in the valley of the River Char, its most notable feature the ancient, square-towered, gray stone church that stood at the center of the modern village. As they let themselves into the church lych gate Owen said, "I'm pretty sure it must be alongside one of the main paths because I was cutting through the churchyard when I saw it and it struck me as so odd."

"What was odd about it?"

"Because some of it was in French and I thought all the French were Catholic, so I wondered what it was doing in here." Owen hovered undecidedly before launching out along one of the paved pathways.

"Could have been a Huguenot, I suppose," Toby observed. "You look on the right and I'll check the left." They drew a blank on the first pathway, but on the second, when they were almost at the exit gate at the opposite end of the churchyard, Owen exclaimed, "Yes, here it is!" and pointed at a tilted gray headstone blotched by vivid orange lichen. "See, the name pops out at you."

Toby whipped out his notebook and peered closely at the stone. In French the inscription read "Here rests Marie Merlin de Thionville, widow of Pierre. Died of misery at St. Gabriel, December 15th, 1795, aged 30 years." Underneath in English was added "An unhappy victim of the French Revolution." While he was digesting this a mild-faced man, sporting a clerical vest and collar under a shabby tweed jacket and pushing a bike, entered by the adjacent gate and smiled shyly at them. "Ah, I see you have discovered one of our curiosities," he said.

Before Toby could open his mouth, Owen was off and running. "Yes, vicar, we were wondering how this came to be here, being French and all, and not from this parish. St. Gabriel it says."

The vicar was shyly diffident. "I'm afraid I can't tell you a great deal. She must have been one of the group of emigrés who came into Weymouth in 1792, escaping from the French Revolution, you know? Most of them went on up to London I understand, but a few did stay in these parts. It is possible the vicar of St. Gabriel refused the burial because she was a Catholic, or, more likely, that there was no vicar at Stanton at that time. As a very small parish it was sometimes unattended, and I do know the church there has been in disuse for over a century and is quite ruined now. Anyway, Whitchurch has in its registers frequent entries for Stanton St. Gabriel over the centuries. Maybe the county library in Dorchester could help you? Doubtless it's a sad story; 'died of misery' indeed—poor soul." And with a sigh he pushed his bike off along the path to the church.

Owen looked inquiringly at Toby, who shrugged. "I can't see what it has to do with anything, but I suppose it's worth checking on further just in case. Odd coincidence about the name. I have a friend who has written several books on the Revolution, so I'll try him."

They headed back for Dorchester and Toby once again sought the phone. This time he called his club, the Athenaeum. "Tobias Glendower here. Is Dr. Stubbs in the reading room by any chance? He is? Good, ask him to come to the phone, please." After a considerable interval, the breezy, wheezy voice of Stubbs came on.

"What are you up to now, you old toper? Not called to inquire after my health I'll be bound."

Toby explained what he wanted and there was a wheezing silence at the other end. Then, "Pierre Merlin de Thionville eh? It does ring a vague bell but I can't bring it to mind. I'll look him up and get back to you. How do I do that?"

Toby told him and then went off to the county library until it was time to rendezvous with Penny. Apart from confirming what the clergyman had told them about the refugees coming into Weymouth, he learned little else except the fact that some of the men had subsequently returned to France leaving their families behind, and that many of them had slipped surreptitiously across the Channel to Royalist Brittany "with the aid of smuggler friends." Penny would love that bit, he reflected.

Next he applied himself to *Crockford's*. All he learned from the brief entry on the Reverend Squires was that he had been born in Wolverhampton 55 years ago and was a widower. No mention was made of his academic training apart from the seminary, so he concluded that Squires was neither a public school nor college man. The only small point of interest was that, Wolverhampton now being part of the greater Birmingham area, there was possibly, though not probably, some connection with the Westcott-Smyths. Feeling he was merely clutching at straws, he decided to pack it in for the day and went in search of Penny.

He found her by the bandstand, hopping from one foot to another in impatience. At sight of him she burst out, "I need an ordnance map of the Charmouth area in the worst possible way. I can't talk now or I'll forget half the names that have been flung at me."

"I have one back at Woolaston Lodge. Let's go pick it up. You *should* take notes," he reproved, but on the way back he regaled her with the events of his day. As they entered the Lodge Gwen popped her head out of the living room. "Oh, Sir Tobias, that Mrs. Westcott-Smyth has been after you again. Most insistent that you call her back, she was, even though I told her how busy you were."

He groaned and shook his head, but received a sharp elbow in the ribs from Penny. "Go on. It could be useful," she urged. "Call her! If she wants you for dinner, tell her you have to bring a visiting colleague or it's no go. It's too late today anyway, so tell her you can come tomorrow."

"Do I have to? She really is frightful," he protested.

"If we're ever going to get anywhere on this, yes. Anyway what can happen to you if I'm there?" she demanded. "She can scarcely drag you off to her boudoir by your silvery locks, can she?"

Reluctantly he phoned and his hopes rose slightly when at the mention of a colleague there was a marked hesitation at the other end. But hope was soon dashed when Brenda said brightly, "Well, I *did* hope to have you all to myself but *tant pis*, as the French say, let's make it a full-fledged dinner party then. I'll try and get hold of some people you and he will find interesting. Let's say 7:30 tomorrow then? *So* looking forward to it!"

He did not disillusion her and, duty done, turned back to Penny, who had retrieved the map from his room and was studying it anxiously. "Well, I hope you're satisfied," he grumbled. "She'll probably have a fit when she sees you. She's expecting another man. And what's so urgent about that map?"

"I didn't want to stop the flow and admit I hadn't the faintest idea what they were talking about," she said. "I've had a long and very rewarding day, and, what's more, I've only just scratched the surface. My fondest wish came true. I met Mrs. Abby Flyte of Cain's Folly Cottage and may God bless her busybody soul! Feed me and I'll tell you all about it."

Chapter 12

"Mrs. Flyte says something is definitely going on, and when Mrs. Flyte speaks, most of Charmouth and I believe her," Penny stated, as she waited for her roast beef and Yorkshire pudding dinner, idly watching the engorged River Frome rushing by the windows of the White Hart Hotel in the valley at the bottom of High Street.

"Then who *is* she, and what's she got to do with Vi or Vi's sister or the matter in hand?" Toby said, with what he considered monumental patience.

"Ah, that's a big question. Mrs. F knows all, sees all, and, if in the mood, will tell all that goes on in Charmouth and vicinity, though her tentacles stretch a lot farther than that, as you'll see. You could call her the local opposition to Job Squires and his cronies, whom she cordially loathes, since, though a loner, she is in much the same line of business: local soothsayer, fortune teller, advisor to the lovelorn, marriage counselor, family advisor, etcetera. When we got to Charmouth Vi's sister—Prim for Primrose—was in an uproar because the local school had just informed her that her youngest was dyslexic and hyperactive, so we all rushed off to Mrs. F to find out what to do. Abby Flyte and I hit it off from word one, so, having soothed Vi's sister, she packed them off home and kept me. Over a delicious pheasant stew, supplied I'm sure by one of her poacher clients, we got down to cases." She was interrupted by the arrival of their dinners, Toby having absent-mindedly ordered the roast lamb. "Didn't you have that last night?" she said, peering at his plate.

"Did I?" He looked at it blankly. "Yes, come to think of it I did. Oh well, go on."

"I'll try to take things in order. First, Job, of whom she thoroughly disapproved, being a strict teetotaler herself. She thinks he was either blackmailing or putting the squeeze on someone important locally, although as of yet she does not know who. He was *definitely* following Orchard around, although the old boy was the closest thing to an upper-crust friend he had. At the time of his murder Job was working as a part-time gardener for Mrs. Westcott-Smyth. And, over the previous three months, he had been seen in the company of Roper, Squires, Margaret Orchard, and, most significant of all, spent an entire evening in Silas Gulliver's house—the one and only time that happened. Old Mrs. Defau, who works for Gulliver, is a steady client of hers . . ." She paused to gulp some of the excellent St. Emilion Toby had ordered.

"On Gulliver she waxes eloquent," she went on. "He is one mean son of a bitch; has been sponging off and has had designs on Mrs. W-S for years, but so far has had little success because he is short on both charm and money. In the past two years he has made frequent short trips to France and has been a little better fixed than formerly. Mrs. F is convinced he's a smuggler. 'It's in the blood,' says she, 'and he's a crooked one.'"

Toby grunted and refilled both their glasses. "So far it's all hearsay. Not a single solid fact."

"Yes, but significant hearsay and it gets better, if more confusing," she assured him. "Take Squires, for instance. Mrs. F is not a churchgoer, as you may well imagine, so has escaped his local hypnotic effect. She's worried about his influence on the parish, which she thinks is dangerous. So she really has been delving deep on him. Item one: he started life as an actor in his local repertory company, then moved on to slightly bigger things in Liverpool. Item two: wife number one was a patron of the Little Theatre there, a childless widow and 15 years older than he. She didn't last long. Five years after they married she dropped dead, apparently of a heart attack. Item three: wife number two, who appeared five years alter, was the spinster heiress of a candy manufacturer and lived on an estate in North Wales. She only lasted two years: the brakes failed on her car when she was driving down a mountain road. The police sniffed around a bit on that one because he was sole legatee, but nothing came of it. After that he disappeared for a number of years and Abby Flyte thinks he may have gone overseas. Then some ten years ago, he turned up in Bristol with wife number three, 'a foreigner,' but she doesn't know where from, and she only lasted three years after the return. Mrs. F is still delving into how and where she died, but she did find out he was then in some export-import business, though in what merchandise she doesn't know."

"How in the world does she know all this?" Toby broke in. "Are you sure she hasn't made it all up?"

"I'd make book on it. I was hoping, now we have some dates and places, your police pals could do some checking. I mean three dead wives *is* a bit fishy!" She grinned impishly at him. "And the answer to Mrs. F's omniscience is what in America we'd call networking. The source of her network I leave to your imagination. Anyway, let me finish on Squires. As I think I told you, Abby Flyte lives in a cottage situated on top of Cain's Folly cliff, overlooking both the sea and the Dorset coastal path that runs from Charmouth to Stanton St. Gabriel—and further, for all I know. When Squires had settled into the parish, she'd see him cycling along the path several times a week, presumably to get at his horse in St. Gabriel's. Two months ago this stopped, presumably when he got his boat and had to drive over because he had to tow it to the beach. At first he was trying out the boat between Stanton and

Lyme Regis, and she spotted him in it together with Margaret O, Gulliver, and, on one occasion, Roper. Recently he has become more daring and has been making solo trips straight across the Channel, sometimes overnight, although he hasn't been out since Orchard's death. Where does he get to if he goes straight across?"

"Straight would take him to the Brittany coast, but the *nearest* landfall if he went slightly northeast would be the Cherbourg peninsula of Normandy or the Channel Islands," Toby said after some reflection. "And that would make more sense for a navigator."

"Umm, well, wherever he goes, Mrs. Flyte is convinced he's up to no good."

"She doesn't appear to think anyone is up to any good," Toby observed.

"On the whole that's true; she doesn't have a high opinion of human nature, but she does have some surprising exceptions—Orchard for one."

"Oh? Did she know him then?" Toby was surprised.

"Quite well. He often used to drop in for a cup of tea and a chat when he was on his explorations, of which she thoroughly approved, being a proponent of ley lines herself. She says her cottage lies slap dab on one of them that comes out of Golden Cap. She really liked him: thought him a good old soul and consequently is anti-Margaret, whom she thought treated her father shamefully and 'is no better than she ought to be, always aleading men on.'"

Toby shifted uneasily. "Did she have anything to say about Stephen?"

"On him, no, but she liked his grandfather a lot, and volunteered that Stephen's father was 'a thoroughly bad lot, a real throwback to the old Farwells.'"

"Good God, his grandfather! How old is she?" Toby exploded.

"Oh, I'd say between 80 and 85," Penny said, and added

hastily, "But she's got all her marbles, I assure you. I only hope I'm half as with it if I get to her age."

"Hmm." Toby was dubious. "And did she have anything good to say about anyone else?"

"All she had to say on Mrs. Westcott-Smyth was that she was a born 'victim,' and Roper wasn't on her hit list either. Says his only real weakness is greed, but apparently he looked after his invalid mother for many years in style and that rated high with Abby Flyte. She's very much into family solidarity: one of the things she has against Squires is the commotion he has caused in Charmouth family circles."

"Scarcely criminal!" Toby sniffed. "But to get back to Orchard. If she was that pally with him, did he say anything to her to indicate any kind of recent problems?"

"That's what I'll get on to first thing tomorrow when I see her," Penny said tartly. "For a first go I think I covered one hell of a lot of ground. Now I'd like you to take me out to Eggardon and the scene of the crime. Maiden Castle, too, if there's time."

"What? Tonight?" he said, hastily polishing off the last of the wine.

"Why not? It stays light until after ten. Got anything better in mind?" she demanded.

"Well, if you insist, but I don't see what good it will do and there's nothing much to see," he grumbled, settling the check and following her out. "We may as well do the Maiden first since it's closer."

Once inside the Iron Age fortress, which they had to themselves, apart from a couple of people walking outsize dogs, he demonstrated his movements and the happenings of that first traumatic day. When he was through, Penny looked concerned. "I can quite see why you were so set on Farwell," she muttered. "I'm afraid I've been rather discounting him, but that series of events *is* suspicious. And you say he could have done the Eggardon Hill one also?"

"In the sense of not having an alibi, yes, but otherwise, no. It just makes no sense, for the mask and notes are genuine, as I am also convinced was his own concern about them. If he'd murdered Job Squires for whatever motive, why wouldn't he have just suppressed all of that? No one would have been any the wiser," he stated.

"You've got me," she shrugged. "Let's go on to Eggardon and see if enlightenment strikes."

But after they had toiled up the farm track that led to the outer ramparts of the hill fort and reached the quiet, deserted sanctuary of grass sward within its towering earth embankments, she appeared restless and ill at ease. "It certainly is a fine and private place," she observed with a little shiver. "So what can you tell me about it that's special?"

Toby waved a pontifical hand around it. "As you can see it's only half the size of Maiden Castle; 20 acres in here as opposed to 45. But it does predate the Maiden by two centuries and may have been the original Durotriges capital. And, of course, it was easily taken by the same Roman legion that massacred them at Maiden Castle."

"Nothing more recent?" she asked.

"I did read that in the eighteenth and early nineteenth centuries the smugglers of these parts had a signal station up here to give their boats an all-clear to come in," he admitted grudgingly.

"Smugglers, eh?" She brightened visibly, then looked puzzled. "But we're nowhere near the sea. How would that have worked?"

He started to climb the southern embankment and beckoned her. "Come up here and you'll see." She puffed on up to join him at the top and gave a little gasp as the dull silver of the English Channel, glinting in the dimming light, spread out before them. "From up here you can see all the way from Weymouth on our left to Lyme on our right," Toby indicated. "The main customs patrols worked along the beaches and coastal cliffs, so smugglers would have been easily spotted on them, but up here I imagine they could hide their lanterns, telescopes, and probably mirrors as well. When the time was right, they would come up here and signal out to sea as to which beach to use. Even if the patrols did spot the lights, by the time they arrived, the signalers would have been long gone. Directly below and in front of us lies Shipton Gorge, Job's home base; the brighter lights to the left are of Bridport and to the farthest right, across the water, is Lyme. If you follow back from Lyme towards us you'll see the dimmer lights of Charmouth and, closer still, a few scattered lights in Stanton St. Gabriel. See the great lowering bulk of Golden Cap sticking out there?"

Penny nodded. "And the dimmer lights between that and Bridport would be Chideock?" she queried.

"Yes, from here we can see the whole spectrum of the scene of action, possibly of the crime," he said heavily. "I think Orchard was killed much closer to home than where he was found, but with all the rain there's been we are never going to know where exactly."

"Then why trek the body all the way back to Dorchester?" Penny mused, then answered her own question. "Maybe to get the police looking in that direction rather than this, though it was taking one hell of a chance."

"Not if it was handier to his own home base and he wanted to keep the hill fort–witchcraft theme going."

"But that brings it down to Roper or Farwell!" she exclaimed. "And you've already ruled Farwell out so far as the Colonel's logbook theft goes, so that leaves Roper."

"I wish to God I could be certain of that," Toby erupted. "But knowing now that Stephen is so cosy with Margaret Orchard I can't be sure *she* didn't abstract it. Oh, if only I knew why the book was so important."

"Standing around on a Dorset hilltop and moaning about it isn't going to find it," she snapped. "Come on. It's getting cold, so let's go back to the car. It strikes me you haven't even begun to explore the terrain you did make notes on—a far more worthwhile enterprise than propping up rural bars and trying to get the locals to talk to you. You should have known how futile that would be."

"Good God, you've got your nerve! I've been working flat out since I've been here," he exploded. "And what good will wandering along mostly imaginary ley lines do, I'd like to know?"

"Those diamonds—the only anomalous things we've got on the old boy and a possible motive. Not his, so where did they come from? Maybe he dug them up, and if there were seven, maybe there were seventy or seven hundred, who knows? But if you could find *where* he got them it might help." She became belligerent. "If he dug them up there may be signs of recent digging."

"But there have been no recent diamond robberies and old-time smugglers didn't go in for diamonds," he roared back.

"But they exist, and they must have come from somewhere and someone, so it's a starting point," she said stubbornly, and they argued hotly all the way back Dorchester.

As they came into the Top o' the Town, Penny calmed down. "Let's stop off at the King's Head for a nightcap," she suggested, "and make some plans for tomorrow."

"Very well," he said grumpily. "One thing about that damn dinner party you've let me in for, at least you'll get to meet some of our suspects. Maybe with your *great* human insight you can point the finger at once and say, 'He did it, call the police,' and we won't have to bother anymore."

She ignored that as they went into the pub, gave their orders, and settled at a table in the back with their drinks. She then started up in a milder vein. "I'll tackle Mrs. Flyte first thing about Orchard's recent moods and movements and see what she has to say about the other Orchards. If the old man was so fixated on Golden Cap, why don't you start there and work down towards St. Gabriel's House? Maybe we could get together for lunch at the Queen's Arms in Charmouth and swap notes."

"I'm expecting some phone calls but I could squeeze that in," Toby said loftily.

She chuckled suddenly. "What we need, since we are groping in the dark, is one of Jocelyn Combe's plot outlines. Remember how dead on she was with hers? Let's each think one up and see where it takes us."

Toby thawed a little. "I can hardly wait to hear your flights of fancy, but do try and remember the police like the odd concrete fact or two to make a case. If . . ." He was interrupted by a voice behind him.

"Why, Sir Tobias, this is a surprise. I thought you had returned to Oxford." He swiveled around to see Stephen Farwell standing uncertainly, a glass of beer clutched tightly in his hand.

"Ah, Stephen!' Toby glanced quickly at Penny who gave an infinitesimal nod. "Won't you join us? You remember Dr. Spring, of course? Just back from New Zealand and dropped by, so I decided to change my plans."

Stephen slid into a seat opposite him, his face strained, his eyes wary. "Nice to see you again Dr. Spring," he said. "This is quite a surprise. I suppose you are here because of the new development."

They looked at him blankly. "What new development?" they said in unison.

Stephen's look of strain intensified. "It was on the local evening news. Naturally I assumed you were aware of it, since you've been working so closely with the police, and with Dr. Spring now so opportunely on the scene."

"What is it?" Penny demanded.

"Why, Colonel Orchard's murder. Inspector Hardy announced it as such this afternoon. Said that they have been quietly investigating it as such and hope to have a suspect in custody very shortly. By tomorrow this place will be swarming with reporters." His lips tightened. "I would take it as a great favor, Sir Tobias, if you would tell me something."

"What?" Toby was still dazed with shock.

"Am I the suspect in question?" Stephen demanded.

Chapter 13

It had been a wearing day, so that, as they drove towards Chideock Manor and their dinner engagement, neither Penny nor Toby was in a conversational mood. They sat in exhausted silence, both inwardly keyed up for what might prove to be a very uncomfortable evening.

As prophesied, the press was already swarming around like Midian's hordes and Toby had awakened to find one determined reporter camped out by his Rolls. He had been forced to make a surreptitious exit by the rarely used front door of the Lodge and had been whisked away by the obliging Owen in his own station wagon and deposited at the foot of Golden Cap, where he had spent a totally unprofitable day checking it foot by foot and finding nothing. Scanning St. Gabriel's House with his binoculars he had noted the Orchards taking off in their minicar and had taken advantage of this to scramble down and make a hasty inspection of the grounds, particularly in the stable area, again with no result. Heartened by the absence of Margaret's car, he had even ventured to climb up into and inspect Squires's powerboat. He had been impressed by its power and speed potential, although the locked cabin had thwarted his intention of looking at Squires's logbook and sea charts to see where his nautical ventures had taken him.

Only one anomalous thing about the grounds had caught

his quick eye: the front and back hedges, and the hedge bounding the property on the side of Margaret's cottage, had all been trimmed within the past two months, whereas the hedge bounding it on the side of the ruined church was in wild disarray and had evidently not been touched since the present growing season had begun; Job Squires for some reason had not finished his hedging task. Bent on examining this from the church side, he had just started down the lane to the ruins when a familiar figure ahead of him sent him in an undignified scuttle back to the shelter of the entrance driveway. There he peered cautiously out to follow the progress of Silas Gulliver, noting with interest that Silas, after a furtive glance around, plunged into the ruins and did not reappear.

Toby was startled into further evasive action by the sound of an approaching car; he hustled back down the sea lane. Once beyond the back hedge he used its cover to get himself out of sight of the house and, panting, made his way back up Golden Cap. Again his binoculars scanned the terrain hoping to pick up Silas's ongoing tracks, but there was no sign of him until, scanning back towards the house, he picked him up at the exact spot where he had first seen him. He followed his casual stroll back up the lane and was grimly amused when Silas halted and peered intently through the hedge at the police car now parked in the driveway but with no sign of its attending policemen. This had evidently added a spur to Silas's ramblings, for he set off at a brisk pace for the haven of his own home just as another car came out of the T junction. Pulling up at the entrance, it disgorged a trio of men, one laden with a camera and obviously of the horde of reporters. This latest arrival quenched all thought of exploring the ruins, so Toby resignedly had descended the far side of Golden Cap and ambled down the farm track to await his appointed pickup by Owen at Filcombe Farm.

Penny had spent an equally frustrating day, if for different reasons. It was not that Abby Flyte had become uncommunicative. It was simply one of her "busy" days, with the phone ringing every few minutes and a steady stream of clients pounding on her door, so that conversation had been in hurried and disjointed snatches. While Abby consulted her clients, Penny had spent the bulk of the time wandering about outside the small cottage accompanied by Abby's three cats, named, predictably, Grimalkin, Pyewacket, and Asmodeus. If she had not managed to better her acquaintance with Abby she certainly had with Asmodeus, an enormous, coal black tomcat with smoldering yellow eyes, who had taken a violent fancy to her. If she as much as halted in her pacing he would immediately camp out on her feet, purring like a sewing machine.

Between clients, as they tried to take up the thread of their conversation, Abby was apologetic. "It's this murder announcement by the police. Got everyone stirred up it has. Like as not they'll settle down again in a few days, but by the looks of it we'll not get much done today. Maybe I should call you or send a message when things do quiet down. Where will you be?"

Penny thought quickly. "I think I'll be moving into the Queen's Arms if there's room. I'd just as soon be out of Dorchester with all those reporters around, and it'll be handier for our get-togethers."

The old woman nodded solemn assent. "Yes, just as well," she muttered. "For there's one more to come, and I think it is nigh in both place and time."

Penny was startled. "Another murder? Who?"

Abby shrugged. "That I do not know, but I feel it in the air, and three winds up the spell."

But as Penny set out for her lunch date with Toby at the Queen's Arms all she had gleaned from her morning was that Orchard, in the six weeks prior to his death, had first been elated "like a big schoolboy with a treat ahead of him" and then, the last time Abby had seen him, worried. "'Abby,' he said to me, 'life is just too damn complicated these days, always a catch to everything.' And then he stopped himself abruptlike and muttered about having to talk to Roper 'who might know.' Those were the last words he spoke to me," Abby sighed. "But you could tell there was a burden on him."

Penny booked herself into the Queen's Arms and reserved a table for lunch, but her frustration mounted as an hour beyond the appointed time there was still no sign of Toby. In exasperation she called Woolaston Lodge, only to be told the sad story of the Rolls and the reporter and that her partner was marooned on Golden Cap until such time as Owen could fetch him. "Then tell him to pick me up at the Queen's Arms at 7:00. I'm moving over here," she announced, and first consoled herself with a large lunch before driving back into Dorchester, packing and signing out of the lodging there, and returning to her more luxurious quarters at the ancient inn. There she put through a call to her son at his New York office to inform him of her whereabouts and to fill him in on developments.

Alexander Spring was grimly amused. "You certainly do get around, Ma. The twins only just received your post cards from New Zealand. I think I'll suppress this murder news from murder-buff Sonya. Otherwise you may have a crazy Russian assistant to cope with as well as her impossible father. I take it this means you won't be coming here as planned?"

"Maybe later, but not until this lot is settled," she said wearily. "And at the rate we're going that may be never, but here's hoping."

"Well, try and stay out of trouble and all in one piece. Leave it to Scotland Yard," he urged.

"Oh, they're not in on this, thank God. Just the local police, and I haven't even had to cope with them yet. Toby's downright matey with them, so I'll leave them to him. Anyway, love to everyone and give Mala and Marcus a kiss from me. Just wanted to let you know where I was," she said hastily and rang off.

She was still thinking about her amazingly precocious grandchildren as her silent partner turned the Rolls into the graveled driveway of Chideock Manor, drew up before its modest front door, which stood open, and announced with deep gloom, "Well, here we are, and by the looks of all these other cars we're late."

They got out slowly, stretched, and looked around them. Chideock Manor, although appropriate ancient-looking from its weathered stones, was no stately home. It had evidently been much altered and restored over the years so that it gave the impression of an overgrown farmhouse, one wing of which had evidently been a large barn before its conversion into a garage that housed a Daimler, a Jeep, and a small pickup truck. The manor grounds were well kept up but showed no particular character or style; the flower beds were stiffly planted with easy-to-care-for shrubs and perennials, and it was obvious from them that the lady of the manor was no garden lover.

Unable to postpone the moment of truth any longer, they looked resignedly at each other and walked through the open doorway into the black-and-white tiled entrance hall. From the room to the right, its door also ajar, came the murmur of voices. Toby cautiously pushed the door open and peered in to find himself eye to eye with his hostess, who immediately surged towards him with outstretched hands and an overbright smile. "Oh, *there* you are at last, Sir Tobias! We thought you were lost."

The smile congealed when, with a determined push, he inserted Penny's small form between him and the surging bosom and rumbled, "Good evening, Mrs. Westcott-Smyth. Allow me to present my colleague from Oxford University, Dame Penelope Spring."

This announcement visibly flustered Brenda, who sent a look of agonized appeal to Silas Gulliver, who was rapidly crossing the room towards them. "Well, this is an unexpected honor!" she spluttered. "When you said 'colleague' I naturally thought . . ." She trailed off with a little gasp and continued, "But no matter. At least now there'll be three of us since poor Margaret came rather unexpectedly." She shot a venomous glance at the tall, chestnut-haired figure clad in a very stylish navy silk suit, who was firmly embedded between the two massive figures of Squires and Roper. "You've time for one very quick drinkie before dinner." She clamped herself firmly onto Toby's arm and again gave Penny her overbright smile. "Here's Silas Gulliver, one of my *dearest* friends; Silas, Dame Penelope Spring. Silas will introduce you to our little group and I'll take care of Sir Tobias." It sounded like a threat.

Gulliver murmured acknowledgments, a smile on his lips but his eyes hard and wary. He steered Penny towards the sherry then started the round of introductions. She became acutely aware as they circulated that what she immediately thought of as the "inner circle" were all looking at her with the same hard-eyed suspicion. There were five "outsiders," elderly men, all of whom turned out to be members of the museum board who evidently did not know her or her reputation. They showed no such reserve and so she decided to bide her time and pointedly chatted with this group until dinner was announced and they all filed into the ornate, paneled dining room, which was heavily furnished in fake Jacobean style.

At the huge, dark oak table she found herself seated between Roper and Squires, with a very strained-looking Margaret sitting across the table from her. A smug Brenda presided at the head of the table, with Toby on her right and Silas on her left; they in turn were flanked by two museum board members; then came Roper opposite another board member, Margaret and herself in midtable, then Squires and another member facing two more of the board directly opposite. With a little superstitious chill she realized they were 13 at table, Margaret's unexpected presence obviously accounting for this ominous number.

What mainly intrigued her was the fact that Margaret so evidently did not want to be there: she was ill at ease, crumbling her bread with agitated fingers, fiddling with her cutlery, and darting troubled glances at Squires, who chatted in his melodious rumble with his right-hand neighbor. Margaret's presence, she realized ruefully, also put a damper on any conversation about the murder, which otherwise would undoubtedly have been the main topic: accident or design? she wondered.

With the soup course before them Roper, on her left, broke his silence. "So what brings you to these parts, Dame Penelope? Not the weather, I'll be bound." He gave a throaty chuckle.

Penny had a sudden bright thought. "Actually I'm down here looking around for a summer place to buy, big enough to house my son and his family as well as Toby and myself. My son married Toby's daughter, you see, and neither of us has permanent quarters large enough to house them comfortably when they visit England. Toby was so enraptured by how unspoilt and beautiful this part of Dorset is that we're seriously considering something around here."

"Really!" He brightened visibly. "How very fortunate we should be seated together then. I'm in real estate and would consider it a great honor if you'd let me assist you in your search. I have several properties that I think might be ideal for you."

"Indeed? I had no idea!" she exclaimed. "Why that would be most kind of you."

"How big a place? Four bedrooms?" he hazarded.

"Oh, I think a minimum of five, possibly six," she said firmly.

His enthusiasm waxed. "I see, you want a *big* house," and he began to expound the virtues of several large houses.

She let him ramble on for a bit then cut in. "None of those sounds quite what I had in mind. For one thing none of them is on the sea and we did want something with easy access to a beach for the children and for sailing, and also I *do* so like this stretch of coast between Lyme Regis and Chideock. Have you anything around here you could show me?"

He fell silent for a moment, his eyes narrowing, and, glancing across the table at Margaret Orchard, he dropped his voice to a low murmur. "It's possible there might be something shortly that would suit you. Six bedrooms, situated very handy to the sea. You've perhaps heard of the Orchard tragedy? That's Miss Orchard sitting across from you."

"Yes, Toby did mention something about it," she said with calculated vagueness.

"Well, I don't know her plans yet, but her late father's house at Stanton St. Gabriel is a big place to keep up, and I doubt whether she will have any desire to do so. It may well be shortly on the market. I've already had a word with her about it. Are you in a hurry for a house?"

"Oh no, not at all. We're prepared to wait for just the right property," she exclaimed. "That sounds interesting, so would you tell me about it?"

And as he did so at considerable length, she became aware that Squires's deep rumble had ceased and sensed that he was listening intently. She gave him a quick glance and saw his massive head bent over the entrée which, to her inner amusement, was roast lamb and potatoes with green peas once again. His handsome profile was fixed and stern and told her nothing.

"Oh, so it's an old house?" she prompted Roper. "How nice! Do you know anything of its history? My son would be fascinated to know."

Roper positively bloomed and launched into a detailed history of the house that amazed her. "How colorful! French emigrés, a smuggler's headquarters, a secret tunnel to the beach! That's fantastic!" she enthused. "My son will just love it. How well you put things, Mr. Roper."

Colin Roper preened. "Always had an interest in local history, being a Bridport man myself. You should talk to Silas Gulliver here; he's an expert in that field. I got a lot from him. The tunnel of course has been long since blocked off."

"Genuine smugglers, how exciting!" She glanced in wide-eyed innocence at Squires who was now frankly listening to them. "The only thing I'd heard about them up to now was your famous smuggling parson who ended up as a pirate, Vicar. Wasn't he a vicar of Charmouth?"

Squires gazed steadily at her, his eyes soulfully earnest. "Ah there I'm afraid you have me at a disadvantage, dear lady. I'm from the Midlands myself, a relative newcomer to these parts, and I've been so busy with the present affairs of my parish that I regret to say I am woefully ignorant of the history of my predecessors," he said and gave her a lingering smile that set her atingle. The animal magnetism he radiated was so intense that she wondered if he turned it on and off by some inner tap. She was no longer surprised at the three wives.

He deftly turned the conversation to more general topics as the meal progressed at a snail-like pace, but when Brenda finally rose and said, with some reluctance, "Ladies, let us withdraw and leave the gentlemen to their port and cigars," Roper laid a hand on Penny's and whispered, "It's not the best time just now, but I'll see what I can arrange about St. Gabriel's. Will you be staying on here?"

"Oh yes. I can be reached at the Queen's Arms in Charmouth and will be here for as long as it takes," she returned, conscious of the hard, significant look that passed between him and Squires.

When the three women reached the drawing room, her hopes for an intimate chat with Margaret Orchard were quickly dashed. No sooner had they finished their coffee than the latter burst out, "Brenda, I know this is terrible of me, but I'm afraid I must go. I have a splitting migraine coming on, and if I don't take care of it right away I'll be useless tomorrow, and I do have an important business conference in Poole. So please excuse me." She did indeed look pale and wretched, and, while her hostess did murmur appropriate platitudes, it was evident that Brenda was more than a little relieved to see the last of her.

This left the two of them in strained companionship, but after a few generalities Penny managed to steer Brenda into the subject of household help, and this unleashed a flood of complaints about the difficulties thereof and her present "couple" in particular, who were Yugoslavian refugees "and quite incomprehensible most of the time." As that topic showed signs of petering out, to Penny's surprise the door opened to admit Silas Gulliver and Nicholas Squires, Silas remarking as they entered, "Too much for us nonsmokers in there, so we've come to join you."

Brenda brightened on the instant and patted the large sofa on which she was ensconced in invitation. "How lovely! Silas *and* Nicholas, how sweet of you!"

Nicholas looked around as he settled in his indicated place beside her. "Where's Margaret?"

"Gone home. The poor girl wasn't feeling at all well. Can you wonder with all the stress she's been under? I'm surprised you even managed to get her here at all." Brenda's tone was acid.

A quick spasm of anger flashed across his face but was instantly smoothed out. "A change of scene and company is often a great solace in times of grief and stress," he commented and stood up. "I too must leave, I'm afraid. I must go up to London early tomorrow. Thank you for a delightful evening, and it was a great pleasure to meet *you*, Dame Penelope. I trust we will meet again very soon." He came over to where she was sitting, gave her hand a gentle squeeze, and gazed deeply into her eyes.

Brenda positively pouted. "Oh, how naughty of you, Nicholas, to leave so early. I hardly *ever* see you nowadays and I was hoping we could arrange for my promised trip in your lovely new boat."

"Soon, very soon," he promised and stalked out.

Brenda turned in a flash to Silas, who had been sitting with a slight smirk on his pallid face. "Now I suppose *you* are going to tell me you have to dash off because of another jaunt to France." Her tone was spiteful and she turned in appeal to Penny. "I don't know what's come over everybody lately. I could *always* depend on Silas, but for the past few months he's been dashing up to London and over to the continent constantly on God knows what errands."

Silas looked none too pleased but said, "I've told you often enough, Brenda. I'm researching a book on French history and you can't do that sitting in Stanton St. Gabriel. You know full well it's a major passion of mine."

"How interesting. What is your subject?" Penny chimed in, but before he could answer, the door opened and the rest of the group, headed by a lugubrious Toby, straggled in, and they were forced to rise and mingle.

As soon as he decently could, Toby edged up to Penny and muttered under his breath, "Let's get out of here. I've had it." Feeling a little exhausted herself, she nodded and they began their round of good-byes, ending up with their hostess, who had latched on to Roper and who evidently was delighted at having all the remaining men to herself.

Once outside, Toby let out a relieved sigh. "Thank God that's over. What a waste of time!"

"Not entirely," she said and shared the meager fruit of her own labors as he drove her back to the inn.

"The French connection does seem to be a recurring theme," he said as he dropped her off. "Maybe there is something to that Merlin business after all. You follow up on Roper and I'll concentrate on Gulliver."

"They all seem to be so interconnected. You don't think they *all* could be involved?" she queried.

He shook his head. "No. Two of them, almost undoubtedly, but which two? There are so many possible combinations."

"But only one obvious one," Penny said grimly. "Stephen and Margaret. She was in a fine old state tonight, but I never did get a chance to talk to her and find out why."

"I noticed," he said tightly, and drove off after setting an afternoon telephone rendezvous for the morrow. On his way back to Dorchester he sorted out his own priorities, foremost of which was to contact Hardy and find out what lay behind the police announcement, then to contact Barnaby White for an update on Gulliver, and to have another shot at Stubbs on the French connection. After all that he decided he would carry out his proposed inspection of the ruined church.

As he let himself into his silent lodgings and plodded wearily up to his room, he muttered crossly to himself, "Talk about grasping at straws. I'm damn well grasping at thin air!" He switched on the light and spotted a white envelope sitting on his pillow. Inside was a note in Gwen's round handwriting. "Dr. Stubbs called and said contact him, 11 A.M. Athenaeum. Has information. And there's been a theft from the police station you ought to know about. The wooser mask has disappeared."

Chapter 14

"Damnedest thing that's ever happened to me, having a piece of evidence disappear right under my very nose!" Hardy's voice came over the wire, shrill with indignation. "I had asked Farwell to come in, as I was not completely satisfied that I'd got the whole story from him. Had a hunch he was keeping something back. Told him to bring in the mask to go with the rest of the stuff. He was very unwilling, but I insisted. Well, we had the interview—not a very satisfactory one, I may say—I saw him out and off, and when I got back the mask was gone, vanished."

At his end of the phone, Toby stirred uneasily. "You don't suppose, er, Farwell just took it back?"

"Not unless he's a bloody magician and can be in two places at once. I tell you I saw him off in his car and he didn't have a thing on him, and the bloody mask was right there on my desk when I left the office. I was gone, oh, say 10 minutes at most. Got stopped on the way back to the office by one or two bits of business, but when I opened the door it was gone. I had the whole damn place turned inside out *and* everyone on duty searched: nothing! No one had heard or seen anything or anyone untoward. It's like a damned conjuring trick. Now, of course, the chief constable is right back on the witchcraft angle, and the worst of it is that one of my own men here almost *has* to be involved. Fair makes me sick. Mind you, I should have thought of what's coming up and taken more care."

"What is coming up?" Toby was puzzled.

"St. John's Eve, Midsummer Night. One of the big witch festivals I'm told. For some reason of their own, whoever did all this drew Farwell into it with the mask nonsense and now they've pinched it back, for God knows what reason. One thing I'm sure of is that this time it's gone for good."

"It may have something to do with your own announcement of Orchard's murder," Toby interrupted. "Why the sudden change, and who is the suspect, if I may ask?"

A heavy sigh floated over the wire. "All my men from the various villages were telling me that everyone was talking about 'the Colonel's murder.' The murmurings of the vox populi had even reached the chief constable, so we decided it was time to end the charade. As to the suspect business, that was just to placate the press and possibly to spook one of your most likely group of suspects. In short, I haven't anything concrete, have you?"

"Not really, but I'm following up on a couple of leads and may have some more soon," Toby said, and related in some detail the Merlin find and his own conjectures.

"Pretty far-fetched," Hardy said mournfully. "All except the bit about Job Squires and the Colonel. Your idea is that the Colonel caught him snooping on his activities and gave him the boot? And that all that ready cash he'd been spreading around was from someone who had paid him to keep an eye on Orchard?"

"Yes, I do, and that after Orchard had found Job out, our murderer had no further use for Squires and so silenced him."

"Any ideas on who?"

It was on the tip of his tongue to mention his suspicions of Gulliver, but without more to back him he could not bring himself to do it. "No, no idea until I get more information," he stated firmly.

"Well, be sure to keep me informed." Hardy sounded weary. "If we don't get a break soon we'll have to call in the Yard," he said, and he rang off.

Toby immediately called the museum. "Stephen," he barked. "I want a straight answer from you. Did you have anything to do with the theft of that damned mask? I assured you the other night you were not a police suspect, but, by God, I'm beginning to have serious doubts myself."

Stephen sounded harassed. "I swear to you, Sir Tobias, that I had absolutely nothing to do with it, although I was afraid something like this might happen. Hardy has never taken this witchcraft angle seriously but I have and that's why I was so unwilling to let the mask out of my care. It's probably gone for good again, although at least we do have pictures of it now." After a short pause he went on, "Do you know what's the matter with Margaret? Have the police been badgering her? Just when I thought all was well, now suddenly she doesn't want to see me and seems terribly upset about something."

"I haven't the faintest idea," Toby said with absolute truth, "but the last time I saw her she did not look at all well. It may just be the aftermath of all this stress, but if you want my advice I'd say it's just as well you don't see each other for the present, for your own mutual protection."

"You can't mean you suspect *her*!" Stephen cried angrily. "That's absurd."

"At present I suspect everyone, and no one in particular," Toby told him sternly, "so bear that in mind." And he hung up on him.

He was briefly interrupted in his telephone orgy by Owen, who bounced in with a bright idea of his own. "I think I'll do another bar crawl around the area," he informed Toby. "It occurred to me that on this Merlin and Mother Crowns business it may be something that old Job *overheard* in his snooping, didn't understand, and so shared with some of his cronies in the hopes they would. Think that's worth a try?"

"Good of you to volunteer your time like this, Owen," Toby rumbled. "And, yes, anything at this stage is worth a try. But for Heaven's sake don't put yourself into any jeopardy on my account."

"What, a wily Welshman like me? No way!" Owen grinned as he left.

Toby reapplied himself to the phone, this time to Oxford and an apologetic Barnaby White. "Sorry, old boy. Haven't a lot for you. Just more tales of Silas the Scrounger. Oh, but just one thing: apparently if he's into French history it must be a late-blooming passion, because when he was an Oriel fellow his emphasis was on French-Canadian history vis-à-vis British-Canadian history. In fact, I'm told that when he left Oriel he went off to Canada—McGill I believe. No idea how long he lasted there, because somebody else said he was on the faculty of some potty little American midwestern college. Ohio I think, but no clue as to where. Shall I keep asking?"

"If you would, and many thanks, Barnaby," Toby said. "I owe you," and went on to call Stubbs who, by contrast, was bursting with information.

"Your Pierre Merlin wasn't a major figure, but he did have quite a track record while he lasted," he wheezed. "He was a municipal officer for Coulommiers, quite well-to-do, and had a place in Paris on the Rue St. Malin. He also played a part in financing Royalist moves in France during the attempted Counter-Revolution. Apparently, from letters recently published from the French archives, which of course that old scoundrel Fouquier-Tinville never sent on to the families involved, Pierre Merlin was eventually nabbed in the Coulommiers affair and got the chop in 1794. So the families of all those poor devils never knew what had become of them. Prior to that he had escaped from France late in '92 with his wife and young child, a boy I believe, to England, but then he returned alone in 1793 and went underground. He was involved in several of the counterrevolutionary plots to finance the Royalist guerrilla forces and to undermine the French economy by spreading counterfeit money . . ."

Toby interrupted him. "Forgive me, Stubbs, but you've got to realize I am almost totally ignorant of all this history. Where did the money come from to finance all these things?"

Stubbs dithered a little, then went on. "Oh, a variety of sources. Some of it from the emigré princes and foreign bankers, but very often those fortunate enough to get out prior to Louis XVI's execution already had placed many of their movable possessions and money in safety abroad and contributed much of it to the Royalist cause. A lot of them busted themselves flat for the royals and then went back to salvage some of their landed properties. That's when many of them got caught and executed."

"And was Pierre Merlin one of those?" Toby queried.

"No, I don't think so, and this is where it gets interesting, because I believe you mentioned something about diamonds?" Stubbs's wheezing was increasing with his excitement. "I came across something that indicates he may have been directly involved with one of the actual thieves who participated in the great robbery of 1792, and acted as one of the carriers."

"What great robbery?" Toby said blankly, but his interest quickened.

Stubbs chuckled hoarsely. "Boy, you *don't* know much about French history, do you? Still, I don't know anything about the Age of Pericles, do I? All right, I'll try and make it as short as possible. After the capture of the Royal family, the Republicans rounded up all the Crown Jewels and put them in storage located in one of the two pavilions in the Place de la Concorde—the Jeu de Paume, I think it was—sealed and under heavy guard. Then, when all Paris was in an uproar during the September Massacres of '92, thieves, who included some acrobats, took advantage of all the tumult to break into the building via the lampposts of the Place, onto a balcony in the upper story, and through the unbarred windows there. Over four or five nights they systematically looted *all* the Crown Jewels. They even had wine-and-sausage picnics in the building as they worked. It wasn't until the fifteenth of September that a patrol finally nabbed one of the acrobats in the act of climbing in. The rest had got clean away with their booty: 8,000 diamonds, almost 10,000 pearls, and God knows how many other precious stones and objects. Of these only 1,500 diamonds were ever recovered, including the Regent, which you *must* have seen in the Louvre. But that means that 6,500 of them are still sculling around somewhere in the world, not to mention all the royal crowns and all the other goodies. Makes you think, doesn't it?"

"It most certainly does," Toby agreed, as clearly in his mind's eye there rose the image of that expensive and obviously new volume on the French Crown Jewels he had seen at Gulliver's. "Is there a list or detailed description of them?"

"Well, no, not all of them. Tell you what, if you can hop on up here I can show you what I have on the jewels and on Merlin de Thionville. But if you just want a general idea I bet there's a book available right there in the county library—by Prince Michael of Rumania on the Crown Jewels of Europe. Very handy little reference book that."

"Maybe I can get up in the next day or so, but there are several things I have to check out down here first." Toby was almost incoherent in his growing excitement. "Can I reach you when ready at the Athenaeum? I can't thank you enough for this, Stubbs. It may be the break I've been looking for."

"Get me here or at home any time. Glad to have helped out," Stubbs chuckled and gave his home number.

Toby, to head off any lurking reporters, had been careful to park the Rolls in the adjacent Roman baths parking lot, and he almost sprinted to it in his new enthusiasm. He even drove around Dorchester for a bit to make certain no press car was tailing him before zooming off down the now-familiar route to Stanton St. Gabriel. To further mask his movements he parked the car with the amiable farmer at Filmore Farm and hiked over the flank of Golden Cap until he came down at the rear of St. Gabriel's House and worked his way around to the overgrown ruins of the church. Here he cursed himself for his precipitate move and for not having taken the time to gather up his equipment and change into digging clothes, as he was faced with a formidable defense system of wild bramble thickets and enormous stinging nettles that masked the tumbled masonry and unevenness of the ground. The earth was humped and pitted into molehills in some spots and deep holes in others, which he surmised were rabbit warrens or possibly even those of some larger wild animal like a fox or a badger. One thing he was certain of, they were not man-made.

He worked systematically foot by foot over the small abandoned graveyard surrounding the church, where the broken stumps of gravestones stuck up through the weeds like rows of rotted teeth. In one corner he came upon a pile of these gravestone fragments, evidence of some effort to clear up after some long ago vandalism, and an anomaly in the pile struck his expert eye. Whereas most of the shattered gravestones were weathered to a uniform grayness, a fragment of a small gravestone made of the cheapest kind of slate bore along its lower edge a much darker line, indicating that it had been wrenched from the earth at a far more recent date. Teetering precariously on the uneven flanks of the pile, he tugged it from its resting place and flipped it over.

The letters inscribed on it were so faint that even through his pocket magnifier he could scarcely make them out. What he did manage to decipher made his heart pound. The stone had been split diagonally so that all that remained of the name on it was "LIN," but underneath were two dates and two placenames: "born Paris 1791, died St. Gabriel 1793." He peered around frantically for the rest of the stone and then noticed a pile of small slate fragments scattered in the long rank grass at the base of the mound. With infinite care he gathered every scrap he could find and, helping himself to a large flat piece from the pile, started to assemble and fit together the fragments with all the patience and expertise that 50 years in his chosen profession had taught him.

The sun rose higher and it was quiet in the churchyard, the only sounds the rustle of the undergrowth as small animals went about their hidden life, the hum of roaming bees searching for nectar in the wild flowers, and the cheeping of fledglings from their nest in the ruins of the old church. He labored on, oblivious to everything but the puzzle before him. Finally, he rose painfully to his feet to ease the cramps in his spindly shanks, groped for his pipe, and let out a long quivering sigh. Some of the fragments had been smashed into illegibility, but from what remained the message was clear enough: "Here lies the crown of our love, our beloved son Jean-Pierre Merlin de Thionville, born Paris 1791, died St. Gabriel's 1793."

His round blue eyes narrowed as he contemplated the stone. Someone recently had wrenched this humble memorial from the head of the tiny mound it had marked and had taken the trouble to smash it to bits. Why? The words "Seek Merlin, find Merlin" floated in his mind: the grave itself had to be important, so its exact location had to be hidden, its marker removed. He glanced ruefully around at the tangled desolation and his tiny rosebud of a mouth clamped tightly around the stem of his pipe. Difficult to find it would undoubtedly be, but he'd faced a lot worse in the past. He would find it.

Another thought came to him as, his imagination quickening, a picture arose spontaneously in his mind: an old man confronting and challenging the vandal, who raises this small stone and cracks him across the back of the head with it, felling his foe and splitting the stone. "Possible. They can check it against the grit in the wound. Or maybe a stone of some kind?" he said to himself and, fishing a glassene envelope from one of his bulging pockets, carefully stowed samples of the slate chips in it. He then carefully demolished his own piecing-together, piling the bits into a rabbit hole nearby and replacing the main fragment in the pile. He would return later, either with or without the police, and gather up these vital fragments. Then he waded through the undergrowth towards the main fabric of the church and started to scan the ruined walls for evidence of a recent scar, taking a sample of the ancient cement that bonded the stones.

In the southern corner of the church, nearest to the tangled hedge that screened it from St. Gabriel's House, he found what he was seeking: a stone had recently been wrenched from its bed in the crumbled wall, leaving behind its sharp imprint in the surrounding cement, which was partly filled with rainwater. He started to scan the ground in the vicinity foot by foot until he was almost at the hedge, and there, lying tangled in the roots, he found it. He gingerly eased it out and examined it: the upper face showed nothing, but on the lower face there were some darker specks on the remaining crumbs of cement that just might be blood.

Cursing himself again for rushing out in such an unprepared state, he decided he could not possibly leave this until later. Wrapping it carefully in a slightly grubby handkerchief he had located in the pocket of his slacks, he marked the finding place with another, smaller stone he found nearby and started to trudge back over Golden Cap to his car.

He let his imagination flow back in time as he walked. Suppose Stubbs was correct in assuming Pierre Merlin had been one of the carriers for the vanished Crown Jewels? Suppose that Merlin then escapes to England with his booty, settles here in this quiet hamlet, but then is recalled to duty in France. He would take some of them back with him to finance his daring and doomed ventures—but not all. He would then have to find a safe and secret hiding place for the rest, and what safer place than the grave of his own dead infant son? A place to which he could return again and again without arousing suspicion. Would he have confided such a secret to his wife?

Toby doubted it, given the heaviness of the secret, her youth and stricken condition, and the prevailing attitude of that time as to feminine capabilities.

So then what? Pierre Merlin carries the secret to the grave with him, and the cache remains where he has hidden it in a lonely churchyard. The church falls out of use, the churchyard returns to the wild, and hither comes an old man in pursuit of his ley lines. An old man who stumbles across some diamonds, thrown up out of their hiding place no doubt by some burrowing animal. A grim smile of amusement touched Toby's lips as he thought of the vital role burrowing rodents had so often played in archaeology, as if they were bent on drawing human attention to the treasures beneath the earth. He well remembered how, wandering on a dusty hillside in Greece once upon a time long ago, he had kicked at a molehill and a thin golden bracelet of exquisite early Mycenaen design had appeared at his feet. Yes, that was one bit of his scenario that he would bet on.

The old man would be thunderstruck, excited, seeing before him visions of further and much-needed wealth. He grubs around but finds nothing more, so sinks the spoils from his windfall into a gadget for finding precious metals—for where there are diamonds, might there not be gold? Along the way he confides in someone he trusts, trying to find out more about his astounding lucky find, and that someone counsels, watches, waits, and finally strikes when the unwary old man reveals the all-important "where" of his find.

Toby reached the car and carefully stowed what he firmly believed to be the weapon that had instigated the murder in his trunk. Closing it, he looked up into the pale blue sky and declared, "If I am right on this, there is only one person it could be. It has to be Silas Gulliver. Now, how the hell am I going to prove it?"

Chapter 15

"This be private property. You'm trespassing. Be off with you!" The old man's words came harsh and angry and were underlined by his black scowl and the anger in his small dark eyes. Penny rolled her window down a cautious inch. "I have an appointment here with Mr. Roper to see over the house. We were to meet here at 11:00 but something must have detained him." It was already 20 minutes after the hour.

"I know nought about that, and he has no more right here than you," the old man growled. "Be off with you I say, or I'm acalling of the police."

"But I assure you this has all been arranged and agreed to by Miss Orchard. Call her at her office," Penny urged, hoping it was true and watching warily as his rheumatism-gnarled fingers scrabbled at the window: beyond the anger she could sense the fear in him and her heart constricted a little at the thought of what her playacting would do to the old couple. But it was too late to withdraw now.

His head jerked up at the sound of another car and his hands dropped away from the window as he stepped back a pace, facing the drive entrance, his fists clenched and braced against this new intruder. A flashy red BMW screeched to a halt inches from him and to Penny's relief, Roper leapt out of it, roaring, "What the hell are you trying to do, Orchard, trying to get yourself killed? I nearly ran you down, you old idiot!" He was red in the face and sweating heavily. Turning his back on the furious old man who had not budged an inch, he leaned down towards her. "I am most terribly sorry to keep you waiting like this, Dame Penelope. Got unexpectedly detained, and by the time I tried to reach you on my car phone you had already left the hotel."

"I think perhaps the first thing to do is explain the situation to Mr. Orchard here," she said wryly. "We were evidently *not* expected and are certainly not welcome."

Roper wheeled back towards the old man, towering intimidatingly over him, though his reedy voice detracted from his menacing stance. "Now look here, Orchard, this is nonsense. Miss Orchard has already told you that she will not be able to keep this place going. It will have to be sold. From now on people will be coming to see the house, so you'd better get used to it. Normally I'd have a written order to view but there simply was not time. So check with Miss Orchard if you wish, but stand aside. What's more, I won't have you upsetting potential buyers, is that clear?"

"You'm nothing but a damned vulture, Colin Roper, hovering over the newly dead for the pickings." There was pure hate in Joe Orchard's eyes as he looked up at the big man. "Show the damned house then, you bloody parasite. And I hope you rot in hell!" he croaked, but his shoulders sagged as he turned and shuffled blindly away towards the stable.

Roper turned back to Penny and opened her door, the apologetic grin on his lips sitting ill with his flushed face and angry eyes. "I do so apologize for this unpleasantness. I promise you nothing like this will happen again."

"All very understandable in the circumstances," she said, struggling out of the driver's seat. "What will become of the poor old souls, I wonder?"

"Ah, that indeed is a very big question," he said heavily as he led the way towards the back of the house where they found

Martha Orchard pinning out some wash on the clothesline. Again his manner changed in a flash to its usual breezy cheerfulness. "Ah, there you are Mrs. Orchard! I'd like you to meet another distinguished visitor, Dame Penelope Spring from Oxford University. Had a lot of them recently, haven't we? Miss Orchard called and wanted me to show her over the house, but don't disturb yourself for us, I know my way around." The old woman, her hands full of wet clothes, nodded uncertainly at Penny, her eyes blinking rapidly. "Well go you in then," she muttered and turned back to her task.

Once inside and the back door closed, Roper became all business. "Doubtless the first thing you'd do would be to have this old kitchen modernized," he said, opening doors into pantries and cupboards and waving an explanatory hand around. They progressed quickly to the rest of the ground floor as he expanded on the pleasant aspect of the big rooms. "A good sound house," he insisted. "All it needs is some cosmetic work—fresh paint, new wallpaper, maybe central heating."

"And with so much interesting history attached to it," Penny added, hoping to get down to her real interest. They had reached the study where the big table, now denuded of its papers, stood bare in the center of the room. Roper leaned both meaty fists on its empty surface and for the first time looked a little uncomfortable. "Well, er, to this *site* yes, but you must realize that this is not the original house. That was torn down sometime in the early years of Victoria and the present house built in what was then the height of modern fashion, with bathrooms and indoor toilets and so on—making it much more manageable and saleable now, of course."

She managed to look very disappointed. "Oh, so there's nothing left of the original house?"

"Well the cellar and foundation of the old house were reused and date back to at least the early eighteenth century," he said hastily.

"Oh, then I'd like to see the cellar," she exclaimed.

"We'll leave that till last, if you don't mind. I'd very much like you to see the rest first so you can get a good idea of how spacious and pleasant it all is. I think it would make a perfectly splendid holiday home for your purposes." But as they continued their tour and in spite of his enthusiastic listing of all the good points, Penny felt more and more oppressed by the overall atmosphere of old age and drab meagerness that pervaded the sparsely furnished rooms. It was all she could do to keep an interested look on her face as he enthused on. It was only when the very last attic had been duly inspected and they had returned to the ground that her lack of response finally penetrated, and he said with false heartiness, "Well, now for the cellar, eh? Wonderful place for hide and seek for your young 'uns on rainy days," and they descended by a door leading off the kitchen into its dimly lit depths.

Roper, who evidently did know his business, had provided himself with a high-powered flashlight to illumine the murky corners, but to her disappointment all it showed was dust-covered household bric-à-brac, an old chest-type freezer, and some rough shelves lined with home-canned vegetables and preserves. There was no indication of any recent activity on the dusty floor.

"Where exactly was the smuggling tunnel?" she asked.

Roper shone his flashlight around on the lime-washed stone walls and shrugged. "I'm afraid I haven't the faintest idea. As I said it was blocked up long ago, probably when the house was rebuilt. It may possibly show up on an old plan of the property, but I imagine if such existed the police would have it now. I'm told they've removed all of Orchard's papers. I suppose Gulliver might know." He switched off the light abruptly. "That's all the inside. Would you care to see the grounds and outbuildings? I'm afraid Miss Orchard's cottage is 'off-limits' for now, and she may even be keeping that."

Penny emerged thankfully into the fresh air, which a brisk onshore salt-laden wind was making even fresher as it blew before it ominous-looking rain clouds. "By the look of those we'd better make it fast," he remarked.

"Then let's go down to the beach first," she suggested. "I'm anxious to see how suitable that is for the children."

"Very well." He started down the graveled lane at a fast pace, and she noted, as she scuttled to keep up with his long strides, that there was no sign of the vicar's boat or trailer, although she could see where they had been parked.

"I thought," she panted, "that the vicar of Charmouth had a boat here."

Roper shot her a startled glance. "Er, yes. Come to think of it it should be here. Must be out in it for a spin." But when they reached the beach all that was apparent was the trailer, parked a little above the high-water mark. Roper looked at it, his brow furrowed. "That's odd. Where's Squires's car? He usually leaves it hooked up to the trailer."

"Maybe he's off on a longer trip and had a friend drive him down and then park the car in a more protected place," she said with a slight shiver, for the wind was cold off the water.

"It wasn't in the stable," Roper muttered, but then appeared to collect himself. "As you can see the top beach is light shingle but at low tide there's plenty of sandy strand for the kiddies to play on and it shelves gently."

Penny was scanning the cliff face. "How about the smuggler's tunnel from this end? Where would it have started?"

Again he gave an impatient shrug. "No idea. These cliffs are very unstable like the ones by Lyme Regis, and the opening has probably been covered over long since by slippage. Why is this so important to you, Dame Penelope?"

"As I told you last night, my son would be thrilled by it. If I am to interest him in this house, the more information I have the better," she said tartly.

"Then you are seriously considering it?" he pressed.

"I am, but you must realize it will take much family consultation before I can give you anything definite on it," she said grandly. "I do not wish to waste your time, Mr. Roper. I'm sure you have much business to attend to, so why don't you just leave me to wander around and I'll get back to you later. I may also examine the neighborhood a bit—look at the ruins of the church, maybe pop in and see Mr. Gulliver while I'm here to see if he can fill me in a little on the history."

Roper stopped in his tracks. "I don't advise you to do either," he said curtly.

She looked at him in surprise. "Why not?"

"The church is much overgrown and you'd ruin your clothes, and I may point out that Gulliver is a writer and probably would *not* like being interrupted during working hours. I feel strongly you should make an appointment to see him." He managed an unconvincing chuckle. "After all, you don't want to get off on the wrong foot with what may possibly be your nearest neighbor, do you?"

She let that go. "How about other neighbors then? Isn't there another farm around here?"

"There's West Hays, farmed by a man called Timmins. Not local, from Wiltshire I believe. Knows nothing about history and cares less, I'd say. On the other side of Golden Cap lies Filmore Farm. Swaine there is a local man, but I doubt he'd know much either. It looks as if it's going to pour at any moment. Shall we get back?"

They toiled back up the cliff and when they reached the house she noted that the old minicar was gone and so made up her mind on the instant. "Well, thank you for your tour, Mr. Roper, and I'll be in touch as soon as possible." But as he opened her car door she shook her head. "I don't want to hold you up any longer, but I think I'll just take a turn around the stable and grounds to get the layout firmly in my mind."

Thus dismissed, he stood uncertainly for a moment then shrugged and got in his own car. "As you wish. And I'll be in touch as soon as I settle on an asking price with Miss Orchard."

With a screech of tires he reversed, turned, and sped off.

She waited until the sound of the car had died away before making towards the stable, which yielded nothing of interest beyond what Toby had already so vividly described. She tried to peer through the untrimmed hedge at the ruins to no avail, then wandered back up the driveway to the road where she looked uncertainly in both directions: "Ruins or Gulliver?" she debated. "I'll leave the ruins to Toby, that's his department," she muttered to herself. "I may get something more out of Gulliver even though my recent smuggling idea does seem a complete bust. And it may be fun to see his reaction to the prospect of having Toby and me as near neighbors. If there is anything odd going on around here, that should stir things up a bit in the inner circle." Tickled with this idea, she made her way back to the car, for although the distance to East Hays was negligible she did not want to risk another unpleasant scene if the returning Orchards found her still parked in the driveway. Besides, turning up in the car would make her visit seem more official however busy Gulliver might be, and she doubted very much that he was that busy. Silas had struck her as a singularly unenergetic individual, certainly when it came to real work of any kind.

Driving the short distance she found the rusty iron gates to Gulliver's weed-strewn driveway firmly closed, so parked on the grass verge just beyond them and walked back to the equally rusty front gate and up the cement path to the front door. There was no bell so she applied the lion's-head knocker vigorously, sending what to her sounded like thunderous hollow echoes within: nothing happened. Nonplussed, she stepped back and looked up at the sea-facing windows, but they were all firmly closed against the keen wind and the rain that had just begun to fall in a steady drizzle. "Damn!" she growled. "Just my luck, nobody's home." But then she spotted the shadowy outlines of Gulliver's car in the small garage whose doors stood partially open. She decided to try her luck at the back of the house and followed the narrower cement path around the house on the opposite side from the garage. Here she found some tired-looking wash flapping damply in the wind and the back door standing partly open. Heartened, she rapped sharply upon it and called, "Hello there, anybody home? Mr. Gulliver, it's Penelope Spring. I wonder if I might have a word with you?"

Her rapping caused the door to swing wide, revealing an empty but very neat kitchen, equally as old-fashioned as the one at St. Gabriel's. "Hello, is anybody at home?" she called again, a trickle of unease running down her spine, for a glance at her watch had confirmed what her prompt stomach had already told her, that it was after one and lunchtime, and yet here there was no sign of any kind of preparation for it.

Surely the old woman who worked for him—what was her name again, Mrs. Defau?—should be here. Abby had said she was a daily and this was a weekday. She hovered uncertainly by the open door, her sense of foreboding growing as she glanced back at the now rain-drenched wash. Surely if she were here she'd have taken in the wash? And though she knew country people in isolated places were not as meticulous about locked doors as their urban counterparts, even so an *open* door indicated somebody within. Increasingly perplexed, she continued around the walk, this time peering in through the windows as she went. When she got to the pleasant corner room that boasted two windows on this sheltered western back of the house and another on its southern side that gave a good cross light, she finally found something that set her heart pounding. A desk sat in front of the southern window and in front of that a high-backed armchair from which an arm dangled limply. Two trousered legs stuck stiffly beneath the desk. The window through which she was looking was opened a crack at the bottom so, alarm bells clanging in her mind, she leaned down and yelled through it, "Mr. Gulliver, are you all right? It's Penny Spring." The figure did not stir.

She whirled around and dashed back into the house, through the kitchen and out into the central hallway where she headed for the end door and, flinging it open, exploded into the cosy book-lined study. She dashed up to the silent figure slumped in its armchair and recoiled instinctively as she caught sight of the congested livid face, the wild staring eyes, the protruding tongue. She staggered back, closing her eyes and willing her unruly heart to cease its tumultuous pounding. So Abby had been a true prophet: the spell was wound up, the third murder had been done. Silas Gulliver, no longer suspect but victim, strangled as he sat.

She willed herself to open her eyes and look again, even to touch the flaccid hand that, though rapidly cooling, still held faint traces of warmth: he had not been dead long. While she had played her silly game at St. Gabriel's, murder had been done in this quiet spot. Steeling herself, she plucked a sheet of paper from the desk and, picking up the phone, dialed. "Dorchester police station? Inspector Hardy, if you please. This is urgent."

"I'm afraid Inspector Hardy is not available," a young female voice informed her. "May I help you?"

"How about Sergeant Wood then?"

"Out with the inspector. How can I assist you?" the voice chirped.

Penny said tightly, "This is Dame Penelope Spring. I am at East Hays Farm, Stanton St. Gabriel. I wish to report a murder. The owner, Mr. Silas Gulliver, has been strangled. I suggest you send a task force here immediately." There was a gasp at the other end and then the phone went dead as a hand was clamped over it. After a few seconds the voice, now squeaky with excitement, came back on. "Stay right where you are, madam, and please touch nothing. A car is already on its way. What was your name again?"

"Penelope Spring," Penny repeated woodenly. "And I'll be waiting for the police in the kitchen. The back door to the house is open." Hanging up, she dialed again. Gwen's lilting voice answered. "Gwen, can you get hold of Sir Tobias fast?" she demanded.

"Oh, dear me. I've no idea where he is at the moment. But if he calls in I can for sure give him a message. What is it, Dr. Spring?"

"Tell him to get over to East Hays Farm on the double," Penny charged. "There's been another murder—Silas Gulliver—and I think I may be in for a very sticky time. I found the body and the police are on their way."

"Oh, dear Lord, how terrible!" Gwen sounded frantic. "And my Owen not here, or I'd send him to you. At such a time it's best to have a man around, isn't it?"

Penny looked down at the mortal remains of Silas Gulliver. "Not always," she said, and hung up. Stiffly she walked away from the horror and, once in the kitchen, slumped down into a wooden chair and stared unseeingly out of the open door at the pouring rain. An ugly picture was forming in her mind, of a man curiously late for an appointment, a man who had arrived red-faced and visibly shaken, a man who had been extremely anxious to keep her away from Silas Gulliver. With a quivering sigh she sat up straight. "If the police want a suspect I've got one all ready for them," she thought. "Colin Roper has a lot of questions to answer. He fits the bill very well."

Chapter 16

With this third murder, all hell broke loose in official circles, and in spite of Hardy's strenuous objections the chief constable had called in Scotland Yard. Now, as they waited for the arrival of the squad from London, the weary Penny reflected that if she had had any conceivable motive for offing Silas Gulliver or had been six inches taller, she would probably already be under arrest herself.

She had told her story of the finding of the body five or six times already to policemen in ascending order of rank culminating in Hardy, and at each retelling her diligent snooping had sounded more unbelievable even to her. The eventual arrival of a perplexed and curiously silent Toby had not helped matters a great deal, although his own hurried colloquy with Hardy had electrified the latter and had resulted in a frantic flurry of activity. Since she had been kept carefully apart from her partner she had no idea what this was all about.

Of developments there had been plenty, some of which had been fortunately in her favor. The hastily summoned medical examiner had established the time of death with fair exactitude at between 10:45 and 11:15, and this had fitted nicely with her own suspicions, but he had then complicated the issue by proclaiming this not a manual strangulation, but one executed by a garrote, a thin strap of some kind, and that

Gulliver had been taken unawares and from behind as he sat at ease, so that no great strength would have been required to render him unconscious. This opened up the possibility that the murderer could be male or female. The one proviso here that had been in her favor was that the murderer had to have been tall to overcome the obstacle of the high-backed chair in which the victim sat. Apart from scuffing of the carpet from the kicking feet of the dying man, there was no sign of disturbance in the house, and nothing, apparently, had been taken.

The police had been none too pleased with her when, on her insistence, they had searched the grounds in the pouring rain for the missing Mrs. Defau. Penny had been convinced that something had also happened to the old woman as no sign of her had been found during the house search. A squad of cross and very wet policemen had reported no sign of her in the grounds either. So the mystery of the missing Mrs. Defau lingered on until the downpour had tapered off to a steady drizzle, at which time she appeared, apparently out of nowhere, at the kitchen door, shocked and much aggrieved at the sight of her kitchen aswarm with police who had tracked mud all over her nice clean floor.

The fact that her employer was dead seemed to have much less impact on her than that her wash was soaked and nobody had bothered to take it in. When they had at last calmed her down enough to question her, after the inevitable antidote of a strong cup of tea, she had an interesting story to tell, a story that brought a curious gleam to the silent Toby's eyes and opened up some interesting possibilities.

She was still in a state of high indignation as, under the gentle prodding of the patient Sergeant Wood, she took up her tale. "Never was there such a morning," she complained. "Got in at 8:30 I did and cleaned up the kitchen first, same as usual, and was in the middle of me first wash load when that dratted phone went. That man from the museum, that Mr. Farwell it was. Wouldn't take no for an answer when I told him the mister was still abed and to call back later. So I wakes the mister up and then of course he gets up and wants his breakfast right away. *Never* up before ten usually, so I'd planned on having me wash all done and out, but no! So I gets his breakfast, goes back to me wash, and had the first lot apinning out when out he comes and sez, 'I want you to take this package into Charmouth for me right away and mail it at the post office. And while you're there you can pick up a few things for me,' and he gives me a list and a tenner. 'What about me wash?' I sez. 'Leave the damn wash. This can't wait,' he sez all lofty like. So off I goes. Clear as a bell the weather was then, so I never even thought to tell him to take the clothes in."

"Did you walk in?" Wood interjected.

"What, me walk with that heavy package and with all those things to bring back?" She looked at him scornfully. "Got me tricycle, haven't I? National Health got it for me when me sciatica got so bad. So I rides in and does me business."

"This package—what was it like and where did you send it?" Hardy had come quietly back into the room with Toby.

"Heavy it was, about the size of a shoe box. Cost a fiver to send. But I never looked to see where it was going. Just gave it to the man, he weighed it, and I paid it," she snapped. "None of me business, was it?"

"And were there any other phone calls before you left?" Hardy persisted.

"Not that I took. But when I brings him his breakfast he was on the phone, and as I was ahanging me wash I heard the bell again. He was up and about so it wasn't none of me business to answer it," she said sulkily.

"So what time did you leave?" Wood pushed her gently back to her main theme and she turned back to him with relief. "That'd be somewheres around ten-fifteen or ten-thirty. I got to the post office just after eleven, I remember."

An eager-eyed young constable broke in. "You left at ten-thirty but you didn't get back here until nearly three o'clock—

where were you all that time?" He shot a triumphant glance at Hardy.

She looked at him with withering scorn. "What, come back in all that rain and set up me sciatica? Not likely. Had no cause to send me off in the first place, me with me work to do. He could have got his car out and been there and back in a jiffy, couldn't he? So when it started aclouding up I thought to meself 'let him wait,' so I goes and had a bit of lunch and a chat with some friends till it began to taper off. Got wet enough as it was."

Hardy gave Wood a quick look. "What I'd like you to do now, Mrs. Defau, if you feel up to it, is to go through the house with the sergeant and see if anything is out of place or has been taken. You know the house and what's in it so well that it would be a very great help to us."

For the first time her old mouth quivered and she looked in appeal to Wood. "He's not still here, is he?"

"No, it's all right. He's been taken away," Wood soothed.

"Well, all right then." She heaved herself to her feet and shuffled out, followed by the sympathetic sergeant. As soon as they were gone Hardy snapped into action. "Dickson, get into the museum and take a statement from Mr. Farwell about that early call and then check on his movements for the rest of the morning. Roberts, you get into Charmouth post office and see if the clerk there remembers the address on the parcel. It may still be there and, if it is, impound it as police evidence. If they give you a hard time on that, refer them back to me here. Smith, you get on to the phone company and see if either of those other two calls were long distance, and when you've done that there are some things in the boot of Sir Tobias's car that need to be taken to the forensic lab for analysis. The rest of you lot can get on back to the station and, if the Scotland Yard squad turns up, send them on here. Two of you better come back with them." The kitchen rapidly emptied of its bluecoated horde, and Hardy turned to Toby. "So what did you make of all that?"

Toby grimaced. "Well, since I was on my way to you to put forth a case against Gulliver as being the murderer of Orchard, naturally it's been a shock, but it hasn't altered my opinion. It's pretty evident that one of those calls spurred him into action and that he deliberately got the old lady out of the house, first to get rid of some evidence in that package, and second, because he was expecting someone, most probably his partner in crime, and that someone killed him."

Penny, who had been steadily ignored in all this and was beginning to feel like the Invisible Woman, broke in. "And I have a pretty good idea of who that someone is." They looked at her in consternation. "Who?" they said in chorus, and she went on to relate her own morning's adventures. At the end of her recital Hardy heaved a weary sigh. "It's beginning to build into a very nasty picture, isn't it? Now would you mind writing out all that you've just told us, Dame Penelope? I can have it typed up later."

"Not before I've had something to eat," she said hastily. "I've had no lunch and I'm starving, and I don't think well on an empty stomach."

"Well, neither have we," Hardy muttered. "Can't you hang on a while longer?"

"Why don't I raid the refrigerator and get us all something?" she retaliated. "If the Yard men are coming directly here we may be hanging around for hours yet."

"Sounds good to me," Toby said in support and Hardy gave a reluctant nod.

Her foraging yielded some cold ham, cheese, tomatoes, and a large bottle of Strongbow cider, so while she slapped together substantial sandwiches and the two men settled at the table with their glasses, Hardy muttered to Toby, "So what do you think was in that package?"

"Until that grave in the churchyard has been located and excavated I can only guess," Toby said. "But it looks to me as if Silas had found something and was about to double-cross his partner who in turn double-crossed him. If the package is located I'm betting it will contain the missing logbook and possibly more jewels. What I'd like to do, with your permission, is to go through Silas's papers and books, which I hope may confirm these rather outlandish theories of mine."

"And while you're at it see if he had any old plans of St. Gabriel's that show the location of that tunnel." Penny had been avidly eavesdropping as she worked. "It strikes me that it would be an even better place to hide valuable stuff than some old grave, and, since it's been closed up for over 150 years, if anything were there, it should still *be* there." Their deliberations were briefly interrupted by Smith poking his head tentatively in. "No long distance calls in or out," he stated. "And no way of knowing about the local calls, but I did find this by the phone, Inspector. It may be something." He came in holding a one-a-day leaf calendar. "This was torn off to today's date and it's got this on it." He held it out to Hardy, who looked at it, sighed, and handed it to Toby. Scribbled across it was "11 A.M. B?"

"Only B I know of involved in this is Brenda Westcott-Smyth, but I suppose it could be Bentham-Bailey who is also on the museum board," Hardy observed gloomily. "More checking to do. She certainly is *big* enough," he added under his breath.

"Shall I get on that then, sir?" Smith demanded.

"No, but I do have something else for you. The forensic lab is your first priority—analysis of those samples to see if they match the particles from Orchard's scalp and the one indicated for bloodstains. But then while you're in Dorchester see if you can have a word on the quiet with the girl who works in Roper's office. Check what time he left, whether he made any calls from the office this morning, and when he got back there. Then get over to the Queen's Arms in Charmouth and see if there was a message left for Dame Penelope—at what time?" he asked Penny, who already was nibbling away at her sandwich. She hastily swallowed the mouthful and cleared her throat. "Our appointment was for 11:00 at the house so I left the hotel at 10:45. He didn't get there until between 11:20 and 11:25, and he told me that I'd already left when he called from his car phone."

"Got it, Inspector," Smith said, busily scribbling in his notebook. "Shall I come back here?"

"Yes indeed," Hardy said, looking with happy anticipation at the huge sandwich that Penny had put before him. For a while there was silence as they all munched away. But their impromptu lunch was not destined to be tranquil. The door opened to admit the substantial figure of Sergeant Wood, obviously laboring under suppressed excitement. He bore before him a small, square, black-leather-covered box that he carefully placed on the table before Hardy, who instantly demanded, "Where's Mrs. Defau?"

"Got a bit upset, sir, and is having a good cry, so I have her lying down in the spare bedroom for a bit of a rest," Wood said placidly, and flipped open the box to reveal a jumbled collection of men's jewelry: gold evening studs and cuff links, an old-fashioned gold pocket watch complete with gold chain and fobs, and a heavy gold ring.

"So what's all this then? Something missing?" Hardy demanded.

"No, Inspector, something *added*." The sergeant was breathless with excitement. "Something Mrs. Defau says she never did see before. Tell me, sir, was there a signet ring on the corpse?"

Hardy quickly flipped through his notebook. "Yes. Gulliver had a signet ring on the little finger of his right hand."

Wood seemed to swell. "Remember, sir, when we first found the old Colonel and I mentioned he didn't have on the ring he usually wore? Well . . ." With a hand that trembled slightly he took the gold ring from the box, "If that's not a regimental crest on this one, I'll eat my helmet. See for yourself."

"I'll be damned!" Hardy said blankly. "It looks as if you were dead right, Sir Tobias. We may have another dead man on our hands but we may have solved our other two murders. Fancy keeping a thing like that! This should be one in the eye for the Yard."

"Er, on Orchard's murder there is a case to be made, but I'm not so sure about Job Squires." Toby was cautious. "As I indicated from the first, two people had to be involved with the very strange disposal of Orchard's body, but Silas was a small man in every sense of the word, and I just cannot see him going to a lonely place like Eggardon, taking on a man bigger than he, and slashing his throat open. Our other killer is bigger in every way, daring, and ruthlessly cold-blooded."

"I'd say keeping a souvenir like this is pretty cold-blooded," Hardy observed.

"I don't think it was quite like that," Toby said. "I don't think Silas even knew the ring was missing until after the inquest, where I do recall it was mentioned in evidence and in the papers. In fact, I'd say he has been looking for it ever since at the scene of the crime and found it only recently. Maybe the very day I saw him at the ruins and his visit stimulated my own interest in them. Why he kept it instead of just chucking it away from the crime scene is anybody's guess, but, since no finger of suspicion had been pointed his way, his own jewelry box would have been as safe a place as any."

Hardy grunted and looked at Wood. "Anything else? Did you finish the house before the old woman gave out?"

"Yes. Nothing she could see amiss, Inspector, and no disturbance as far as I could see either."

"Then you may as well get her up and take her home. You know where she lives and we can get a fuller statement from her after the Yard arrives and she's calmed down. For that matter the same goes for you, Dame Penelope. You've had quite a day, and, once the Yard gets here, I'll be tied up for hours, so if you want to go back to your hotel it's all right with me. Just so long as you don't leave the area, for they'll be after you for a full statement."

Her lunch finished, Penny was feeling a lot brighter. "Toby too?" she queried, for she was dying to hear exactly what Toby had been up to.

"Don't you want to get at Gulliver's papers?" Hardy asked Toby who had withdrawn with a deep reverie. He roused himself with a start.

"If the house is to be sealed and guarded, it can safely wait until tomorrow, so I'll go back with Penny. You'll have your hands full with the Yard for the rest of today and I've a lot of thinking to do and, when they arrive, lots of questions to answer, which I would rather do after I've assembled a lot more information than I have now. I may have to go up to London. Would that be all right?"

Hardy grinned at him. "Why not? It's a free country and *you* didn't find this body. Let 'em wait!"

Sergeant Wood departed to collect Mrs. Defau, and they were putting on their raincoats when there came another sharp rapping on the back door. It was flung open, and on the threshold towered the figure of a woman, ramrod-straight, black-haired, dark of skin, and with large, dark, magnetic eyes. Only the loose wattles under her chin and her shriveled clawlike hands betrayed her great age. The dark eyes clamped on Hardy's. "I've come for Mrs. Defau," she announced in a firm melodious voice. "She has need of me."

The men looked at her in startled amazement, but Penny smiled. "Hello there, Abby. So the news has reached you I see. Need a lift back?"

The dark eyes fixed on her with a hint of reproach. "The Orchards were with me when the news came. Fair upset they were. They brought me here, but yes, we must talk. I will see to Clara first."

As if on cue the door opened to admit the shuffling figure of the old, red-eyed servant, who let out a little moaning cry as she saw the tall woman and rushed to her. "Oh, Abby, he's dead, murdered, whatever shall I do now?" she wailed.

Abby Flyte enfolded the small woman in her arms. "Now, now there, no cause to fret. All will be well. For a good worker like you there's half a dozen more worthy than he who'll be thankful to have you, but we'll think of that tomorrow." Her voice sank to a low croon. "Now you come along o' me for now. Today you will rest and forget. For your own good you must forget." Her black eyes glittered a defiant challenge at the startled and silent bystanders as she stared at them over the old woman's head. "There has been enough murder done. There will be no more," she stated.

Chapter 17

Toby was feeling faintly aggrieved and somewhat at a loss as he drove back alone to Dorchester, for Penny had elected to drive the two old women back to Charmouth after a hurried promise to get together with him over dinner at 7:30. His watch showed just after four as he reached the Top o' the Town, so he decided to cut his losses and make for the library, where the reference librarian, who was beginning to look on him as a steady customer, amiably directed him to Prince Michael's book on the Crown Jewels of Europe but with the warning that "We'll be closing in an hour, Sir Tobias."

He settled himself at one of the blond wood tables, took a quick skim through the book to see what it covered, then flipped back to the French section and began to take notes. Part of his mind was still going over the events of the day and worrying quietly about Stephen Farwell's urgent early morning call to the dead man, so that the significance of a phrase that leapt at him from the printed page took a moment or two to sink in. When it did, it so startled him that he let out an exclamation, causing two old men, who had been drowsing over the daily papers at the same table, to come awake with a start. "The crown of Charlemagne known as the 'Mother of Crowns' was first produced by Philip-Augustus in the twelfth century based on the original design of Charlemagne's time," he read.

Electrified, he stared at it. "Mother of Crowns—Mother Crowns," he muttered. "Could it possibly be?" He read on to find that this Mother of Crowns had been remade by that avid patron of the arts, Francis I, in the early sixteenth century, in more lavish style with more precious stones, and that it had served in the coronation of 23 French kings ending with the coronation of the ill-fated Louis XVI, who had complained bitterly on that occasion because the crown was "uncomfortable." Along with the rest of the Crown Jewels it had been impounded by the Republicans and had been stolen during the great September Massacres robbery. No trace of it had ever been found.

He read the entire chapter with avid attention, so that by closing time his photographic memory had absorbed every detail. In a slight daze he headed speedily for Woolaston Lodge and the phone, for he had to get to Stubbs without further delay. In this he was thwarted, for no sooner had he put foot inside the back door than he was pounced on by an excited Gwen, almost on the point of tears. "Oh, it's worried sick that I am," she gabbled. "It's Owen. No sign of him and he should have been back hours ago. Promised me faithful he did that he'd be back just after two, to see the new lodgers in, isn't it? And here it is after five and not a word from him. Not like him at all, it isn't. Whatever can have become of him?"

He groaned inwardly at this new development but did his best to be soothing. "Now, Gwen, I'm sure he's all right. Probably had car trouble in some remote spot and hasn't been able to reach you. Have you any idea where he was headed?"

"On *your* business it was!" she shrilled. "Said he was going to the pubs you'd visited to ask more questions. Oh dear, with that terrible murderer at large, dead in a ditch he may be with his throat cut from ear to ear. Should we call the police?"

"Not yet," he said hastily. "Let me check on those pubs—maybe get a line on him or his whereabouts. They should be open again by now." She followed him anxiously into the living room where he searched out the number of the Shipton Gorge pub and dialed.

"Yes," said the barkeep. "I know who you mean, the little Welshman. He was here about noon and had a pint and a ploughman's. Went off again about one. No idea where."

"Was he alone?" Toby queried.

"Yes, all by himself."

His heart sinking, Toby rang the pub at Chideock and here also received an affirmative. "Yes, came in and stayed about an hour. Left about two when we closed, with a couple of old gaffers he'd been standing rounds for. Feeling no pain, I'd say."

"Do you know who they were or have any idea where they headed?"

"One's a regular. Never seen the other in here before. The Welshman bought a bottle of Scotch at our off-license when we closed up. Did say something about Eggardon."

An icy chill went up Toby's spine as he thanked the man and hung up, then turned with false heartiness to the anxious Gwen. "He's been drinking with a couple of pals, so nothing to worry about, my dear. I have an idea where he may be, so I'll just take a run out and pick him up, shall I?"

"I'll go with you then," she insisted. "But why didn't he call?"

"No, you stay here," he said quickly. "After all, he may be coming home under his own steam. Maybe he was waiting to sober up a bit before driving. You know how it is sometimes."

"Indeed I do *not*." Gwen gave him an icy stare. "And if it's drunk he is, a good piece of my mind he'll be getting." Suddenly she went rigid. "What was that?"

"Men of Harlech in the valley, onward to the fight!" charged a thin but mellifluous tenor, and she flew to the door and flung it open to reveal her husband wobbling in from the courtyard. "Owen Ap Jones!' she shrilled. "It's dead ashamed of yourself you should be! Drunk you are."

"Not as drunk as I was, Gwen vach," he grinned. "And is it the great man himself I see there? Good news, good news!" He staggered happily past his enraged wife and slumped on the sofa. "Oh, I'll sing you a merry tune-oh, I'll sing you a merry tune," he caroled.

"Now you just look here, Ap Jones . . . ," his wife began, when the relieved Toby broke in.

"Now then Gwen, you can see he's all in one piece and quite all right, but he does need sobering up. Why don't you go and make a nice strong pot of coffee? I'll keep an eye on him." With an outraged snort she turned on her heel and flung on out to the kitchen.

Owen tittered. "Oh, am I ever in for it now. But it was worth it, haven't felt this good since I was a boyo. But those two must be made of blotting paper. When we'd finished the bottle, they poured me back into the car and left me to sleep it off, while they went marching off over the hills and far away. Heads like rocks on 'em. Must be something in this magic stuff after all."

"Owen, for Heaven's sake pull yourself together," Toby charged, his patience wearing thin. "Who were they and what did you get from them? This is very important and I have to get on up to London."

Owen straightened himself up with an effort and blinked rapidly. "One of 'em was the old pal of Job's we met before. The other I've no idea, but I think he may be Job's replacement in their doings. Anyway, you were right. Job *did* try out some things on 'em to see if they meant anything to 'em, 'cos he was fair puzzled. He mentioned a Merlin, 'French Blue,' 'Queen's Lace,' and 'Mother Crowns.'"

Toby's brow furrowed, for in his reading he had gathered that French Blue had been the original name of the ill-starred Hope Diamond that now nestled in solitary splendor in the Smithsonian, and this made no sense to him; nor did Queen's Lace. "So *did* they make anything of it?"

"One thought it was flower names, t'other butterflies or birds," Owen said solemnly then giggled again. "Doesn't make much sense either way."

"Did Job indicate where he got those names from or who told him about them?"

Owen wagged his head. "Nary a word. Old Jack—that's the one you know—thought he may have heard it from the Colonel, but you could tell he was guessing."

"Or that he overheard it," Toby murmured, deep in thought. The door opened to admit the angry Gwen who came over to the sofa and hauled her husband unceremoniously to his feet by his collar. "Come you along with me and get this coffee into you, Ap Jones," she snapped. "And if that doesn't do it, it's your head under the tap until you come to your senses. We'll leave Sir Tobias to his phoning."

Owen clasped her fondly around the waist and squeezed, planted a kiss on her rosy cheek, and chuckled, "Oh, what would I do without you, me darling?" To Toby's surprise this elicited an answering giggle from her, and they staggered off fondly entwined to the kitchen.

Vastly relieved, he turned back to the phone and got Stubbs. "I can be in London by 7:30. Could we have dinner at the club, and you can fill me in on all you've dug up?" he asked anxiously. "I think I'm onto something so incredible that I need a sober judgment on it before I make an utter fool of myself at this end. I *think* I may be on the track of Francis I's Mother of Crowns. Have you any idea how much monetary worth that might represent?"

Stubbs's wheezing attention ended in a startled gasp. "Why *priceless*, old boy! Yes, for God's sake come as soon as you can. I'll bring all my stuff along. The Athenaeum at eight then?"

"Oh, one other thing. Does the French Blue or Queen's Lace mean anything to you?"

"Should be the French Blues, a matched pair originally. The only one extant is the Hope Diamond. The other one is long gone," Stubbs wheezed. "No idea on Queen's Lace. You're sure you haven't been drinking, old son?"

"Not a drop, but I certainly could use one," Toby said. "See you later."

"Oh, don't know if you want to check on this before you come," Stubbs added. "You probably won't have time. But there's an old geezer in Weymouth, name of Francis Charles, who has done some work on the French emigrés in Dorset. May be useful." And he rang off.

On his way to the car Toby made a brief stop at the kitchen, where he found Owen meekly slurping black coffee as Gwen stood sternly over him. "Gwen, I'm off to London now and may not even get back tonight. I'll be staying at the Athenaeum if anyone wants me. And later on would you call Dr. Spring at the Queen's Arms and tell her I won't be able to make our dinner date?"

Gwen looked critically at him. "You're surely not going up to London like that, Sir Tobias?"

He was surprised. "Why ever not?"

"Well just look at yourself! Your trousers are all over mud and grass stains, your jacket's ripped, and you've got threads hanging out all over the place—a proper sight you are!" she said with heavy disapproval.

He looked down at himself and for the first time noticed what havoc the brambles and bushes of the churchyard had wrought on him. "Er, I see what you mean," he said, and went upstairs to change into a dark suit, making a mental note to enlist Hardy's aid in clearing the churchyard before going after the Merlin grave. There was so much to be done and there was a growing sense of urgency in him that time was running out.

On the trip up to London, which he accomplished in record time, he managed to calm himself down enough to appear his usual aloof and imperturbable self to his fellow members of the august club. The red-faced, roly-poly Stubbs, who was there to greet him, by contrast was positively bouncing up and down in excitement and clutching a large file of papers from which bits were constantly falling out and floating away as he bounced. "I say, I've had an idea on the Queen's Lace business," he bubbled, as they settled over drinks. "Tell me, did you get all those names you threw at me first hand?"

"Far from it, more like third hand," Toby sighed. "The man who reportedly said all these things was murdered before I even came into this affair. What's more, I think he overheard the words in the first place."

This appeared to please Stubbs. "Then is it possible he was a little deaf so he didn't hear clearly?"

"He was an old man so it's possible. Why?"

"Then instead of Queen's Lace how about Queen's *Necklace*?" Stubbs enthused. "*That* would make a lot of sense—the famous necklace of Marie Antoinette, made up of a series of heavy diamond studs, and the subject of that terrible scandal involving Cardinal Rohan and the Comtesse de la Motte just before the monarchy fell. The necklace was supposedly broken up by the Comtesse in 1791 after her disgrace. Other members of her family later became heavily involved in the Royalist plots and another Comtesse de la Motte got the chop in '93."

"Was she involved at all with Merlin de Thionville?" Toby asked, his own excitement growing.

Stubs nodded. "After he returned, yes. But as I said he was always on the fringes, not a main player, as it were. And some of the studs were recovered and remade into a necklace. I believe the Comte de Paris has it, but I'm not sure. It was such an elaborate thing that about half the studs are still missing."

"So it *wasn't* among the things stolen in the '92 robbery?" This puzzled Toby.

"No, as I said it was broken up earlier. Now tell me about this Mother of Crowns business. That really *is* exciting." Stubbs leaned forward eagerly.

"I'd better tell you the whole business up to now," Toby said, and did.

At the end of it, Stubbs appeared deflated. "You've built one hell of a lot on a small handful of diamonds flogged by a batty old man," he said bluntly. "Are you sure you haven't let that Celtic imagination of yours run away with you?"

"It's not just the diamonds. It's all these other coincidences. How could an almost illiterate old man come up with these terms out of the blue if he hadn't heard them from someone? And the latest murder victim was evidently on the same track. He *was* knowledgeable and had very evidently been researching the French Crown Jewels. He may even have found the cache. Tell me, how big was that crown? Could it have fitted in a shoe box?"

Stubbs looked at him in horrified disbelief. "Oh, come on! Not unless it had been broken up." He gave a little shudder. "Which God forbid!" He groped wildly into the overflowing file. "No photograph exists of it, of course, although there are a few woodcuts that give you a general idea, and its dimensions are known, but I did bring this along to give you some idea." He emerged triumphantly with a photograph that he plonked down before Toby. "This is the crown of Louis XV made in Paris in 1722. Perhaps, like his grandson, he found the old one uncomfortable so he had this made to fit. Anyway, this was preserved because it was hidden away in the abbey of St. Denis, and it gives you a general idea of what the Francis I crown was like. It is 24 centimeters by 22, far too big for any shoe box."

Toby peered at the somewhat garish collection of sapphires, rubies, emeralds, and pearls interspersed with large yellow and white diamonds that made up the crown. "And the base of it, was it gold or something else?"

"Some crowns are of gold, but it's such a soft metal and so bendable that a lot of them were made either of some alloy, like electrum, or with a silver base and a gold overlay—like this one. Some of the really early ones were even made of iron or steel," Stubbs informed him.

"So they would be picked up on a metal detector?" Toby mused.

"Certainly." They were interrupted by a steward summoning them to their table in the dining room, and when they were settled and had ordered, Toby changed tack. "This is immensely useful to me, Stubbs, so indulge me for a little. Let's do some supposing. Let's suppose I am Pierre Merlin, a dedicated Royalist. I manage to get out of France with my wife and child after the September Massacres and with a portion of the Crown Jewels that have been stolen back from the Republicans. I come to England, settle in a remote house in Dorset, and, to add to my griefs, my child then dies. I am summoned, or volunteer to go back to further the Royalist cause and to bring funds. What would I do then? How would I go about it?"

"Well, presumably you are fairly well educated or would have taken some kind of expert advice, so you'd start with the less valuable pieces. You're still hoping for a restoration of the monarchy, aren't you? So you certainly would not take anything of great historical importance. Don't forget that old magpie Louis XIV had an incredible collection of loose stones. In one year alone he bought 45 large and over 1,000 smaller diamonds from Tavernier and another 14 large and over 130 smaller ones from another jeweler, and he kept that up all during his reign. Not all were made up into jewelry. So, obviously you'd flog the loose ones first and then go on to the breaking-up of the smaller pieces like tiaras and necklaces."

"So you'd take your loose stones and proceed to sell them, where? Here or on the Continent?" Toby asked.

"Abroad. Don't forget England was flooded with French emigrés at that time, all flogging their jewels like mad just to stay alive. The prices here would have been very depressed," Stubbs pointed out. "In France itself, when the currency started to go to pot so rapidly, a small diamond would be a hefty bribe and a good bargaining tool. However, don't forget also that here's a man in daily fear of being picked up and imprisoned and with no *safe* place that we know of where he could stash any large quantities of stones."

"So he'd just take some and hide the rest," Toby concluded. "But hide them in a place he could easily get at them. In this case, if I surmised correctly, his child's recent grave."

"Maybe." Stubbs was evidently a little dubious. "But I certainly would not have hidden any of the really important pieces out there in plain sight, as it were."

A short silence fell as Toby mulled this over. "My colleague, Dr. Spring—do you know of her at all?"

Stubbs chuckled. "Who doesn't? You two seem to make the papers on a pretty regular basis."

"Well, she is very set on the idea of them being still stashed in the house Pierre Merlin occupied, a house that, over its history, had been used by smugglers and is reported to have had a smuggler's tunnel to the adjacent beach. I've already established that smugglers were involved in returning a lot of these emigrés back to France, so could they have been at all in on this?"

"Speaking for a patriotic Frenchman like Merlin, I very much doubt it," Stubbs stated. "He may have had to pay them off in small stones, but he certainly would have hidden the knowledge of the more precious stuff from a bunch of cutthroats. As a stranger in an alien country the only person he'd have been at all likely to have confided in would have been his wife. I suppose she may have passed it on to someone when he didn't get back."

"But she died 'of misery' not long after," Toby said. "I suppose the next thing to do is to find out more about her. I must contact this, er, Mr. Charles, is it? Thanks for the tip."

"Come to think of it he must be incredibly old, so I hope he isn't gaga," Stubbs confessed. "But yes, I should. I'm beginning to believe you, Toby, and in my opinion the big stuff may still be there. You're going after it?" Toby nodded. "In that case," Stubbs held up his glass of vintage Bordeaux, "happy hunting and the best of luck, old man!"

Chapter 18

"You're worried about her?" It was more of a statement than a question as Penny faced the tall, grim-faced Abby Flyte across the table used for her "consultations." They were alone in the tiny Cain's Folly Cottage, for a suddenly stubborn Clara Defau had insisted that she wanted to go home and rest in her own bed. Abby had reluctantly agreed, but had summoned a great-niece to stay with her and had instructed the startled girl to let no one approach the old woman save the police and herself.

"I take precautions. Someone may think Clara knows more than is good for her."

"About the murder or the parcel?" Abby's remarkable grapevine had already informed them that the parcel had left Charmouth and that all the clerk remembered for the police was that it had been self-addressed to Gulliver at a London address, but he could give no further details about that.

"About everything that's gone on. Yet she knows nothing."

"You think Roper might try and harm her?"

Abby snorted her scorn. "Roper's no murderer! Wouldn't have the stomach for it."

"Then how do you explain his very odd behavior this morning?" Penny was a little irked. "And you said yourself he's consumed by greed, and the stakes in all this could be very high."

"How high?" Abby demanded bluntly.

Penny could see no harm in confiding Toby's theories, so she did. A strange gleam came into the dark, magnetic eyes, and Abby nodded in satisfaction. "If it is as you say, then yes, for that a man like Gulliver could easily be drawn into murder, but a man like Roper, no. It's not his line. He may cheat on land deals, he may pounce on bankrupts and milk them dry, but to take three lives for a bunch of old jewels, no. He wouldn't have the guts."

"Then if not him, who?" Penny said hotly. "Brenda Westcott-Smyth, who apparently had a date with him at the time of the murder?"

Again Abby snorted her derision. "I told you, she's a victim not a victimizer! Can you honestly see her slashing a helpless old man's throat and togging him out as a Druid, or creeping up behind her best friend and strangling him? Even if tempted, no: it would tarnish her precious ladylike self-image and would be too much of a risk to her even more precious reputation."

A horrible thought came to Penny as she gazed at the tall, commanding form opposite her; still she had to find out. "Abby, I know Silas Gulliver was a murderer and in a sense deserved what happened to him, so a final justice has been done. Er, you didn't by any chance take it into your own hands?"

This time Abby laughed aloud and held up her shriveled claws. "With these? No, not up to it, I'm afraid."

"He was garroted," Penny persisted. "Not much strength would have been required if one were tall enough."

Abby continued to chuckle. "Don't you think if I *wanted* to kill Gulliver I could have come up with something cleverer than that? I would much rather have seen him rot in jail for the rest of his life; that would have been a far more appropriate torment for him. Besides . . . ," the black eyes twinkled, "I have an ironclad alibi. I had clients all morning here until the Orchards arrived with their sorrows and the call came in about the murder. If you want to check I can give you the names."

"No, I believe you, but I had to be sure," Penny said hastily. "So who do *you* think killed him?"

Abby gave her an unfathomable look. "I'm not sure—yet," she said, and changed the subject. "What's all this about you buying St. Gabriel's?"

Penny looked ashamed. "I had to see the house and when Roper suggested it, it seemed like a good idea. I'm sorry if I upset the Orchards. As it was I didn't find what I was hoping for."

"And what was that?" Abby prodded.

"Some signs of the old smuggler's tunnel that supposedly ran from the house to the beach. I thought maybe it had been used again recently. But there is no sign of it or even where it was at either end."

Abby frowned and shook her head. "I've never heard tell of such a thing. Is it important?"

"With these latest developments it might be. At least it'd be worth checking."

"I'll ask around. There's one person who may know of it," Abby mused. "Martha Orchard."

Penny was surprised. "Why her?"

"She's a Squires *and* a direct descendant of the Squires who was the right-hand man to the Stephen Farwell of the high time of smuggling." Abby's voice sank to a croon. "Squires and Farwells, what a bunch of cutthroats they were! And old memories here live long." There came a sharp rapping on the door that startled both of them. "Who on earth can that be?" Abby exclaimed, glancing out at the rain that was again pelting down. "I canceled all my appointments."

She got up stiffly and answered the summons: on the threshold loomed the dark-caped, dark-hatted figure of Nicholas Squires. Heedless of the rain, he doffed his hat politely and said in his most dulcet tones, "I understand Mrs. Defau is here and have come to offer her my consolation and help after her terrible ordeal."

Penny could see Abby stiffen. "I'm afraid you have been misinformed, Vicar," she said in an equally sweet voice. "She's not here."

His face tightened. "Then where is she?"

"Safe and protected with a relative," Abby said blandly. "And in no need of *your* consolation, Vicar." Somehow she contrived to make his title sound like a rude expletive. "She is not of your faith, and of consolation she has had plenty. So leave her alone." This last was rapped out.

His handsome face convulsed in sudden anger, so that for a second it looked like a demon mask. "How dare you speak to me in that fashion! Kindly remember who I am and keep your place, old woman!"

"My place and my care is here and always has been," she hissed. "Yours is not nor ever has been. You do not have us all bedazzled and there are those of us who watch and wait. So leave now and remember my words."

"You crazy old hag, how dare you threaten me!' he roared. "A thousand pities they don't burn witches anymore. You're a danger to this community and I intend to do something about it. You'll see."

"Oh, no, a danger to the community I am not," she said softly. "But mark me well, Nicholas Squires, I am and will be to you." And she shut and bolted the door in his face.

Penny had gone unnoticed in the shadows of the dark cottage and had kept resolutely silent, fascinated by the behavior of the cats that had grouped in a silent semicircle behind Abby, their tails bushed, hair bristling, and crouched to spring. With the slamming of the door she burst out, "Oh Abby, was that wise? You've challenged him and you can see what a nasty temper he has. Besides, what good does it do to show your hand like that?"

Abby tranquilly drifted over to the stove and put the kettle on. "Because I think it is now time," she said evenly. "And something has to be done about him. You see, I haven't yet told you what I wanted to see you about, and with what you have just told me I think the picture becomes clearer."

"And what was that?" Penny said, getting out the cups and saucers, for she was beginning to feel curiously at home in Cain's Folly.

"I found out what export-import business he was in: cut and uncut gemstones from Brazil, so when it comes to jewels he's something of an expert. I think the third wife was Brazilian too. Her name was DaGoa, though of her or her fate no trace has been found. She may have left him and returned there. If there was a divorce he had reason to keep quiet, for the C of E may welcome a widower into the clergy but would be a lot more leery of a divorced man," Abby stated.

"Good Heavens! Are you sure of all this?" Penny was so excited she almost dropped the milk jug.

"I can get proof of it on paper if needed," Abby assured her as she made the tea and they settled back at the table.

"Well, that should give Toby something to chew on," Penny said with a contented sigh. "Oh, and I've been thinking, since he was now so fixated on this French angle, Clara Defau, is she a descendant of one of those emigrés?"

"Clara? No, she was a Lyme Regis Gaich. Her husband could have been, I suppose, but he's been gone these 30 years and not much loss to anyone. A farm laborer was all he was, lazy and shiftless as they come and always thinking himself too good for it. He was a Catholic. They used to go into Dorchester every Sunday to the Catholic Church on High Street."

Penny abandoned that. "Would you get in touch with Martha for me about the tunnel?" she began when the phone rang. With an exclamation of annoyance Abby reached a long arm for it. She listened for a moment or two, grimaced, and handed it to Penny. "For you. The police."

It was a very subdued Sergeant Wood. "Sorry to trouble you, Dame Penelope, but Scotland Yard has arrived and wishes to take a statement from you about this morning. Inspector

Gray says would you please be at the Queen's Arms at 7:00 sharp for an interview."

"Oh Lord, him of all people," she groaned. "Has Sir Tobias seen him?"

"Not that I know of." He sounded depressed. "What shall I tell them?"

"Tell him I'll be there." She sighed, cradled the phone, and looked at Abby. "Damn! Inspector Gray of Scotland Yard is in charge and I am *not* one of his favorite people. He's got it firmly into his head that I'm a CIA agent, which of course I'm not. Mind if I call Toby? I believe he's quite a good pal of Gray's now, so if he's there that should help."

Abby smiled grimly. "Go ahead."

But the call only yielded the information from Gwen that Toby was in London and would probably not be back that night. "Never around when you need him and always underfoot when you don't," Penny grumbled, getting up. "Oh well, I've crossed swords successfully with Gray before. Thanks for everything, Abby, I'd better be on my way. Do be careful about Squires, won't you? Oh, by the way, did I mention his boat has gone from St. Gabriel's?"

This seemed to electrify her companion. "No, when?" she demanded.

"No idea, but the trailer was the only thing left there at the beach. No car and no boat."

"Then things are moving faster than I thought," Abby said, seeing her to the door. "When Sir Tobias gets back, tell him that he must move fast or it may be too late."

"That's not all I'll tell him," Penny exclaimed. "But you haven't been holding anything out on me, have you?"

"I've told you everything I know for a fact. And I'll get right on to Martha; if she knows anything you'll be the first to hear." And Abby sent her on her way.

Back at the hotel Penny braced herself with a stiff drink for the coming interview. One look at Inspector Gray, when he appeared, flanked by two assistants, told her that she ought to have had two. Jaunty and dapper as ever, his dark blond hair was now a uniform silver-grey and there were deep lines in his tired boyish face, but the gray eyes that bored into hers were as shrewd as ever, and, although he greeted her with cool politeness, he was looking belligerent. After introductions to his two aides, one an inspector, the other a young detective sergeant, he got right down to business. "Not wishing to waste your valuable time, Dame Penelope, shall we get right on with your statement?"

Her heart sinking, she did so as succinctly and expertly as possible, so that when she had finished, his two companions were looking impressed. He was not. "Now before we discuss some of the points in your statement, there is something I want to make very clear." He leaned forward in his easy chair towards her. "I was pulled off a very important terrorist case in London to come down and sort out this mess. Why? Because the commissioner had heard that Toby and you were involved and on the scene, and that that probably meant trouble—for us. I was not too surprised on arrival to find that you and he have done a fine job of leading the local police by the nose and up the garden path. I even have a pretty shrewd idea as to why, at least in Toby's case, and am not surprised he left town so suddenly when he knew I was coming. So let me tell you here and now that with the Yard in charge, this is at an end. You are both *out* of it. I will brook no further interference, is that clear? In fact I don't know why *you* are involved in this at all. The Russian affair, the terrorists of Rome, even the Hawaiian murders I can understand, but what possible interest this purely domestic case can have to the CIA or your government baffles me."

Penny was provoked out of her startled silence. "Really, Inspector, how many times do I have to tell you? I am not now nor have I ever been connected with the CIA: that was all a terrible misunderstanding. And I'm here because Toby asked me to come. After all we have, may I point out, a remarkable success record on *domestic* murders. And I deeply resent this hectoring tone of yours. Toby's already solved Colonel Orchard's murder for the police, and is well on his way to wrapping up the other two, so why all this hostility from you?"

"On Orchard's murder that remains to be seen," Gray snapped. "But what he *has* done is to misdirect the police, so that the two prime and obvious suspects had the time to make their plans and get away."

Shocked into silence Penny gaped at him. "What on earth are you talking about? What prime suspects?" she finally managed to get out.

"Why, the ones who *should* have been under close police scrutiny from the outset, Margaret Orchard and her lover, Stephen Farwell, who, I understand, is a former student of Toby's," he said quietly. "All indications are that they fled the country on learning of the Yard's imminent arrival and if *that* isn't a dead giveaway I don't know what is. Thanks to your interference they have a head start, so they may have got over to the Continent—for the moment. But we'll get them."

Her thoughts in chaos, Penny played for time. "But how can you have jumped to such a rapid conclusion when there are so many other suspects? What about Roper? And Brenda Westcott-Smyth? And, for good measure, the Reverend Nicholas Squires, who has had a *very* strange life that the police have not bothered to look into up to now."

At this last, Gray looked a little startled, but held up an admonitory hand. "Roper has already been questioned and now, on the basis of your statement, will indeed have many more questions to answer. Mrs. Westcott-Smyth, on learning of Silas Gulliver's murder, went into violent hysterics, had to be heavily sedated by her doctor, and cannot yet answer our questions. As to the Reverend Squires, well, this is actually the first I've heard of him and he seems a most unlikely suspect. But may I point out that *they* are all here. Farwell and the Orchard girl have fled."

He paused, then went on. "At this juncture I am prepared to grant that Toby may be right in thinking Gulliver was a party to Orchard's death and that he was also involved in whatever scheme those two were involved in. That the motive for his murder was the classic case of 'thieves falling out.' Item one: the urgent early morning call from Farwell to the deceased. Item two: an equally urgent and very long call from Farwell to Margaret Orchard at her office in Poole, after which she announced suddenly she had decided to take a few days vacation. She left the office, packed two bags, and disappeared after making a hefty bank withdrawal. Item three: Farwell was not seen in the museum after opening time; a lot of his clothes were missing from his apartment, which showed signs of being vacated in a great hurry. He showed up at his bank long enough to withdraw nearly all the money from his account, and then he too disappeared. We think he went over to Stanton St. Gabriel, strangled his partner in crime and went off to meet his mistress at a preestablished rendezvous. As you can see from all this," he leaned back in his chair with a satisfied air, "we've not been wasting *our* time. So what do you say to that?"

Despite her own deep misgivings, Penny was not giving up the fight, for a glimmer of an idea had come to her. "Then I would say that things are not always what they seem, Inspector. That you have a long way still to go on this case. Now that you have your very efficient team here and will be continuing your expert questioning, may I suggest you ask the Reverend Nicholas Squires where the powerboat that he keeps at St. Gabriel's House is at present? It wasn't there when I was at the house this morning, and it just may be the boat in which your suspects took flight. That in turn would mean one of two things: either that they are innocent of Gulliver's murder, because they would have left prior to that event, or that the Reverend Squires was their accomplice both before and after the fact in all this. And what do *you* say to that, Inspector Gray?"

"It will be looked into in due course," he said stiffly. "The Yard will take care of it. It is none of your business."

Chapter 19

Toby's blood was up as he headed for Weymouth and his early morning appointment with the aged Francis Charles. The voice on the phone had been thin and reedy but the old man had appeared clear minded and quick to understand his urgent need. "Come as early as you like," he had piped. "At my age I don't waste much time on sleep."

He himself had not had much sleep, for, driven by his sense of urgency, he had returned to Dorchester after his dinner with Stubbs and there had found a desperate message from Penny to contact her at no matter what hour. He had taken her at her word and well after midnight had awakened her from her own restless slumber and had been brought up to date on the dismaying news of the day. Upset as he was by the apparently damning flight of Stephen and the Orchard girl, his reaction had nevertheless surprised his partner. "Then the cards must fall as they may now. This thing has to be settled," he stated. They had both agreed that the longer he stayed out of Gray's way the better, but he had vetoed Penny's offer to run interference with Scotland Yard. "No, you lie low also, and see if you can get anything on that damned tunnel," he growled. "I simply have to have more confirmation than I have now before I unload all this on Gray."

To that end, and after much agonized thought, he had also

put in an early morning call to Sergeant Wood. "Look, Wood, I know Hardy can't give me any more official help now the Yard's here, but I desperately need some, so I wonder if, unofficially, you can give me a hand. Can you find a couple of local men and hire them for me to clear the undergrowth in the churchyard, starting with that area around the back of the church and near the overgrown hedge? I have to get out to Weymouth, but I'll be along as soon as I can, so could you possibly get them right to work and keep an eye on them until I get there?"

"Can be done, sir, and come to think of it I do feel a bit poorly myself this morning," the sergeant's rich voice assured him. "Think I'll take a sick day, so you've no need to hurry. Would you be needing a sieve?"

"Good thinking, Wood. Yes indeed, a fine mesh if you can find it," Toby approved. "And many, many thanks."

"No need for that, glad to do it, sir. I don't like the way things are shaping, no not at all I don't," the sergeant confided. "Mighty uppity, those London men. I'd like to take them down a peg or two, I would, and you're just the man to do it."

Remembering this brought a wry smile to Toby's lips as he reached the narrowing streets of downtown Weymouth and edged cautiously through them to his destination of Newton's Road that was right on the sea front paralleling Newton's Cove. He located the small, semidetached house indicated by Charles, with some difficulty found a parking space large enough for the Rolls, and with mounting anticipation walked back to the house and rang the doorbell.

It was opened by a small, gnomelike man, made more gnomelike by the ravages of extreme age. He was completely bald but, as if to compensate, had extremely bushy white eyebrows from under which two faded blue eyes twinkled out with lively intelligence. "Come in, come in, Sir Tobias," the gnome commanded. "This is indeed a pleasure. I have everything ready and waiting." He shuffled into a back room that overlooked the sea. It was packed from floor to ceiling with overflowing file cabinets and bookcases. "Sit down, sit down." He indicated a chair on one side of a plain oak table standing in the middle of the clutter and sat down on its partner on the opposite side in front of a pile of yellowing folders. "Now, what do you wish to know?"

"Anything you can tell me about the emigré Pierre Merlin de Thionville," Toby said with equal briskness.

The white eyebrows rose a fraction. "How remarkable! For years no one has shown the slightest interest in my humble research, and now within a short period of time I have two Oxford scholars interested in one and the same man."

Toby's heart stepped up a beat. "When was this, and who?"

Charles cogitated. "Oh, must have been about two months ago, I'd say. And he lives around here—a Silas Gulliver. Do you know him?"

"Er, yes." Toby hesitated, then asked cautiously, "Do you follow the news at all?"

The old man shook his head vigorously. "No time for it, no time: newspapers, radio, television—terrible waste of time and none of it matters to me. Let's see . . ." He flipped through a folder. "Yes, here it is. Not much on him, I'm afraid. Came into Weymouth from Cherbourg on October 15, 1792 on the Bonaventure, along with wife and infant child, and 35 other refugees. Stayed around here and rented St. Gabriel's House, Stanton. Returned to France the following year but left his family here. Apparently never did come back. That's all I have."

"He was caught and executed in 1794," Toby murmured, his heart sinking.

"Oh, poor chap, poor chap. Terrible time that was," Charles sighed.

"How about his wife, Marie Merlin de Thionville?"

After more flipping, the old man brightened. "A little more on her. Oh, goodness me, yes, a coroner's inquest." He read it through and shook his head sadly. "Terrible, just terrible! Found dead in the house by its owner. Verdict was death by starvation and cold. It seems the poor woman was destitute, couldn't speak the language, and so could turn to no one for help. The owner, Robert Farwell, blamed her servant, who apparently had deserted her, and he accused him of stealing what little she had. The servant claimed she had given him a couple of her rings in lieu of wages, but they jailed him for five years anyway—just in case he had."

"Well, I'll be damned. Farwell! Anything else on him?" Toby said eagerly.

"Oh, Farwell was very well-to-do. Owned St. Gabriel's and quite a number of other places around the Chideock and Shipton area. He kept his nose clean, but, since he was brother to the notorious Stephen, one can surmise he was the 'front' man for the smugglers. I've often thought he may have been the anonymous 'Colonel' who did their organizing, although he never went beyond being a captain in the militia to my knowledge," Charles mused.

"And the Merlin servant?"

"When he came out of Dorchester jail, amazingly enough he went back to the area, married a local girl, and had a family. Worked for the Colvilles at Chideock Manor as their French chef. Came in the same boat as the Merlins, from Paris originally. Name of Louis Defau."

"Well I'll be double-damned!" Toby said. "Er, may I ask if you gave all this to Silas Gulliver?"

A wheezy chuckle erupted from the old man that ended in a coughing spell and he choked out, "Never got beyond Pierre. He kept pressing me about when Merlin went back to France and who took him, so I asked why he wanted to know—not that I could have told him anyway—and he told me it was none of my business. At my age you get a little touchy, so I told him to go about his business as I'd told him all I knew. Didn't much fancy him anyway—a pushy sort of man. Not a friend of yours, I hope?"

"No, not a friend," Toby said honestly. "You seem very well informed also about the local smuggling scene. Tell me, do you know anything about a supposed tunnel from Golden Cap beach to St. Gabriel's House?"

Charles's reply staggered him. "Oh, there *was* a tunnel. I remember well when the coast guard blew up the Golden Cap entrance. First year of World War One it was, when we were all thinking the Boche might smuggle in spies to Dorset and they thought it might be used. A prep school friend of mine used to play in it regularly when he was down on holiday at Stanton. Was in it myself once or twice. That was . . ." the old man cocked his head in reflection, "oh, must have been '08. Anyway I was about 10 or 11."

Toby gaped at him. "You mean you're . . ."

"Ninety-six going on 97: not bad eh?" The old man grinned widely at him displaying two sets of brilliantly white false teeth.

Toby collected himself with an effort. "I should say not. Remarkable! Er, do you recall anything at all about the tunnel?"

Charles closed his eyes and for a horrible moment Toby thought he had dropped off into a nap, but after a short interval he opened them again and said, "We played pirates—wonderful place for that. First there was this natural cave, quite small it was, and the entrance to the tunnel was in back of it. You had to turn into it past a big rock. The tunnel was stone-lined for at least part of the way. I remember it branched into two after a while . . ."

"And where did it lead?" Toby pressed.

"Oh, it didn't *go* anywhere. There was earth fill blocking both tunnels, fallen or filled in long ago, I imagine. After the coast guard blew it up I suppose the whole thing caved in. May I ask what this has to do with Pierre Merlin?"

"Probably nothing, I just hoped . . ." the discouraged Toby trailed off. "In any case I can't thank you enough for all this information. You've been extremely helpful, Mr. Charles. Scholars of local history like yourself do invaluable work and are rarely appreciated."

The old man preened a little and waved his hands at the overflowing cabinets. "My hobby, particularly since I retired. Let's see, that's almost 30 years ago. I was a solicitor here, you know. My wife died shortly after I retired. . . ." He in turn trailed off. "It's good to talk to someone who understands."

Toby got up. "I may come back, Mr. Charles, and when I do I'll be able to tell you what all this was about. You see, the Mr. Gulliver you talked to was murdered yesterday and I think his murder was connected to Pierre Merlin and St. Gabriel's."

Charles looked at him quizzically. "So it's serious, isn't it?"

"Very, but I won't burden you with it now. I'll be back," Toby said.

The old man shuffled after him to the front door. "Then don't take too long about it," he charged with another wheezy chuckle. "Or I may not even be here! Good-bye, it's been a pleasure, Sir Tobias."

"For me also," Toby said, and dashed back to the car and took off for what he thought now to be his final hope. He reached the churchyard in record time to find a bucolic scene under a sky that was once again a cloudless blue. Three men with scythes and billhooks were moving in a timeless graceful rhythm along the line of the hedge, under the watchful eye of Sergeant Wood, who was perched on a wall fragment in the sun, clad in a short-sleeved shirt and faded jeans, and puffing contentedly away on a large briar pipe. A considerable area had already been cleared, and, as Toby loped up to his lieutenant, his quick eye picked up amid the broken remains of larger stones a line of small headstones at right angles to the hedge—the graves of children.

"Going well, sir," the sergeant greeted him affably and waved his pipe stem at a small pile of plastic bags, digging tools, and a couple of sieves. "Brought along the things you wanted I did." He dropped his voice. "Just one thing. Old Joe was snooping on the other side of the hedge for a while. He's gone now. I didn't say anything to him: thought it best not to."

Toby nodded his approval and made his way quickly to the line of small headstones, scanning the ground anxiously. Sure enough there was a noticeable gap, and he knelt down to ascertain if there was any indication of a missing headstone: there was. He got up and went back to Wood. "I think we've found it," he said in a low voice. "Come with me, will you, and bring one of those plastic bags?" and they made their way around the front of the church to the pile of broken headstones. Toby quickly found the main fragment and showed the name on it to Wood, then delved into the rabbit hole in which he had stashed the rest of the fragments, pouring them into the plastic bag. "If the bottom of this fits I think we can stop the clearance and start digging," he said. "Is there a pub around here you can send the men off to for a while? The fewer people who know what we're doing the better, I think."

"No pub closer than Chidcock, but Cyril brought his pickup truck with the tools, so we could send them off in that. They've been at it for three hours so could use a break. Shall I tell them to take a couple of hours for a lunch break and come back this afternoon?"

"Good idea, their drinks and lunch are on me." Toby got out his wallet, extracted some notes, and handed them to Wood. "And how about you, Sergeant, would you rather go off with them?"

"With all that's happened here I wouldn't feel right about going off and leaving you alone," Wood said stoutly. "I'm a fair hand with fork and shovel. Grow all me own vegetables in me garden. You just tell me what you want done."

Toby smiled at him. "Thanks again. I must say I'd welcome some company. But first we'd better see if this thing fits." They made their way back to the row of small headstones and with a quick look to see which way the inscriptions faced, Toby got out the two major fragments and fitted them into the small deep slot he had found. "Yes, this is it," he breathed, getting up and dusting off his slacks. "Do your stuff, Sergeant."

Wood scurried off to his work force, who looked pleasurably surprised as he doled out the money. They sketched a salute of thanks to Toby, and sloped off with their scythes on their shoulders towards the truck. "I told them to come back in two hours. That time enough?" the sergeant asked anxiously.

"Should be," Toby said, handing him a sieve. "I'll dig and you sieve, and if I wear out we'll swap places." He produced a supply of small glassene envelopes. "Anything you find, put in these."

"Sure you don't want me to dig?" Wood protested.

"Not just now," Toby said and stamped his fork into the grass near the headstone. His heart plummeted, for the ease with which it went in told him that the ground had already been disturbed. With a groan he knelt down and tested the sod, which peeled easily away under his questing fingers. He proceeded to peel sod after sod until an area measuring four feet by three had been cleared. "Damnation!" he hissed. "It's been dug recently and then carefully camouflaged again. Hell's teeth, I've missed the damned boat. Chances are that whatever was there is gone. Still . . ." he got up with a sigh, "it has to be dug out, just on the faint chance there is *something* left behind that would confirm all this." Loosening the undersoil with the fork, he began to dig rapidly so that soon he had to take the other sieve to help the sergeant with the growing pile of loose earth. As the small grave grew deeper they worked on in grim silence, until suddenly there was an excited exclamation from Wood.

"Here's something, sir!" He whipped out a large white handkerchief, rubbed his find, and held it up.

The sun's rays struck tiny red glittered from it as he handed it to Toby, who said with fervor, "God bless you, Sergeant!

No doubt about it—it's a small ruby."

They went back to their task with renewed vigor and it was Toby's turn to hit pay dirt when his sieve trapped two small stones, one a yellow diamond, the other a cloudy sapphire. By the time they reached the rotten wood of the small coffin, Wood had added to their yield another small diamond and an emerald and Toby another sapphire and some fragments of rotted canvas, indicating their original container. Wood was round-eyed with excitement. "So you were right. The treasure *was* there," he panted. "That's one in the eye for the Yard, all right."

Toby straightened up with a sigh. "We'd better start filling in. Now we've reached the coffin there's no point in digging further. We've got enough to prove what was there, but now the big question is, did Silas Gulliver get the lot or had he already split it with his accomplice?"

Wood looked downcast. "Put like that this don't mean a lot, do it?" He gazed sadly at the contents of the glassene envelopes.

"Even this lot would have been enough to save a young widow from starvation," Toby replied as they began to fill in the grave. "*If* she had known about the treasure. It's evident from what happened that she had no idea of its existence. And that means the really important things, the real treasure, may still be here. I'm pretty certain that what Gulliver and his accomplice found was only Merlin's 'ready cash' hoard. That's why the Colonel had to be got out of the way, why the metal detector and the logbook were stolen. They were biding their time until things simmered down to go after the big stuff, but something happened, something that panicked Gulliver and led to his murder."

They both suddenly froze at the sound of female voices beyond the hedge, but when a small, dumpy figure followed by a tall, gaunt one appeared, Toby heaved a sigh of relief. "Oh, it's only you. What are you doing here?"

"Well, I like that, 'only you' indeed!" Penny said, coming

up and gazing with avid curiosity at their handiwork. "I was tracking you down and got lucky. Abby and I just brought Martha back to the house. We got something, but not much. Maybe it'll help. Find anything?"

"Enough to confirm some of the jewels *were* here," he muttered, carefully replacing the sods and smoothing away the last telltale signs of their activities. "But someone got to the main cache ahead of us."

The sergeant had been gazing uneasily at the silent Abby Flyte, who was glaring balefully back at him. He cleared his throat. "Er, if you'll not be needing me further, I was thinking I might run over to Charmouth and have another word with that postal clerk. I know him well and I might be able to prod his memory a bit on that parcel. Then I could come back here and pay the men off. No sense in going on with the clearance now, is there, sir?"

"Good idea, Wood," Toby said absently, getting out some more notes and handing them to him. "For form's sake, you can have them clear around the front of the church. It'll look less obvious that way. This should cover it, I think, and I'll contact you later at your home, shall I?"

The sergeant handed some of the notes back. "This is too much. The rest is handsome enough for that lot. And yes, I'll be home by four at the latest. What about them jewels?"

Toby grinned at him. "You hang on to them. They are now official evidence for the Dorset police. The Yard might not be happy about it, but Hardy should be. Thanks again."

Wood grinned back. "A pleasure. Haven't enjoyed a sick day this much in years." With another uneasy glance at Abby, he tramped solidly away.

"So what did you get?" Toby asked, getting out his pipe and lighting up.

"I didn't get anything," Penny said, looking in admiration at Abby. "Abby's the one to thank. I just did the driving. You tell him, Abby."

But her silent companion was gazing fixedly at a spot near the hedge. "It was here it happened, here he was murdered, wasn't it? Damn their rotten souls to hell. He was a good man at heart and did not deserve to die like that." The black eyes blazed at them for a second; then the flame died and she came back with a start. "Oh yes, Martha," she muttered. "To put it shortly, she did know of a tunnel and that it had two entrances this end. She doesn't know where they were. The only thing she was sure of was that they *weren't* in the big house. I believe that. I'd been asking around and it seems that it was common 'round here to have more than one bolt hole in case the Revenuers came. And Dorset wasn't like some parts where they'd unload the boats on the beach right onto packhorses. Here, because of the exposed nature of the beaches, they'd keep the horses out of sight somewhere and trek the goods through the tunnels to them."

"Abby has pointed out that the two oldest buildings next door are the stable and Margaret Orchard's cottage," Penny broke in. "So it seems to me that's where we should look."

"In that case," Toby said solemnly, "my next move is very clear. Margaret Orchard has gone, so we'll have to have search warrants. It's time I confronted Gray. And I'm not going to take 'No' for an answer."

Chapter 20

Always on the side of prompt action, Penny was intensely aggravated when Toby proceeded to take his time about setting up the confrontation with the Yard. "It's no use carping," he told her sternly. "I have to do this my own way and do it right; otherwise it'll come to nothing." But two days had gone by and there was still no sign of it.

It was not that he was inactive. Most of the time, in fact, she had no idea of his whereabouts as he hopped around like a demented flea, rushing up to London and Oxford, conferring with Hardy and the stalwart Wood in out-of-the-way places, but still maintaining a tight-lipped silence on his eventual plans. She knew that on the day of his impromptu excavation he had, again with Wood's connivance, gained entry to Gulliver's house and had spent the rest of the day going through his files. From that he had emerged with a satisfied air and a file of papers he had immediately bestowed on Hardy, but the only statement he had made to her was a baffling one. "Our second murderer doesn't read French, so that seems to let Stephen off the hook." When she had protested his cloak-and-dagger attitude, he had explained airily, "Because, if Gray gets after you, which he probably will, you can say with all honesty that you don't know anything. You'll know it all in the end, so bear with me a little longer."

"But what if he wants to go after you?" she demanded.

"No reason that he should. I've given everything I have on the first two murders to the police, and I wasn't even involved directly in the third," he pointed out. "If he wants to see me, it'll be when I'm good and ready and not a minute before."

Irked by his obstinacy, she had to fall back on that lively pipeline of information, Abby Flyte, and what she gleaned from her indicated that Gray and his men were not having an easy time of it. Colin Roper had been questioned several times, had been inconsistent in his statements, had finally flown into a towering rage and demanded a lie-detector test—and had failed it. At that point he had demanded to see his solicitor and had withdrawn into a sulky silence. With no concrete evidence against him, and with his two prime suspects still unfound, this left Gray in a quandary, so, for the moment, Roper was still a free, if frightened, man.

Clara Defau had again been questioned but had nothing to add to her original tale, save to confirm the early meeting between Job Squires and Silas. And in the wake of this, Abby had whisked her off to Whitchurch, where an American family had taken a house for the summer, was desperate for some help, and so was thankful to engage Clara until Labor Day. "The house came with a couple of guard dogs," Abby said with an enigmatic smile. "She'll be safe enough there."

Brenda Westcott-Smyth, "on doctor's orders," had taken off for a spa hotel in Harrogate before the Yard had had a chance to question her, but, according to Abby, she was considered so unimportant that they had not bothered to send anyone after her. There was still no sign of the missing parcel and Abby had been unable to find out if the Yard had anything on the missing young couple.

It was from Gray himself that Penny got the first inkling on them although it did little to raise her spirits. He came ostensibly to go over some points in her own statement again, but this time he was in a far more subdued and placatory mood, and after it was out of the way he inquired casually, "So what is Toby up to these days? Haven't seen him around."

"I haven't the faintest idea," she stated. "We're not Siamese twins, you know, and we do have very disparate interests." But not wishing to pursue this dangerous subject, she continued, "And what did the Reverend Squires have to say about his missing boat?"

Gray looked nettled. "We saw no need to pursue that since Stephen Farwell's car has been located at the long-term parking lot at Heathrow. It is evident that they've fled the country and we are still checking airlines to see in which direction they've gone. It takes time."

"I would have thought that any atypical behavior would be worth at least some investigation, particularly since Squires was formerly into the import-export of precious stones, which *do* seem to figure in this case."

He looked startled. "How do you know that?"

"A local and very trustworthy informant," she said blandly. "But then, as you so forthrightly pointed out recently, it's none of my business."

"I suppose it might be as well to have a word with him, just to cover all bases," he muttered.

"It's not as if it's the first time the Reverend Squires has been interviewed by the police." She managed to keep a straight face. "I believe he was questioned quite intensively by the Welsh police after the mysterious death of his second wife. You may want to check that too."

"Second wife?" he echoed, his tone hollow.

"Oh, yes, he's been married three times. Has a habit of losing his wives rather quickly, if profitably," she said with acid sweetness.

He looked at her in exasperation. "I told you to keep out of this."

"I had this information before the Yard even came on the scene," she retaliated.

"Then why didn't you say something before this?" he exploded.

"You never asked. You were far too busy telling me to get off the case," she snapped, and, at loggerheads as usual, they parted.

She had to admit, when the confrontation eventually did take place, that Toby had a fine flair for the dramatic and when he set things up he did so in style. He had gone straight for the top, namely the chief constable, to demand a meeting, on neutral ground as it were. This ground had turned out to be the council chamber of Dorchester town hall. It had been a good choice on all counts, for the chief constable, underneath his official cloak of authority, was a man who panicked easily and had a great yearning to be on the right side of the "right" people. And the town hall, while having an official cachet, nevertheless was alien ground to both the Dorset police and the Scotland Yard men, and in the case of the latter the venue evidently caught them a little off balance.

She was part of the "Home" team, which consisted of Toby, Owen Ap Jones, and, to her amazement, Dr. Septimus Stubbs, who by repute never could be enticed away from London. But here he was, clutching an overflowing portfolio of papers and positively bouncing with excitement. The chief constable was looking apprehensive, the Yard men wary, and the Dorset police, headed by Hardy, a little smug, so she deduced they had already been apprised of Toby's tactics and approved of them.

The phase of the proceedings where introductions were made all around was awkward in the extreme, since Gray had made the mistake of trying to assert his own authority by breezily greeting Toby with, "So here you are at last, Toby. You've been dodging us so successfully that I thought we might have to send out a search party to bring you in."

Toby was at his most formidable. "Inspector Gray," he said icily, "I asked the chief constable to allow Scotland Yard to be present at this meeting out of courtesy, although it has nothing to do with your current operations but may have some bearing on the possible outcome of your murder investigation. And may I say that I strongly resent your frivolous accusations of interference by myself and Dame Penelope, since all along we have been working in the closest cooperation with the Dorset police with positive results."

"Quite so," Inspector Hardy chimed in, with a sly glance at the uncomfortable chief constable. "Their assistance has been invaluable in the solution of the first two murders. We appreciate expert help when it is offered."

With a little bow to the inspector, Toby took back the ball. "What I am about to request is so vital and so unusual that, in order to make the situation clear, I feel it is necessary to go step by step over what we have found up to the present to show why my request is so vital, and I have brought along witnesses and documents to corroborate some of these important findings."

"Er, what exactly *is* your request, Sir Tobias?" the chief constable said uneasily. He was seated at the head of the long council table with Toby at the other end. The police representatives ranged along one side; Toby's team, along the other.

Toby glared at him. "All in good time, sir, for it is essential you understand the whole sequence of events," and then he launched into his recital. He had always been a great lecturer, on occasion a real spellbinder who could captivate his audience. This was one of these occasions, Penny reflected, as his melodious voice droned on and she could see vivid scenes of the drama that unfolded. The lonely old man who had stumbled over his unexpected windfall in the remote churchyard and delightedly confided in his friend and neighbor. The neighbor who set another old man to spy on him and did his own research on the source of those jewels. "Silas was a mean man," Toby rumbled on. "He needed money both to keep Job on the job and to underwrite his trips to France, so he in turn confided in a third party—one who could provide such funds and be of assistance in other ways. The person who would eventually murder him as he had already murdered Job Squires—who had found out too much for his own good, had become too demanding, and was no longer necessary.

"Once Gulliver had established the provenance and enormous potential value of the treasure, once he had discovered the location of the old man's find, Orchard also had to be got out of the way, so Gulliver and his accomplice could go after the grand prize," he continued. "And to tell you about that I have brought along England's leading expert on the French Revolution, Dr. Septimus Stubbs, who will explain what this grand prize was."

Stubbs was a sad anticlimax to Toby's magical delivery but, as he bumbled on, his excitement and the content of what he had to say equally captured them. When he had concluded, after spraying his listeners liberally with sheaves of paper to back up his statements, Toby followed him with Owen, who confirmed his findings concerning Job's knowledge of the treasure and made a good job of that, while omitting the drunken binge. Penny followed him with the joint findings about the tunnel, and Toby once again took up the recital. "As you have already heard from Dr. Stubbs, the grand prize may consist of Francis I's Mother of Crowns, the missing mate to the Hope Diamond, and possibly the missing segments of the infamous Queen's Necklace, and you have heard his very cogent reasons for believing that they would not have been hidden in the grave of Merlin's infant son, or that Merlin took such treasures with him back to France."

He paused for a second and then added solemnly, "We both believe they are still hidden on the St. Gabriel's property. We even have a fair idea as to where. Which brings me to my request. In the absence of the owner, Margaret Orchard, I wish for a search warrant to examine her cottage and the outbuildings and, if we find what we are seeking, permission to excavate."

The room was deathly silent as the chief constable looked at him in stunned disbelief. Toby went smoothly on. "And speaking of Margaret Orchard, while I admit her flight with Stephen Farwell looks highly suspicious, I myself find it hard to believe that *she* was the accomplice who supplied Gulliver with funds and who connived in her father's murder. Although she certainly did not like her father, she did not hate him to that extent, nor does she strike me as the right psychological type to commit three such cold-blooded murders for sheer greed. Even more so do I find it incredible that Stephen Farwell, who undoubtedly is in love with her, could be her fellow accomplice, when it is he who called *me* in the first place to look into the Eggardon Hill murder and indeed supplied me with all the data that eventually led me to all these other remarkable developments. He may be foolish, but he certainly isn't *that* stupid."

Again he paused. "My purpose for the excavation therefore would be twofold, for, whether we find the missing treasure or not, it would demonstrate to the accomplice that we know what is behind it all and that his own hopes along this line are doomed to failure. We may even provoke him into making a break for it with whatever he has of the treasure, or making some desperate move. I understand from Dame Penelope that several other people involved in this case have also been acting in a suspicious and atypical fashion: namely, Colin Roper, whom I believe has given an unsatisfactory account of his movements the morning of Gulliver's murder; Mrs. Westcott-Smyth, who also has left the area hurriedly *before* being questioned by the police; and the vicar of Charmouth, who has a missing boat, who has been inquiring after the package sent by Silas Gulliver on the morning of his death, and who has just spent the past two days in London 'on business.'"

This last was news to Penny and she perked up as he went on. "But doubtless Scotland Yard is on top of all these things and would tell me that it is none of *my* business." He looked wryly at Gray who had clearly been jolted by this last bit of information. "But I do consider my request both reasonable and necessary in the circumstances, chief constable, and one to which Scotland Yard could scarcely have any objection."

The chief constable squirmed uneasily in his chair. "Well, I don't know, Sir Tobias. It certainly is most extraordinary. I shall have to give it some thought."

"Time is of the essence," Toby boomed back at him. "And I may add that I am quite prepared to go to the very highest levels of government if necessary. I have so far restrained Dr. Stubbs from contacting his friends in both the French Embassy in London and in the French government with this news, which of course will be of vital interest to them. If obstacles are thrown in our way, that *will* be done, and I am sure the French government will then put pressure on our government for action and this may have unfortunate repercussions at lower levels."

This was too much for the chief constable, who said hastily, "Well, since Margaret Orchard is a suspect, I am sure a magistrate would feel justified in issuing a search warrant, providing Scotland Yard has no objections?" He looked hopefully at Gray.

"Oh, by all means let Sir Tobias have his little treasure hunt," Gray said ironically and added in an audible aside to the assistant beside him, "At least it will keep him busy and out of our way."

"And you, Hardy?" the chief constable demanded.

"I'm all for it," Hardy said instantly. "My men have a good lead on that package, and with that and what Sir Tobias proposes we should have a very strong case when it comes to a trial." He shot a triumphant glance at Gray who was looking quietly murderous.

"In that case I agree to your request," his chief muttered. "When would you want it for, Sir Tobias?"

"No time like the present," Toby said. "How about today? I'm all ready to get started."

Chapter 21

"How in the world do you ever expect to find a tunnel that has probably caved in, let alone what's in it?" Penny demanded, as Toby drove them the short distance between Charmouth and St. Gabriel's. He was dressed like a tramp in his oldest digging clothes and was looking extremely happy.

"Magic, modern magic, not Abby Flyte's kind. I've sent for the Barnett twins and the Gipper. With any luck they'll be there waiting for us." He was in the highest spirits since every aspect of his gamble had paid off and the search warrants and permit had been granted.

"Who?" She was baffled.

"The Barnett twins are the new wave of archaeologists, both of them doing graduate degrees in the high-tech archaeology that will soon make me and my kind more redundant than the horse and carriage. And it doesn't hurt that their father is one of our leading oil geologists," he added.

She snorted in utter disbelief. "And the Gipper?"

"Ah, now that you just have to see for yourself. Oh, and by the way, Stubbs will be there later. He's so excited about it all that I hadn't the heart to send him packing. And a couple of Hardy's men will be on hand to keep a general eye on things and turn away anyone who has got wind of it—which, in this part of the world, unfortunately seems all too likely. If Wood can get away he'll be along also. He's already explained to the Orchards and warned them to keep out of our way." They had reached the T junction and, turning into the St. Gabriel's driveway, drew up behind a white panel truck bearing a chaste design in dark blue on its side with the Oxford University shield surrounded by lettering that announced "OU Archaeological Field Laboratory." Two extremely healthy- and energetic-looking young people, one male, one female, were flanking it.

"Excellent!" Toby boomed, climbing out. "Penny, I'd like you to meet Miss Paula Barnett of St. Anne's and her brother Paul Barnett of Trinity; Dame Penelope Spring." Apart from Paula's long dark hair, Penny felt she was seeing double as her hand was seized and pumped in turn. "Give Dr. Spring a quick rundown on the Gipper, would you, Paul, while I show Paula what little I have on probable location and where you'd best start the search. Need a hand with anything?"

Paul shook his head and opened up the truck as Toby and Paula moved off towards the cottage. As Penny watched in growing amazement he off-loaded two folding chairs, a bridge table, and then rolled out what to her appeared to be an oversized luggage trolley on which reposed a box, bristling with wires and gadgets. It looked like a leftover prop from a science-fiction movie. Paul pointed at it proudly. "Our ground-penetrating radar machine, or GPR for short. It allows us to identify subsurface features without digging. Works on the same principle as both sonar and radar but hooked up to this . . ." he produced a second bristling box, "it can actually give you a visual display that gives an immediate view of what lies below—walls, cavities, even artifacts if they're big enough. From the patterns formed by the antennae to the stylus on the recorder paper, you get a continuous cross-section of what is underneath and at what depth, and a trained person can rapidly interpret this to know where to excavate. This tunnel should be a snap."

She could scarcely take in what he was saying. "Does it really work?"

"Of course it works!" He looked mildly indignant. "My father helped develop it for oil exploration, but it's God's latest gift to archaeology, I assure you. Every respectable dig uses one nowadays."

His sister came bounding up. "All set? Sir Tobias wants us to start on the seaward side of the cottage. As soon as we pick up the line he wants to know, then we can carry on and trace the rest of it down to the beach and map it all later. We may find another branch that comes off it and he wants that as well."

Toby came up behind her. "Give us a signal when you pick up the line and I'll start to investigate this end. Oh, did you bring the metal detector?"

Paul scrambled back into the van and emerged with another sci-fi apparatus: a small disc at the end of a long rod hitched up to a small black box. "This is the nearest thing we have to the missing one you described to me, although I think this is more powerful. You realize it will only pick up different metals, not gemstones?"

Toby nodded. "You'd better run through again what buttons to push," he said cheerfully. "On matters mechanical I am not at my best." The silver head and the dark one bent in deep concentration over the black box, as Paula casually hefted the two chairs in one hand and the table in the other and towed them away to the lane by the cottage where she set them up, returned for the second box and set that up on the table. By the time the men had finished their consultation she was back for the trolley and its contents. She looked at Penny and then out to sea where, after three perfect summer days, the storm clouds were once more roiling over the Channel. "Looks as if it might rain on our parade, doesn't it?" She dived into the van and emerged with two gaily striped golf umbrellas. "For us," she explained cheerfully. "The Gipper is waterproof, thank the Lord!"

"Amazing," Penny murmured faintly. "Did you do your first degree in archaeology?"

"No, electrical engineering and computer science. Archaeology is a late-blooming passion with me. Paul is the arty one. He did his first degree in physics, but he's always been batty about antiquity. Ah, they're done!" Without a word to her brother she seized one side of the trolley, he the other, and they trundled off down the lane. "You see what I mean about the new breed?" Toby asked as they watched them go.

"Indeed I do." She pulled herself together. "So what have you in mind for us antiquated redundant types?"

"Nothing for us to do at the moment, so why don't we take a brisk walk down to the beach and see if Squires's boat has reappeared?" he suggested, lighting up his pipe. "By the time we get back they should have something."

They strolled in amiable silence down to the shore, but the boat trailer was as she had last seen it, and there was no sign of the boat or of any kind of activity. "By the looks of those clouds we're in for one hell of a storm," Toby observed as they turned back. "Glad I'll be out of it and underground."

Penny was busy with her own thoughts. "I know Abby won't believe Roper could be our man, but what do you make of his odd behavior?"

Toby pondered. "It occurred to me that maybe, because he was so late that day, he also had paid a call on Gulliver and actually found the body before you did. He may also have seen something or someone there. He is obviously hiding something, and, granted he is such a greedy man, he may be hoping to gain something for himself."

"You mean blackmail?"

He nodded, then let out an exclamation as they came upon the abandoned GPR machine and saw the twins in earnest consultation at the bridge table. They hurried up to them. "Anything?" Toby demanded.

"Oh, yes." Paul got up, held out a sheet of paper and indicated the seaward wall of the cottage against which two sticks had been planted. "That's where it begins, the top about three feet below this surface. The passageway is approximately four feet wide. After twelve feet the line of the walls drops to about half of the original height."

"Any anomalies?" Toby was a little breathless with excitement.

"Could be." Paul pointed out a small dot on the sketch map. "About ten feet along on the left-hand side there appears to be a small cavity behind the wall. Of course it may just be a stone that has fallen out. There are indications of a lot of loose stuff, probably earth, on the floor. Shall we carry on or do you need a hand below?"

"No, you carry on. I should be able to locate the entrance easily with this to guide me." Toby made for the cottage and opened the door with a key the Orchards had provided, Penny hard upon his heels. He located a trap door under a mat in the small kitchen and this revealed a small flight of rickety wooden steps. He looked around for a light switch, but there was none. "Damn, that means lamps," he groused, and dashed out to the car, returning with a large Coleman lamp and two enormous flashlights. "Can you handle these and I'll get the lamp?" he said and led the way down into a darkness that reeked of damp and mildew.

Their dancing lights lit up an earth floor over which a white mold had spread in cobweblike precision. "One strike in favor of Stephen," Toby muttered. "By the looks of it nobody has been down here in years." His light soared across damp-stained stone foundation walls and fixed on the seaward side. He reached it in three long strides, his footprints clear in the mold. "Hold your lights steady here, will you?" he charged, putting down the hissing lamp and dragging his trowel out of a sagging pocket. He started to tap along the apparently solid line of the wall until, even to Penny's untrained ears, there was a sudden change in sound. "This is it!" he exclaimed and delineated the outline with a piece of chalk. "I imagine it was a recessed doorway and they just faced over it when they blocked the tunnel off. Now I must find some extra muscle to get it down."

To Penny, who was more than a little claustrophobic, it was a relief to get back to the light, but, as she emerged from the trap door, she found herself facing two startled constables behind whom Dr. Stubbs's rotund figure was outlined in the doorway. "Ah, excellent timing," Toby said, emerging like a pantomime genie from the trap door behind her. "It's Smith and Roberts, isn't it? Would one of you mind giving me a hand with a pickax? We have to expose a doorway."

"You've *found* it?" Stubbs squeaked in excitement.

Toby nodded, as the taller of the two constables said, "I'll do it, sir. Smith has a bad back."

"Fine, Roberts. You'll find a couple of pickaxes and shovels in the back seat of my car, and bring the other flashlight there, will you? And Smith, would you stand guard at the drive entrance and see that no one comes in, save your own people?"

"Does that ban include the Yard men?" Smith asked with a grin.

"For the moment, yes," Toby grinned back. "But I doubt they'll be around. Penny, will you and Stubbs handle the lights for us below?" And when the laden Roberts returned they all trooped back down, the reluctant Penny very much in the rear.

With the two men wielding pickaxes the rotting mortar between the stones was demolished in a matter of minutes, and as they pried out the blocks, the outline of a door was revealed, secured by a heavy wooden bar. The bar removed, they prised at the door with their pickaxes and it sagged open, admitting a gust of foul-smelling damp air. Peering into the darkness they could hear the ominous dull clump of falling earth. As Toby took a step inside Penny cried, "Toby, for Heaven's sake don't go in there! It sounds as if the whole thing is coming down. You've found what you're after, so be sensible and wait until it can be shored up or something. If anything is in there it can wait a few more hours or days if need be."

"It's just stuff we've jarred loose with our hammering," he said impatiently, shining his lamp up and around. "I'm not waiting."

"Then get Paul here," she cried. "You've no right to risk your neck like this. Think of the family."

"I'm certainly not going to risk anyone else's," he retaliated.

"I don't mind, sir," Roberts volunteered. "Won't you need someone to hold the light?"

"It would be a help," Toby admitted. "You married, have a family?"

"Yes sir, two young 'uns."

"Then thanks, but no. How about you, Septimus?"

"I thought you'd never ask," the fat man wheezed, gathering up the flashlights. "Lead on, Macduff!"

Toby looked at Penny's concerned face. "Don't worry, we'll be all right. If Roberts hears anything caving in he can hightail it for help. Would you mind going on up and making sure no one comes down here? No one at all, not even the Barnetts."

She hovered uncertainly for a second, then gave a grudging assent. "But for God's sake be careful," she urged, and stumped angrily back up the rickety stairs.

"Keep well back of me, Stubbs," Toby said, "and if you hear a rumble, run like hell." And they launched themselves into the sour-smelling darkness, their feet sinking deep into the morass of loose earth that littered the narrow passageway. At twelve feet, as the Gipper had predicted, Toby's light picked out the point where the height of the walls suddenly dropped from seven feet to four, and he immediately backtracked a couple of feet.

"Hold the light steady on this, will you?" he said, hefting the black box attached to the metal detector. "I hope this damn thing works." A tiny green light sprang up as he activated it, and he started to run it up the wall in front of him. As it rose breast high it suddenly emitted a shrill ping, startlingly loud in the close confines, and with a gasp he hastily marked the stone facing and continued his probe, but apart from that the detector stayed silent. He switched it off, took a deep breath, and looked at Stubbs as earth fell nearby, showering them as it landed. "Well, this is it. I dare not use a pickax. I'll have to trowel it out, so just keep the light trained on the wall."

Stubbs nodded, his wheezing labored in the clammy silence, and Toby began to work carefully around the stone, the rotting mortar crumbling easily beneath the probing trowel. He worked on, only pausing to wipe the sweat out of his eyes, until the stone suddenly shifted under his touch. Using his fingertips he gently urged the two-foot-square block out of its bed and gently lowered it to the floor.

Heedless of Toby's warning, Stubbs surged eagerly forward and shone the light into the cavity beyond: for a moment they stared in dumbfounded disappointment, for it appeared to be empty. Then Toby thrust in a questing hand, and, almost at arm's length, his fumbling fingers encountered something soft and faintly slimy to the touch, which crumbled beneath them. His straining eyes caught the faint gleam of metal. With a tremendous effort he willed himself to be calm as his fingers began to trace the outline of what he had found. "It's a bag of some kind of fabric, velvet I think," he muttered to Stubbs, who was now wheezing excitedly in his ear. "There's something a little more solid at its base, about a foot square. I'm going to try and get both hands in and ease it out gently. Give me as steady a light as you can." With agonizing slowness he started to inch the slimy object forward, for the slightest pressure was causing it to disintegrate faster, but after what seemed an eon of time he brought it out of the dirt and onto the solid surface of the wall stone, and, green and rotten with damp and age, what had been a black velvet bag was revealed. He tried to remove it, but it just fell apart under his touch, exposing what lay beneath.

"Oh, my God!" Stubbs groaned, as a rainbow of jewels

flashed their fire under the dancing light in his trembling hands. The Mother of Crowns sat serenely on the rotting remains of a black velvet pillow, but what brought sudden tears to Toby's straining eyes was what lay within the inner circlet of the crown. The French Blue twinkled in the middle of a group of large diamonds arranged in a pathetic attempt to make a fleur-de-lis. Clustered around them were large sapphires to make the blue background of the Royalist flag, and in a circle around them were rubies, some as big as pigeon eggs. Pierre Merlin de Thionville had kept the faith and had left a final testament to his long-lost cause.

"Never did I think I'd live to see a day like this," Stubbs croaked, tears trickling down his cheeks. "It's so incredibly wonderful, so . . ." his hand touched the crown tenderly, "beautiful."

Toby cleared his throat and blinked the tears out of his eyes. "Yes, well, now I'd like to get this out of here just as is in one piece, but I'm not sure it's possible. The cushion is rotted." He fumbled in his pocket and dragged out his minicamera. "At least we'd better get some pictures *in situ*." As he snapped the flash several times there came another ominous rumble, and again they were showered with earth. "Now would you go back to the kitchen and see if you can find something flat, a tray, a bread board, anything I can ease the cushion onto. I'll stay here and, if this collapse continues, I'll just grab and run."

"Right," Stubbs whispered and edged gingerly away, leaving Toby in dreamy contemplation of the jewels. Heedless of imminent danger, he was feeling an extraordinary sense of peace and satisfaction for a job well done.

When Stubbs returned bearing a small plastic tray, he was looking concerned. "There's someone upstairs with Dr. Spring—a man," he said, as Toby eagerly took the tray and began to edge the cushion onto it.

"Any idea who it might be?"

"Not a clue. He appeared to be angry but she seemed to

have the situation under control." Stubbs looked in agony at the jewels. "What should we do?"

"Get these back to the cellar," Toby said grimly, straightening up with the tray and its precious burden. "Get going. We can lie low until she gets rid of him or send Roberts to do it, but how the hell did he get in?"

Penny, in her anxiety for Toby, had been on the jump. She wandered outside the small cottage, walked down the lane until she saw the twins in the distance still busy with their strange task, and noted that the Orchards had evidently taken off, for there was no sign of their minicar. She rambled back to the entrance for a word with Smith, who was stolidly standing in the middle of it. "All quiet?" she asked, as she came up to him.

"Not a soul around," he assured her.

"If need be, how soon could you get a rescue squad out here?" she queried anxiously.

He looked shocked. "Oh a matter of minutes. We have a car radio. Charmouth Fire Brigade be our nearest, ma'am. Why?"

"They're in the tunnel and there's earth falling."

"Oh, don't you fret. It'll be all right, you'll see. They know what they're doing and so do we," he reassured her.

"Well, if I do come running, you jump," she said and retreated reluctantly to the cottage where she left the door standing wide for instant action. She sat down in a wing chair, leaned back closing her eyes, and tried to keep her mind off what was going on below. Calm gradually returned and she was in a semidoze when a slight noise outside jolted her awake. She looked up to see a familiar massive figure, clad in riding clothes, framed in the doorway. The Reverend Nicholas Squires looked every bit as startled to see her as she him. "What are you doing here?" he exclaimed.

She sprang to her feet. "I might ask you the same thing. This place is off-limits pending an official investigation. How did you get in? The guard on the entrance was not supposed to let anyone through."

He continued to gaze balefully at her. "As usual I came along the coastal path to go riding, what else? When I saw this door open I assumed Margaret had returned." He tapped his riding crop impatiently on the palm of one meaty hand. "In her absence, what right have you to be here, and who are those two people I saw in the grounds? You've no right to trespass like this."

"But I have," Penny said smoothly. "As a result of new developments, the police have a search warrant for St. Gabriel's, and the young couple you saw and I are part of the investigating team. The police will be very glad to know that you are back from your recent travels, Vicar. They've been wanting to ask you about your boat that has been gone since the morning of Gulliver's murder."

He tensed in anger. "Not that it's any of their business *or* yours, but the boat needs some repairs. It's over in Lyme. And I resent your implications."

"I was implying nothing, just stating a fact," she came back at him. "Now I must ask you to leave. The stable is also off-limits until this is over, so I'm afraid you'll have to postpone your ride. If you don't, I'll have to summon the constable at the gate."

"I'm damned if I will," he roared, taking another menacing step towards her. "Not until you tell me what's going on here."

She stood her ground. "That's police business and I have no intention of telling you," she snapped. "If you're so concerned call Inspector Hardy in Dorchester. Again, please leave!"

He started back as heavy footsteps crunched in the gravel outside and swung around as the sturdy figure of Sergeant Wood appeared in the doorway. The sergeant came in, his face heavy with disapproval. "What's going on here? Vicar, you're not supposed to be here. How did he get by Smith?" he demanded of Penny.

"He says he came by the coastal path," she replied, thankful to see him. The sergeant stood aside and waved his hand at the door. "Now I don't want no trouble, Vicar. Please go, *now*!"

After furious protests, Squires strode out and slammed the door behind him. Wood turned to Penny, his eyes dancing with excitement. "You can tell me about this later, after I've seen him off the premises. But I've some real strange news. The Yard found where Farwell and Miss Orchard went: to America, Baltimore in Maryland. But that's not all. They bought *return* tickets. They're due back this morning, so Gray went up to Heathrow. What do you make of that?"

Chapter 22

From being a featured player Penny suddenly found herself precipitated into a starring role in the hectic developments that followed upon the finding of the treasure. It all started the next morning, when Gray burst in upon her as she was having breakfast and demanded, "Where's Toby?"

"Still in London, I suppose," she said, swallowing the last morsel of her poached eggs. "Went up with Stubbs, Hardy, and the jewels yesterday afternoon to deposit them in the Bank of England vault and notify the PM and all interested parties. May be there for days."

"Then it will have to be you. Will you come with me?"

Her eyebrows shot up. "You're *arresting* me?"

He almost danced with impatience. "No, of course not. I need your help, since you know your way about and are close to the locals. I owe you an abject apology. I should have listened to you, but I was so certain I was right . . ." he trailed off. "Now I'm working against time and hope to God I am not too late. I have statements that are still being checked but that clearly point in one direction. Will you come? I'll explain as we go."

"Right!" she said promptly, gathering up her tote bag and rainwear from the chair beside her, for the unusual summer storm was still raging outside. "I'm ready."

They hurried out to his car, with his detective sergeant at the wheel, and scrambled into the back seat. "Where are we going?" she asked.

"First to interview the Reverend Nicholas Squires, as you have been urging for days," he said tightly. "You may as well know that I picked up the Farwells at London airport yesterday."

"Aha! Then I was right," she exclaimed. "As soon as I heard where they had headed I thought the object of their journey was matrimony, not larceny. In Maryland you can still get married in a remarkably short space of time." It had also sent her spirits plummeting, thinking that the motive for it might be that a wife need not testify against her husband and vice versa. "So you've arrested them?"

"No," he sighed. "For, apart from everything else, they have watertight alibis for the time of Gulliver's murder. According to them they fled because of threats to Margaret. They were working against time, so he had a friend, name of Bill Sykes of all things, drive him up to London, drop him off, and park the car for him. *She* had a friend drive up in her car and then drive it back to her apartment in Poole. They just made the plane, and their witnesses support their story."

"Threats from whom?" she demanded, as they drew up before the rectory.

"That's what we are going to ask the vicar of Charmouth," he said, as they all piled out, hurried up the pathway, and rang the electric bell at the front door. It was answered by a tight-faced, middle-aged woman with a broad Midland accent, who informed them that the vicar was "not at home."

"Then where is he?" Gray demanded, producing his credentials. "We're police officers and must speak with him urgently." The sight of these alarmed her. "Well, I don't rightly know," she faltered. "Said he was off for a bit of an 'oliday to get away from this awful weather. Didn't say where. Packed his two bags hisself, put 'em in t'car and took off. Last night it was, quite late. Left me some money and said he'd be in touch. That's all I know."

"He told me yesterday that his boat was in Lyme for repairs," Penny explained to Gray. "Maybe he's on it waiting for the weather to clear."

Gray nodded. "May we look through the house then?" he asked the housekeeper, who drew herself up in indignation.

"Oh, no you don't! Vicar left me in charge of t'place. I know my rights. You're not coming in here without a search warrant, you aren't."

"Then we'll get one and be back," he said and they raced back to the car and off to Lyme Regis. "While we check the Lyme boatyards, Sergeant, you get on to Inspector Wicks in Dorchester and tell him to get us that warrant pronto." As they settled back he went on to Penny, "According to Margaret Farwell, Squires proposed marriage to her. I think it was just about the time you arrived here. He also proposed that he move into St. Gabriel's until such time as the wedding could take place to look after it for her. When she said no to both propositions he turned very nasty: said he had information that her father had been mixed up in some very funny crooked business and that he could ruin his reputation. When this didn't get to her he went even further. Said that if she did not change her mind and marry him immediately he'd see that Farwell was ruined and jailed. This frightened her, so she temporized. She obviously wasn't too sure herself at that point about Farwell's activities, but then when Farwell finally got through to her and found out what was going on, *he* thought the obvious solution would be to face Squires with a *fait accompli* and just get married right away. She still dithered. He didn't know what Squires could possibly have on him or the late Colonel, so that's why he called Gulliver, to find out what he knew about it. According to his statement, Gulliver was very evasive, but did say Squires was not a good man to cross and that it would be a good idea for Margaret Orchard to get out of his way. When Farwell mentioned he thought it may have something to do with the jewels Orchard had found, Gulliver appeared to get very excited—'almost incoherent' Farwell says—and hung up on him. But this did the trick so far as Margaret Orchard was concerned, and off they went and got married in Maryland as soon as they legally could."

"But why did they come back so soon? Why didn't they stay on there for a honeymoon?" She was a little puzzled.

Gray chuckled as they slid to a stop before the first boatyard. "Farwell says he has an important excavation to do, so they had to get back. He sounded just like Toby. But what mainly worries me is that just before they left America they sent Squires a Federal Express overnight letter notifying him of their marriage in the hopes of getting him off their backs. He must have received it yesterday."

"Oh, oh!" Penny said faintly. "Yes, that does rather tear it."

At the first boatyard they drew a blank, but at the second they struck lucky. "Oh, yes, the Reverend Squires's boat? Yes, it was here."

"For repairs?" Penny asked.

"*Was*?" Gray growled at the same instant.

"Not repairs, no. Just wanted it checked and overhauled. Was thinking of a long trip," the foreman replied. "Picked it up yesterday evening, he did. Said he'd snug up till the storm died down. Paid me something on account but said he'd settle with me later. Had his trailer with him hitched up to that thunking big car of his, so I helped him on with it and off he went."

"Where?" they chorused.

The man shrugged. "He didn't say."

They looked at each other in consternation. "Maybe he headed back for St. Gabriel's," Penny suggested. "He must have been there earlier to pick up his trailer. Wasn't there a man left on guard after we took off? He should know."

"I don't know. It wasn't my party, remember?" Gray said

with a hint of bitterness. "You say Squires was there with you. Do you think he knew what was happening?"

"About the Crown jewels, no. They kept out of sight until he'd left and Wood had seen him on his way." She herself would never forget the scene, as the small procession had emerged from the cellar: first the awe-stricken Roberts, then two scarecrow figures, plastered with earth from head to toe, bearing tenderly and with expressions of rapturous pride their glittering spoils. Never, in all the years she had known him, had she seen such joy on Toby's face. "However," she mused, "Squires isn't stupid. It's possible that Joe Orchard had told him of Toby's dig in the churchyard, and with me there and the two young ones at work with their gadgets, he may have realized there was no more hope along that line."

"Since we've no idea where else to go, we may as well try St. Gabriel's," Gray said wearily, getting into the car and starting it up.

"What about your sergeant?" she asked, getting in beside him.

"I'll phone and tell Wicks to pick him up here after he's got the search warrant. If we strike out at St. Gabriel's we'll meet them back at the rectory." They both sank into worried silence as he drove at whirlwind speed back to the house, where he drew up in the lane and made for the back door. Before they reached it, it was flung open by Joe Orchard, who glowered at them. "What do you want?"

"Police business," Gray snapped. "I need to use your phone. And did the Reverend Squires come by last evening to pick up his trailer?"

"Never a minute's peace," Joe grumbled, reluctantly standing aside as Penny indicated the way to the phone. "And yes, the vicar did. It was his to pick up, wasn't it?"

"Has he come back here with the boat?" she asked, as Gray applied himself to the phone.

"Not that I know of, but I mind my own business," he snarled.

Gray had just put the phone down when it shrilled again and he snatched it up. "Inspector Gray here. Who? Yes, she's here with me. Right!" He handed the phone to Penny. "A Mrs. Flyte wants to talk with you urgently."

"Abby? Are you all right?" Penny said anxiously.

"Yes, but listen. This dawn I saw a powerboat in Cain's Folly Cove. It wasn't there yesterday, but I think it's Squires's. I've been calling all over for to tell you, and it's too late now. The storm is slackening and he's just pulled out and is heading towards you at St. Gabriel's. I'll do what I can." And on this obscure note the phone went dead.

"Quick!" Penny grabbed Gray's arm and started towing him towards the door. "Down to the beach. Abby's spotted him and says he's heading towards us. We may nab him. Do you have a car phone?"

"No, just a police radio," he said, starting up the car and bumping down the rain-soaked track as she fumbled in her tote for binoculars. The crash of the surf was deafening as they reached the storm-battered beach, the strong onshore wind snatching at Gray's words as they scrambled out. "I must say he's got a lot of nerve going out in this," he shouted, as she handed him the glasses.

"His car and trailer aren't here," she pointed out. "So Abby could be wrong. He may be making a run for it."

"Got him!" Gray cried. "Yes, he seems to be heading straight out across the Channel." He handed her the glasses and indicated the direction. "I'd better get onto the coast guard and see if they'll intercept and pick him up."

She picked up on the dancing boat and the huge figure in yellow oilskins at the wheel, then swept on up to the towering cliff above the boat. "Wait!" she cried. "Look, there's Abby Flyte. I think she's signaling to us." She handed him the glasses.

The tall figure stood erect at the very edge of the vertiginous cliff, a long staff in her hands, which she was pointing directly towards the boat then slowly rotating in a circle. "Must have spotted us on the beach and is pointing him out to us," Gray said, waving both arms wildly above his head in acknowledgment.

"I'm not so sure." Penny took the glasses back, for Abby had not so much as glanced in their direction but continued to motion with the staff. What astounded Penny, as she focused in, was to see the three cats ranged in a semicircle behind her and standing upright like statues in the face of a gale that would have sent any normal domestic tabby scuttling for cover.

Gray waved again, then let out an exclamation of disgust. "Well, if she's too addled to get back to the safety of her cottage, there's nothing I can do. I'm radioing the coast guard." And he headed back for the car.

Penny continued to watch Abby whose swings were gaining in momentum, so that the staff was whirling in her hands, then she switched back to the boat heading into the massive rollers, spray spuming like fountains from its bow but still making good headway. Then, astern, she noticed a strange turbulence in the water and her heart began to thump when, as if magnetized, the bow of the boat slowly swung around towards the whirlpool that was forming. She could see Squires wrestling frantically with the wheel, as waves crashed over the stern and the boat began to wallow. Another wave cascaded over him and she could see the massive head look upwards at the cliff. He shook a defiant fist at the figure above as another roller crashed over the stern and the boat was submerged. For a few heart-stopping seconds it surfaced again like a broaching whale and seemed to right itself; then it was buried under another cascade and it slowly heeled over. With Squires still clinging desperately to the wheel it disappeared from view. Feeling sick, Penny kept her eyes glued to the spot but there was nothing but the turbulence of the massive gray-green rollers. She switched back to the clifftop in time to see Abby entering her cottage, the cats in single file behind her, their tails held high.

"Bureaucracy!" Gray snorted, rejoining her and taking the glasses out of her limp hand. "They'll take action after they've verified my credentials. How's he doing?"

"He isn't," she said weakly. "He's gone. The boat submerged with him in it."

He was scanning frantically. "What! How the hell did that happen?"

"Must have been some kind of power failure. The boat suddenly swung around and was swamped, and that was that."

"Good God! Poor devil! All I wanted to do was *question* him. I wonder why he panicked like that," Gray exclaimed.

"Well, as you said earlier in the case, only the guilty flee, and I believe the Reverend Squires had a lot to feel guilty about. If he did have any part of the jewels with him, they are now at the bottom of the English Channel and gone for good. Anyway, this is one murderer that won't stand trial for his crimes but has paid the ultimate penalty."

"We don't know for sure that he was one," Gray protested.

"I think now that he's gone you'll find your proof," she said quietly.

In this she was a truc prophet, for as soon as the news was released, Roper was on the doorstep of the Dorchester police station, volunteering a statement that he had indeed found Gullivcr's body that morning and, further, that he had seen Squires's Jaguar speeding away as he arrived. He claimed to have been too frightened of Squires to come forward with this: no one believed him, but the matter was quietly dropped. Squires's bank accounts showed that he was indeed in bad financial shape, and heavy cash withdrawals over the past three months matched deposits in Gulliver's account. To cap everything the missing metal detector was found concealed in the attic of the rectory, together with some of Gulliver's preliminary notes on the jewels and Pierre Merlin. And, belatedly, Gulliver's package was tracked down to an accommodation address at a bookshop in southeast London. It contained, as

Toby had predicted, the missing logbook, some gold louis coins and a quantity of loose jewels that were immediately added to the collection in the Bank of England's vault. Other confirmation of his murky past had come from the police in Wales, who verified that they had been certain of his guilt in the murder of his second wife, but that they had not enough evidence to charge him with it.

But before any of this had come to pass, Penny had paid a final visit to Abby Flyte. She found her huddled over a small coal fire in the dark cottage, the three cats ranged in exhausted sleep around her. Penny was shocked by what she found, for it was an aged shriveled crone who looked up at her, the black eyes dim and lusterless. Abby nodded grimly at her. "Yes, negative to negative is always dangerous," she croaked, "and must be paid for."

"Is there anything I can do for you?" Penny choked out.

"Yes, there is. I have enjoyed knowing you, but now we must say farewell and you must leave me be and say nothing of this to anyone." A faint smile touched the bluish lips. "Besides, even if you did, no one would believe you." For a second a gleam came into the dim eyes. "I have no regrets," Abby whispered. "He was an evil man."

This, and not what followed, was the final verdict on the Reverend Nicholas Squires, whose body was never found but to whom a memorial plaque was eventually erected in his church by mourning parishioners, who would believe no ill of their beloved vicar.

Epilogue

Two days later, under cloak of darkness, Toby slipped into the Queen's Arms to rejoin his partner. London had proved no different from Dorchester for, despite all precautions taken, news of his discovery had leaked out. Every headline on both sides of the Channel had screamed it, and the hounds of the press had been in full cry after him. He had gone to ground in the Athenaeum and once again had had to make an undignified escape through its kitchens and by way of a tradesman's van to Stubbs's home where he had left the Rolls. In Charmouth he found Penny busily packing her bags. "You're leaving already?"

"No point in staying, is there?" she said grumpily. "Jewels found, murderer dead, case closed. I'm off."

"What exactly did happen after I left?" he asked, slumping wearily down on her bed. "All I heard from Gray was that Squires had made an unexpected run for it and had drowned. Any idea what spooked him?"

"Oh, I think he realized it was all over. The Farwells were back and talking. Wood, in order to get rid of him the day of the find, told him that Scotland Yard wanted a statement from him, and I think Roper had already, from a safe distance, tried to put the arm on him. So, he took whatever it was he had and made a run for it. He knew his past would not stand up to close scrutiny." Penny brightened and said smugly, "It's nice to be right on target. I felt it had to be him from the start." Toby opened his mouth to protest, then wisely closed it again. They both lapsed into a depressed silence until she asked, "What's happening about the Crown Jewels?"

Toby roused himself from his gloom. "Oh, I think our government is going to milk it for all it's worth, *entente cordiale* and all that. Their foreign minister will probably come over for an official presentation with all flags flying. It'll take a while to set up. There may be complications because the Comte de Paris will probably put in a claim for some of them, like the rest of the studs from the Queen's Necklace. The crown, the French Blue and some of the bigger things will go to join the rest of the Crown Jewels in the Louvre, but I wouldn't be a bit surprised if the present French government doesn't follow the pattern of the Third Republic in 1883 and sell off most of the rest."

"You involved in any of this?"

He groaned and gave a faint shudder. "Good God, yes. I tried to shove it all off on Stubbs, who is just as much responsible for the find as I am, but no one seemed to listen. The French propose giving me the Legion of Honor, first class, making me an honorary member of the Academie, and God knows what else. As if I wanted any of it. I shudder to think what lies ahead after all the whoop-de-do we went through in Brittany. God, I hate those things!" He looked mournfully at her. "Do you have to go right away? Where are you heading?"

"Initially, to Littlemore to see if my odd-job man has been keeping up with the garden. If he hasn't, with all the rain there's been, it'll be a jungle by now. Then in three days' time I'm off on my delayed trip to the family."

He brightened. "Then I'll come with you. By the time I get back the furor should have died down."

"If we're going together I'm not going by Concorde or first class," she stated firmly. They had a brief spirited spat about that and finally compromised on going cabin class. "So will you come back with me to Oxford tomorrow?" she said at the end of it.

"No, I'll meet you at Heathrow. I daren't go back to Oxford. The press will be watching for me there, and besides, that frightful young editor from the OUP will be after me to write another damned book. I'll stick around here for the next couple of days. I have to see old Francis Charles and tell him the whole story, see about the memorial, and get a few things straightened out with Stephen, who seems quite addled by his newly married state. They're moving into St. Gabriel's, by the way. With both their salaries they can swing it, and they're letting the old couple have the cottage."

"Oh, that's nice," she said, then started and demanded, "What memorial?"

He cleared his throat and looked uneasy. "Yes, well, I thought the least I could do in the circumstances was to restore that vandalized headstone of the Merlin infant and include his patriot father on the new one also. I don't think his deed should be forgotten."

She gazed fondly upon him. "That's very nice. Under all that grumpy crust you *are* a sentimental old thing, aren't you?" He gobbled at that, as she went on. "Okay then, I'll get the tickets. I'll be staying a month. Any date you want to return or shall I leave that open?"

"Oh, I can only stay a week. As this is the height of the tourist season, make a firm return reservation. I have to get back."

"Whatever for? What's so urgent?" she demanded.

He looked at her in popeyed amazement. "Why, there's an extremely important henge to be dug! In Stephen's present happily muddled state, I have to be there to keep a very sharp eye on things to see they're done right. After all, it's what I came down here for in the first place and when I say I'll do something, I do it."

She looked at him and started to laugh helplessly. "Tobias Merlin Glendower, you know you're hopeless, quite hopeless, but then I wouldn't have you any other way."